BRATS

MARY R. TRUSCOTT

BRATS

E. P. DUTTON  NEW YORK

Published in the United States by E. P. Dutton,
a division of Penguin Books USA Inc.,
2 Park Avenue, New York, N.Y. 10016.

Published simultaneously in Canada by Fitzhenry and Whiteside, Limited, Toronto.

Library of Congress Cataloging-in-Publication Data
Truscott, Mary R.
        Brats / Mary R. Truscott.—1st ed.
            p.   cm.
        ISBN 0-525-24815-3
        1. Children of military personnel—United States.   2. Truscott, Mary R.   I. Title.
UB403.T78   1989
355.1'29—dc20   89-33506
                                                                                                         CIP

Designed by Steven N. Stathakis

10   9   8   7   6   5   4   3   2   1

First Edition

For my son, Ian,
and for my family

Contents

Acknowledgments

I should like to thank the many military families and brats whose generosity and willingness to tell their stories made this book possible. Throughout my work on the book, my contacts with military family members renewed my regard for the camaraderie that is such an integral fact of military life.

Barbara and Lee Hager, Krys Lilly, Lisa Schwab, Terry McCulloch, and Dan and Joel Nelson were all involved in this project, and I am indebted to them for their help.

Every member of my family contributed to this book, and I can't thank them enough for their encouragement, advice, assistance, and for tolerating my endless questions. My sister, Virginia Butcher, deserves special thanks for her contributions to the book, and my son deserves a medal for his patience and flexibility during many long months.

Roll Call

CATHY ATCHISON	Dep USAF Officer
CAROLINE BAKER	Dep USAF Enlisted
ROBERT BLAKE	Dep USMC Officer
TIM BROCKWAY	Dep USA Officer
MARY CHANDLER	Dep USA Enlisted
RICARDO COTTRELL	Dep USAF Enlisted
MARK DENTON	Dep USA Enlisted
GEORGE DEXTER	Dep USA Officer
GAIL EMERSON	Dep USN Officer
BILL FLYNN	Dep USA Officer
SHARON GILMORE	Dep USN Enlisted
RHONDA HEALEY	Dep USN Officer
ANNE HEYWOOD	Dep USAF Officer
BRAD HOLMES	Dep USAF Officer
PAULA HOLMES	Dep USAF Officer

BRUCE HUTSON	Dep USAF Officer
BARRY JENKINS	Dep USN Officer
NANCY KARACAND	Dep USAF Enlisted
MARSHA KATZ	Dep USA Enlisted
JACK LEMONT	Dep USMC Enlisted
DEREK LOWE	Dep USA Enlisted
RANDY MARTIN	Dep USN Enlisted
JULIE MEDINA	Dep USAF Enlisted
TERRY McCULLOCH	Dep USAF Enlisted
MIKE NEWCOMB	Dep USA Officer
HELEN PIERSON	Dep USA Enlisted
BRENDA ROWAN	Dep USN Officer
JOHN ROWAN	Dep USAF Officer
SHERRY RUTLEDGE	Dep USMC Enlisted
MICHELLE SLOAN	Dep USA Officer
ELIZABETH SPIVEY	Dep USAF Enlisted
MARK STANLEY	Dep USAF Officer
SHERRY SULLIVAN	Dep USA Enlisted
JEFFREY TAVARES	Dep USA Enlisted
BEVERLY TAYLOR	Dep USMC Officer
PETER VARGAS	Dep USAF Officer
DEBBIE WEST	Dep USN Officer
LARRY WILLIAMS	Dep USMC Officer
LINDA WINSLOW	Dep USA Officer
SHEILA WRIGHT	Dep USA Enlisted

BRATS

Introduction

When I moved again recently, people innocently asked me "Where are you from?" That question has always been difficult for me to answer; I was born in one state, lived in several other states, lived longest in yet another. Rather than recite the litany of states and explanations, I choose the easy reply, and shrug, and say, "I was an Army brat." Even the most stable civilians require no further explanation. "Oh," they say, with a combination of envy and curiosity, "then you've lived everywhere."

The simple statement "I was an Army brat" offers a convenient summary to questions about my origins, and I never elaborate on my response; people ask me whether I ever lived overseas and leave it at that. No one ever asks me what my father did in the Army, or whether he ever fought in a war, and so I never tell them that by the time I was eight years old my father had been away, at war, for two years. I never tell them that "living everywhere" was a bittersweet adventure, a series of wrenching good-byes and tentative hellos.

1

Both of my parents were Army brats and were raised in Army families. As adults, they followed a tradition that my grandparents had established: my mother married a career Army officer, and my father pursued a military career. My maternal grandfather, a West Point graduate, retired a colonel; my paternal grandfather was a general, and although the details of his career were vague to me, his booming voice and military bearing convinced me that he was no ordinary grandfather. My grandmothers were aristocratic, stylish women who were unaccustomed to having grandchildren underfoot, because we rarely lived near them. I didn't know my grandparents very well, but I knew that they were different from the kindly and ineffectual grandparents depicted in my storybooks.

As far back as I can remember, I was aware that my sisters and brothers and I were second-generation Army brats. It wasn't until much later in my life that I acknowledged my family heritage, my grandparents' legacy. I have always known where I came from; I can start with the year I was born and recite a list of places, and the list is as representative of my family's military background as our ID cards.

My parents, in retirement, have ID cards and are welcome to take advantage of the services on any military installation, and they have maintained contact with the military friends who share their background. I left home and left the military behind. I have only infrequently discussed the details of my background with anyone other than my immediate family. Even when I've met other military brats, once we establish the commonality of our backgrounds, we rarely discuss our experiences: we just assume that they were similar.

In the past few years, I began to wonder about other military brats. I wondered whether they argued with their families over the details of their lives: "That happened in Germany." "No, it didn't; it was New Jersey . . ." I wanted to hear about their experiences—moving, making friends, going to new schools— and their perceptions of the military's codes of behavior, social taboos, and hierarchies of rank, both inside and outside their homes. I wanted to hear their stories about what it had been like to grow up in a military family, and I wondered how they had been influenced by living everywhere and being from no particular place.

One of the women I met launched into her story with the statement "Your parents are your parents, and every set of parents is different, and every set of circumstances is different." In researching this book, I met people from all branches of service, people who had come from large families or who had been only children, people who had lived all over the world. All of them had stories about their own unique set of circumstances; even siblings had completely different versions of identical experiences. Given the dynamics of family life and the highly personal perspective of childhood memories, the people in this book have one thing in common: their fathers had chosen military careers. They had all been military dependents.

Because of their fathers' military careers, military brats had been conscripted into the military at birth. It is not uncommon for a father's career to influence the daily life of a family; ask any doctor's family about the long hours required by his profession, or any policeman's family about the risks that are a part of carrying a badge and a gun. A military career, however, defines and shapes the lives of families to an extent that is rarely matched in nonmilitary occupations. Factors that are not unusual when they occur sporadically during the course of a career are, collectively, the way of life for military families. Military life includes frequent moves and the ensuing isolation from relatives and friends, a father's long- or short-term absences from home, and risks that are an inescapable part of military duty during war or peacetime.

The children of active duty military personnel were dependent on their parents and on the United States government; their fathers worked for the military, and the military is committed to provide for the children of its personnel.

In between wars, military posts are like vast, idling engines; all manpower and resources are devoted to keeping the engine primed and ready to shift into high gear. It can be difficult to imagine just what, exactly, goes on in the military until the word is given to mobilize, and suddenly every piece of equipment and every soldier has a purpose, a function. Until that time, though, it

3

is easy to forget that the military *is* the Armed Forces, that it serves both to keep the peace and to wage war.

The military was not established as a retail business or a residential landlord, nor had its personnel plans included the care and education of young children. Doctors and military hospitals were intended to treat soldiers, not deliver babies. But in order to fulfill its obligation to the dependent children of its military forces, the military became involved in the business of families. No matter where the housing areas were placed, the parade grounds on military posts did double-duty as playgrounds and the children who lived on post, with their noise and enthusiasm and their innocent disregard for pomp and circumstance, were part of the military. They were "hangar bats" in the Air Force, "juniors" in the Navy, and "rugrats" or simply "brats" to each other, to their parents, and to the outside world.

Before I began interviewing military brats, I knew that the rate of alcoholism in military populations has been estimated to be three times higher than in other identifiable groups, and that child abuse and wife beating in military and nonmilitary households alike have recently become topics of great concern.

Many of the people I interviewed for this book waited until the tape recorder had been turned off before they hesitantly broached the sensitive subjects of alcohol, abuse, or family problems. Although I am obligated to respect the off-the-record nature of such conversations, it is obvious that alcoholism and domestic violence are, in some families, very real problems. Whether they are endemic or epidemic in military families is not for me to determine. When I conducted the interviews for this book, I made absolutely no effort to obtain a statistical sample; I simply talked to military brats about their lives.

What I do know is that military families keep closed ranks; they mind their own business. I believe that the tendency to close ranks is particularly common in military families: life on a post is often compared to life in a goldfish bowl. Any hint of family problems, even in casual conversation, could have an impact on a family's reputation, and ultimately, on a father's career. I can understand the unwillingness to go public with family problems.

4

When neighbors, physicians, and even ministers around a family are all connected to the military, a paranoia develops, a willingness to "bite the bullet" to prevent irrevocable damage to a career. The military certainly does not condone aberrant behavior within its ranks, but its very methods for handling such problems have, no doubt, perpetuated them.

Military brats grew up secure behind the post gates that kept them in and kept the outside world out, and their status as dependents gave them a distinctive point of view about what really went on within the inner sanctum of the military.

The word *brat*, according to my grandfather's old *Webster's* dictionary, originally meant a coarse garment or cloak and "came to mean a child through the sense of a child's bib." It is easy to condense experiences, translate them into two autobiographical words, "military brat," without explaining what it was like to be a military brat. There was more to being a military brat than just the moving, the "living everywhere." The fabric of our daily lives was as military as the olive drab uniforms.

1

Dependents

We look like any American family in our home movies and slides and photographs. There is nothing that catches the eye, no detail that marks us as a military family. Like any family, we trace our history in the images that we captured on film, and we search the background of each frame of the home movies and each slide and photograph for clues and memories. Suddenly the blur of the past takes form, and all of our stories and anecdotes are related, in some way, to my father's career, to the military. We identify the background, the quarters we lived in, before we can remember the specific tales that accompany the pictures. Who's that baby? Oh, that was Japan, so that's my oldest brother. I see snow on the ground; that must have been the year of the blizzard in Alexandria, when Dad worked at the Pentagon. There we are at the beach at Fort DeRussy.

We had a family reunion whenever we saw any of our relatives. They rarely appear in our family pictures. I had usually forgotten about my grandparents, aunts, and uncles in between

7

visits; they were exciting strangers to me, people who always exclaimed, "My, how you've grown since the last time I saw you!" We had our own traditions and rituals for holidays and birthdays, and with so many kids, our family life was raucous and full with or without our relatives around.

My four brothers and sisters and I were all born in military hospitals, unknowing little recipients of the free medical care that the military provided. I heard the term *serial number* frequently when I was a child. I used to study the side of cereal boxes for a clue of any kind, convinced that it had to be related, somehow, to the box of cereal. As I got older, I realized that my father's name, rank, and serial number were the key not only to his identity as a career Army officer, but to our identity as a family. The military called us "dependents of active duty military personnel." My mother was a dependent wife, and we were dependent children.

The U.S. government issued my father's paycheck, and we knew it. It was because of my father's military career that we had a roof over our heads, food on our table, and clothes on our backs.

We had a roof over our heads, but we didn't live in a house; we lived in "quarters," another bewildering military term, which was not related to the coin or the fractional amount. Once my father received our housing assignment on a new post, we hurried off, in the car loaded with kids and suitcases and family pets, to see our new quarters. There was never any choice involved, as far as I knew; we were always told where we would live. It never mattered to me. All I wanted to do was open every closet and cupboard and explore the new territory.

My family was familiar with "close quarters." We could and did get by in cramped apartments with five kids and two adults. Since housing was allocated by rank, our quarters became more spacious as my father was promoted and moved up through the ranks. My brothers left home just as we were assigned quarters that were realistically large enough for a family like ours.

My sister and I shared a room even after it was no longer a necessity to do so. Actually, we shared nine different bedrooms in various quarters and houses over the years. We slept and played and fought and were sternly sent to those rooms when we misbehaved. We always had a night-light so that we could find our way if we got up at night. Each new bedroom was exciting during the day, but in the dark, every shadow was fraught with perils and nothing looked familiar.

The food that we ate came from the commissary, and that word still evokes memories of a drafty, poorly lit warehouse. First we flashed our ID cards at the door to gain admittance, and a clerk approved my mother's check by scribbling my father's serial number on the back of it. Then we ventured into the aisles, which were always crowded with women and overflowing shopping carts.

In addition to the usual supermarket items, the commissary carried the military's "generic brands," government issue food, usually canned goods, in jumbo size meant for mess halls and perfect for large families. The GI food, as we called it, had plain white labels with block letters: GREEN BEANS, 64 OUNCES. New brands of food that we saw in advertisements took months to appear on the commissary shelves, after being routed through the channels of government purchasing. If the commissary didn't carry the latest fad food or our favorite brand of cookies, then we didn't get it. We never shopped anywhere else.

The prices were low at the commissary and the lines were interminably long. There was a separate checkout stand that usually sat idle, exclusively for the few men in uniform who shopped in the commissary. The bag boys were a motley crew of teenage boys from the post and older civilian men who loitered against the wall near the exit and worked for tips only.

The table that our food was served on was, quite possibly, issued by the Quartermaster (QM). The post Quartermaster was both a person and a furniture warehouse. The Quartermaster handled our housing assignments each time we moved and provided replacement furniture for items that were in storage and supplemental furnishings to families like ours who were either moving frequently or growing rapidly. In the long run, it was easier and more economical for us to borrow furniture from the military, rather than purchase things that we would have to move all over the country.

We usually had several QM pieces on loan. It was sturdy stuff, constructed to stand up to use by many families over the years, and some of it looked better than our own furniture. QM

9

furniture reminded me of hotel furniture. The drawers had a funny smell. We borrowed the things that we needed from the QM during the time that we lived in a place and returned them when we left.

The clothes that we wore came from the Post Exchange (PX), another inner sanctum, like the commissary, that required an ID card for admission. The PX was the military version of Sears, with something for everyone, from thread to television sets. GIs were always gathered near the record albums and stereo equipment.

Every post had a snack bar, and a shoe shop to repair heavy black military shoes and boots, and a barber shop that specialized in smart military hairstyles. There were a beauty shop for the wives, a post office, a gas station, and a package store, which sold liquor and cigarettes at legendary bargain prices. We retrieved my father's shirts and uniforms from the cleaners, which fascinated me because the racks were filled with rows and rows of identical green garments.

I can remember my mother's sighing a lot when I was a child. It seemed as if we were always waiting, waiting in lines with the other dependents. Our free medical care seemed to elicit the most sighs. We were taken to the post hospital for our childhood illnesses and injuries, physicals, and endless immunizations. We had no jovial family doctor, no paternal pediatrician; we saw a series of anonymous doctors who were transferred as often as we were.

The hospital issued its own green plastic cards, and the ritual showing of the card began at the front desk. My mother had a deck of medical cards in her purse for the five of us, fastened together with a rubber band. Each visit to the hospital meant a potential snafu: our medical records were still in transit from our last station, or they were misfiled, or they were simply lost. We spent many hours in waiting rooms.

I hated GIs because they manned the fateful medical records desk, and all too often they administered the blood tests, poking my arm with grim determination until they finally hit a vein. They also worked in the pharmacy, another waiting room, where we could hear them type out prescription labels one slow letter at a time. My mother would sigh and mutter about "hunt-and-peck typing," and I assumed that the GIs in the pharmacy were named Hunt and Peck.

We were dependents, and the military was all around us. Even families who lived in civilian housing, off post, remained connected to the military. Their rent was paid, at least partially, with a housing allowance, and they were still card-carrying military dependents with fathers who wore conspicuous uniforms to work. Whenever possible, they traveled to the post to take advantage of their military privileges: they shopped at the commissary, not the supermarket.

Military kids were fluent in military lingo: "ID Required," EM Club (Enlisted Men's Club), and BOQ (Bachelor Officers' Quarters). We played on playgrounds and parade grounds. We used scratchy surplus Army blankets to make forts in the yard, spent our allowances at the PX and our Saturday afternoons at matinees at the post theater. The post PA system, used for bugle calls and air raid drills, provided the soundtrack for our lives.

Dependent families were independent units, nuclear families in a nuclear age. The military provided everything that we needed, including a surrogate extended family of other people just like us. Uncle Sam was merely another distant relative, an invisible man who dominated every aspect of our lives. Our fathers were our connection to the military world. They went off to work every day, either in offices and buildings on the post, or on the other side of the world, and we went about the business of growing up. *Dependents* was just another military term that we used, a word that meant us.

JULIE MEDINA

I was born because he came back from Korea, my little brother was born because he came back from Tripoli, and when we stayed three years in Nevada, they had three kids. There were six of us kids. We lost one in Nevada from what is now known as SIDS, so there are five of us left. I am the second oldest.

I remember the night Mom found out she was pregnant the last time. They didn't have birth control back then; there was no way out. I could hear her going, "You bastard, you couldn't wait two days, and now I'm pregnant again! It's all your fault!" She screamed and yelled at him for nine months, never wanted the baby, but when my sister was born, my mom was so happy. That was the last time she got pregnant.

When we were real small, my dad had little dog tags made for my sister and me, with his serial number and "$\frac{1}{2}$," so I have known his serial number since I was three.

PETER VARGAS

My mother used to chide me about my clothes, because they were my "uniforms." I had certain things I wore together, and I would never mix and match things. I remember my father teaching me how to shine my shoes, and how to tie my tie. There was a way to do it, and how to tuck my shirt in. I still find myself, sometimes, doing that military tuck.

At five o'clock every day on the base, they would lower the flag. We all stopped, no matter what we were doing. Usually we were playing a game of tag, or army, or hide and go seek. And no matter where we were, no matter what foxhole we were hiding in, prepared to ambush the enemy, we stopped. "Retreat" would blare out from loudspeakers all over the base. We could never see the flag; it was miles away. But we knew where it was, and like facing Mecca, everyone turned around and put their hand over their heart, and stood there until the music stopped. Then we'd go back to our business. We had all blown our hiding places, and everyone had to scatter to new places, and the guy who was "it" always tried to take advantage of that, that breach of security. But it was something that we all took in stride, that daily routine. There was never even a comment about it, no matter what was going on. It just happened every day.

BRUCE HUTSON

It was interesting; on the base, when they took the flag down, you'd have to stop whatever you were doing. That really brings back an image to me, of walking down the sidewalk, and suddenly everyone would just stop. It was like a B movie, and the aliens had invaded everyone's head. It was weird.

We went to a lot of movies back then, because they were only a quarter. And before the movie started, every time, you had to stand up for the National Anthem. The recording always went, "Ladies and gentlemen," and then a pause, "Our National Anthem." And it was so funny, because you'd be in the theater with all these GIs, you know, seeing movies like *A Shot in the Dark*, so there's a lot of hooting and hollering going on with GIs. They'd either come from downtown, or the EM Club, so they'd had a beer or two, maybe, before the movie. Invariably, someone would wait for that pause, just after the "Ladies and gentlemen," and some GI would call out his name, "Spec Four So-and-So," and then everybody would do it. And then when the National Anthem was over, they would call out, "Play ball!"

JACK LEMONT

I can remember my parents taking me to the NCO Club when I was real young—I guess before my brother came along—and they would have a beer and I would have a Buck Rogers with a cherry in it. That was a big deal.

I remember always having an ID card, always having to show it out at the PX. I wasn't very conscientious about it. To this day, I always stick my money in my pocket. I know I lost it a couple of times, and had to go get a new one. It was always messed up, always put together with Scotch tape. I remember getting in trouble. "You forgot your ID card, and now you can't get into the PX."

ELIZABETH SPIVEY

My parents met when they were both in the Air Force and they were stationed in France. My mom got out and came back to the States. He called from France as soon as she arrived home and asked her to marry him, over the phone. This was in 1957, I guess. They got married when he got back and they moved to Wyoming, out in the middle of nowhere.

So my mother knew what she was getting into. For a woman to join the Air Force then was a hideous thing. My mother had been raised on a farm in northern Tennessee. She was the youngest of six kids. She lived for the day when she could get off that farm because it was so awful and boring. She had received a scholarship to go to college, but the college wasn't far enough away, and she passed it up so she could join the Air Force and see the world and live an exciting life. That absolutely crushed her family.

My dad joined the Air Force when he was seventeen, and I suspect he lied about his age. He was one of eight children, and his father was very ill. He felt it necessary that he leave and be able to send money back home, so that was why he joined the Air Force. And probably there was a lot of impetuousness, too, like he wanted to get away and see the world. So I think my parents had that in common, a great desire to get away from home.

We couldn't afford a second family car. In fact, my dad would ride a bicycle to work when we were living on base. We would walk down the block to meet him after work, and he would pile us on his bike and give us a ride home. He would come home for lunch when I was about five years old. I learned how to tie shoes on his combat boots. I guess it was easier because they were so big, those big, black shoelaces. I would practice on my dad's boots when he was home for lunch.

MICHELLE SLOAN

The first time I ever got to ride a yellow school bus was when I was in high school. Until then, I always had to go to school on those big brown Army buses. They had signs inside that said, DO NOT STICK ARMS THROUGH WINDOWS. I was always trying to decide which kind of arms they were talking about. Probably both.

DEREK LOWE

There were five of us by the time it was all over with. I'm the oldest. Vacations were part of moving, and most frequently that was going back to visit the relatives in Louisiana, at the homestead. There was a real extended family that was a very stable thing for us to enter and leave, enter and leave. They would also come and visit us. My father was in the first group that integrated the Army in the 1950s during the Korean War. In a lot of ways, I think particularly for black Americans in the early 1950s, that was a real privileged status, so consequently it was a fairly esteemed kind of thing for the family to come and visit us on the base. So we had a lot of contact, except when we were in more distant places like Germany and upstate New York.

We wouldn't go back to Louisiana for holidays. Holidays were always when we were together as a family. A lot of times, too, we did things with the company. My dad was in an NCO leadership role, so he was overseeing those kinds of things. He enjoyed his job, so he was on base a lot. There were company Christmas parties and other events. He used to make extra money bartending at the NCO Club, so we were usually on base for those holiday types of functions.

At some point, all military kids become enamored with the junk associated with the Army. I used to shine my dad's shoes for him, and I became aware of tasks that he would let me do related to his uniforms, or the Brasso. He went through this ritual every day to prepare himself for work.

Our food was always from the commissary. I would go with my mom and stand in that line at the commissary with those two or three baskets, filled to overflowing once a month. All that milk and cereal. The uniformity of that experience—we'd have bounty at the beginning of the month, and then hot dogs and pancakes at the end of the month.

My earliest, vague memories go back to Fort Leonard Wood, when I was four. We lived right on the parade ground. Once they were preparing for a parade, and they brought out all of these missiles and launchers and set them up and then left them there until the parade started. So all of us kids were out there, immediately, playing on top of those missiles. Those are my first memories of the huge fields, and the housing, and the block that we lived on with the huge field in the middle, the sandboxes and all that. The experience of being a kid in the Army was really an unmatched experience. Riding my bicycle—that's one of my first

15

memories—riding my bicycle with wild abandon across that large field at Fort Leonard Wood.

In retrospect, it's a really ideal environment for a child. That's what I remember about the Army, aside from the other crazy part of it, the "kill, kill."

DEBBIE WEST

To me, the Navy was more than just a job: it was a life-style, and my father epitomized that. I knew that there were other types of jobs that people came home from. They had a break from it. There was never any break in the Navy.

I'm the oldest of six kids. We were little stepping-stones; you can tell when he was home on leave. I was born in Arizona. At the time, my father was in the Navy, but as an enlisted man, not an officer. My parents were very young at the time. I guess my mother got pregnant right away and had me there. We lived in an empty airplane hangar the first year of my life.

Money was a part of life that we never heard about, and I mean never. My mother always felt that "nice people" didn't talk about money. The only time I ever heard about any kind of financial difficulty was when they were buying a house, and for some reason the loan fell through. I can remember my mother on the phone, on a transcontinental call to my father, who was halfway around the world at that time, telling him that the loan didn't go through, and asking him what she should do. That was the only time that I ever remember hearing her talking about finances.

RICARDO COTTRELL

My stepfather was of Portuguese descent. He was born and raised in a small farming town in Hawaii. When we lived at Vandenberg, there were a lot of GIs on base who were from Hawaii. Hawaiians eat rice, like the Japanese, three times a day. My father never gave that up; he had his rice three times a day. He opened our house up to the GIs from Hawaii, and let them come over and have parties and hang out. There got to be over a dozen of them, and they would come over and play volleyball, and sometimes they would put on luaus. My parents became like parents to them.

PAULA HOLMES

Our situation was a little different, because my father was a chaplain in the military. I always thought that our situation was doubly hard, it was compounded, because we were chaplain's kids. I hated hearing my father preach on Sunday mornings. I hated that. I can't imagine any kid who would enjoy that, being so different.

TERRY McCULLOCH

Payday was always the day when my mom went to the commissary and came back with about twenty bags in the back of the station wagon. It was a big thing—Mom's coming home from the commissary this afternoon, so none of us could leave the house. We all had to be there to help bring in the groceries and put them away. It was always fun, because there were always cookies and potato chips and stuff that we didn't have later on in the month.

I remember her going down the aisles with two carts. She always grabbed two carts, and she'd fill up two entire carts, because you only shopped on payday. You didn't go to the commissary in between. She still has that habit of buying all of her groceries once or twice a month. She doesn't go, just occasionally, to the store. It's the funniest thing. She would buy tons of food. She would buy eight cartons of milk and freeze them. I used to hate that. I'd go, "Mom, you don't freeze milk!" She still does it. She freezes the damn milk.

I was so proud of my first ID card. I'd carry it in my back pocket everywhere I went. I'd go to the movies and I'd show it, and they'd say, "You don't have to show your ID card!" I was really proud of it. It was like a driver's license.

17

TIM BROCKWAY

Army families generally had a lot of kids. We had four in our family, and there were lots of other kids around. One of the things about the military was they expounded that job security, and you always had a place to live. It was not a financial consideration to have a big family.

One of the things I remember was how many jobs I had at a young age. We delivered the *Daily Bulletin*, and my brother and I had a monopoly on *TV Guide* delivery all over the base, and we had a great income off of those jobs. My first job was as a busboy at the Officer's Club, and I set pins at the bowling alley before they had automation. I sacked groceries at the commissary; I loaded the clay pigeons at the rifle range for the skeet shoots. It was really easy to get little jobs, right within the compound, delivering papers, mowing lawns.

RHONDA HEALEY

We had five kids in our family. We span just nine years.

I remember going to the commissary with my mother once, and she wrote a check for seventy-five dollars. At that time, I can remember just standing there and being totally blown away that we could spend that much money on groceries.

While we were in Los Angeles, which was probably our poorest time as a family, Dad was in college, so they had all of his university expenses, and he did not receive the other kinds of bonuses that he had gotten when we had been living on base, so it was really very difficult for them, financially. My mom tells stories about how she stretched recipes and sewed every stitch of clothing for us, and she did some typing for people. They never went out. I can remember once having a baby-sitter because they went out for the evening on their tenth anniversary.

I remember waking up at night and hearing her crying because she was so worried about how they were going to get through. I told her that I don't ever remember feeling like I was deprived. We didn't have a lot of things, didn't do a lot of activities, but we camped and Dad took us to campus football games and whatever, and otherwise we played around the neighborhood on our bikes. I don't remember ever feeling poor.

There was one Christmas Mother describes, and when I look back I realize she was right. My grandparents had flown out to visit us for Christmas. My mom had made us these beautiful stuffed rag dolls. I still have mine somewhere, and she made us some other things, and basically that was going to be our Christmas. She tells us that my grandfather came in and saw that and couldn't believe it. On Christmas Eve he was downtown buying everything he could get his hands on. He just bought everything, really bought Christmas for us, and my mother was so relieved. She tells that story, and just gets real misty-eyed about it, and I never knew as a kid.

HELEN PIERSON

There were four of us children in my family. We always lived on military posts. It's like living in a very small town. Not that you knew everyone, but that you were all the same. For Halloween and stuff, it was nice. There was never any fear of going to someone's house. Part of it was that time, in general, and part of it was the military. There was one incident in Hawaii where a GI did go nuts and was breaking into houses. He slit the screen on a window down the block—a young girl's window—but they caught him and took care of it right away. It's not like the court system now. There were repercussions for doing something wrong, and it was handled right away.

The thing I remember most about being in the military was five o'clock when "Retreat" would sound, and we had to stop. Even in Hawaii, when the rain was pouring, you had to stop. I remember standing in the pouring rain, in my Brownie uniform, saluting the flag.

NANCY KARACAND

There were a lot of things that we couldn't afford when I was growing up. We couldn't shop at the stores I wanted to for clothes. We had to go to Penney's and Sears, and I hated that, because inevitably, I'd buy an Easter dress and go to church or school and see some girl who I didn't like wearing the same dress. I would be mortified. "That girl has my dress on!" I remember crying about that. We never had new furniture, and we never had a new car. So I was aware in that sense, that we always kind of had secondhand stuff, but I was never aware that there wasn't enough money to cover this or that. I think they were real good about keeping that from us. That was not something that we ever had to know about or worry about or think about.

We ate real well. That was my dad's big priority, that we would always have real good food on the table, because he literally starved as a kid and grew up in some awful circumstances. He took a lot of pride in the fact that we were always going to eat well.

MARY CHANDLER

When I was in fifth grade, we had been moved to the Pentagon area, had to pay rent off post, all ten of us were still at home, and my folks had to buy a second car so my dad could commute to the Pentagon, and his pay raise from his promotion was delayed for a couple of months. I found out about all these problems when my father called the four older kids to the living room for a meeting after I had gone to bed, and I heard every word because my bedroom was adjacent to the living room. What he said to them was that there would be no Christmas that year for them because of the pay raise mix-up, and that what money there was would be spent on the four younger kids. Proof positive came two weeks later when my birthday came and went and I got nothing but a birthday cake.

MARSHA KATZ

It's strange to think about it now and realize just how military everything was. Even having a sore throat or the measles ended up being a military experience, because you would get dragged off to the infirmary.

We were always sick with something, probably from moving

around so much and being exposed to so many different germs. Of course we went to the hospital every time we got sick, and it seems to me that the military was very conservative about everything: almost *stingy,* if that's the right word. You *really* had to be sick before they would do anything beyond just examine you and give you a shot or a prescription. Half the time you didn't even see a real doctor, you had to see these medics. My mother just had to drag me in to the hospital sometimes, because I just hated it so much. I guess it's kind of like the HMOs that they have today. They had some rule about surgery; you had to have tonsillitis a certain number of times before they would even consider operating on you and taking your tonsils out.

My mother just went along with it, but, of course, now I realize that it doesn't have to be that way. You don't have to suffer through being sick for two years before you have your tonsils taken out.

It wasn't just the medical care, either. Trips to the dentist were awful, and all of us kids were just phobic about going to the dentist. We used to scream and cry and pitch fits whenever we had to go, even my brothers. When I was older, I had to have a crown replaced, and the civilian dentist I went to was just shocked at what he saw. He asked me if I had done my own dental work. I think the Army dental equipment was all pre–World War II surplus or something. My mom used to joke that they had to hand crank the drills. I still remember the old-fashioned chairs that they had; they were overstuffed, in all the wrong places, and full of lumps and they didn't even adjust.

When I tell people about it now, they just don't believe how different my life was. I didn't even realize it myself, at the time. But it wasn't like we were living in just any neighborhood. I mean, most people don't live in guarded compounds. In Kansas, we were living near the federal prison, and they also had the big military prison on the post. It was really weird, because they had the military prisoners on some kind of work-release program, so they worked at the car wash and the dry cleaners and the stables. We had a horse for a while, so I used to hang around at the stables all the time, and a lot of prisoners worked there, taking care of the horses. They wore these brown uniforms, and we weren't supposed to talk to them or even make eye contact with them. You were allowed to talk to the trustee if you needed something, but we used to try to talk to the prisoners on the sly.

This was also in Kansas—they had a real mosquito problem there, so they sent these trucks around to spray insecticide. The DDT trucks. They were these big tanker trucks that drove around really slowly, spraying this giant cloud behind them. We used to hold our breath and run behind these trucks for fun. It was right up there with the ice cream man, the highlight of a hot summer day. We'd go, "Mom, here comes the DDT truck! Can we run behind it?" And she'd say, sure, just be home in time for dinner. Some of us would just run, and other kids would be on their bikes. It was like the Pied Piper coming through the neighborhood, and we were all running along in these clouds of toxic chemicals. It's amazing that we even had any chromosomes left. I can still remember the way that stuff smelled.

We lived in some really great old houses, with servants' quarters in the basement and enormous, huge rooms with high ceilings that made our furniture look ridiculous, like toy furniture. Of course, when I was younger we also lived in some real pits, with five or six or seven of us crammed into three bedrooms. It was almost unbearable sometimes in some of the places we lived. My dad was always having to fix up bedrooms in the basement for my brothers. As the oldest, they had to rough it, and the rest of us got the "real" bedrooms upstairs. We didn't just have sibling rivalry, we had battles over territory and who was going to have to live in the basement, and this went on every year, every time we moved. When you really think about it, even the things that went on between me and my brothers and sister can be traced back to the military. I kind of remember my childhood by remembering where we were living, and I'm sure my brothers remember theirs by the basement they lived in.

SHERRY SULLIVAN

My parents always said, "We never had a piano. We want you to learn." Isn't that something that all parents do to their children? Even taking piano lessons was a terrible mess; you'd move and have different teachers and different books every other year. That's terribly confusing when you're just a beginner. I'd just dread starting my lessons up again.

JEFFREY TAVARES

When something would break in your house, the post engineers would come out and fix it. When we retired, I was just astonished that you had to fix things yourself. I never knew where all this stuff came from; you'd just make a phone call and put in the order with the engineers, and they were out there.

I remember paydays in Indiana because a lot of the officers' children would be at the end of the pay line with cookies and things that they were selling for Boy Scouts. That's one thing my dad refused to let me do, because he always felt that the troops would buy them because I was a first sergeant's son, and not because they wanted to.

I went to military hospitals. I never knew any different. I had never even heard of going to your own doctor. Going and taking a number and sitting and waiting, I heard of a lot. And the shots we got at school—it was cattle-call time. We walked to a green trailer, and went in one door, got the shots, and came out the other door. They used air guns, and you'd hear stories—"Yeah, some guy in basic training got his arm blown off with that air gun"—and then they'd come out with this thing. They'd take each grade, pow, pow, pow.

LINDA WINSLOW

I was an only child. My parents were twenty-six when I was born, and back then, for a woman to be twenty-five years old before she even married was kind of unusual. I was, of course, supposed to be the perfect colonel's daughter with the white gloves and the Protestant choir. I used to read the *Officer's Guide* for fun. I had a collection of patches and crests. I was in New York, and that was where everyone left to go overseas and came back to be discharged, so there were guys from all over, and they didn't want their patches, and here was this little gap-tooth, pimply-faced girl going, "Hey, mister, can I have that?" I had a hell of a collection.

I must have been in the third grade when my father was the base engineer. His idea of a big thrill for me was to let me ride in the fire truck, because the base engineers were automatically fire marshals. Well, the last thing I wanted to do was ride in the fire truck, because what they were doing was demonstrating napalm. Here came these low-flying jets, making horrible noise and dropping flaming shit all over the place. It wasn't even like a fireworks display; it was just downright creepy. It scared me, and I didn't want to be there, but I had to be there. My father's idea of a good time was not what I considered to be a good time.

Once the phone rang, and I answered it with "Major Bower's quarters, Linda speaking."

"Ma'am, is the base engineer available?" It sounded like an airman second or third.

"I'm sorry, but my father is not available at this time."

"Well, this is the tower. I am required by regulation to inform him that we have a hot load in danger landing on runway seven." What it meant was that there was a nuclear weapon–loaded aircraft that was having a mayday, landing a mile away from my house. So I said, "Thank you very much. I'll inform him." Just so matter-of-fact. Day-to-day stuff. It didn't shock me at the time or upset me.

SHEILA WRIGHT

My dad was in the Air Force. My birth certificate says "Sergeant Benjamin Wright" is my father. When I saw that, I thought, well, that's strange, putting his rank on there.

Going to the commissary with my mom was a treat. We didn't say, "Mom, can we have this? Can we get that?" We were quiet, and we went along with our mom. And I think all the kids were like that; it wasn't just us. The family's the image of the man.

GAIL EMERSON

We didn't have as hard a time financially as a lot of other people in the military, because my mother's family is moderately well-to-do. They helped her out a lot: they bought furniture for her, and when we finally got a house, they helped with the down payment on the house. My parents paid them back, but they were able to do so at a rate that they could afford.

But my aunt told me how she made "end of the month soup." Her husband was an officer, but even officers had a hard time with their families. With a big household, it was hard. It only cost ten cents for a big can of salmon then, so she would take a ten-cent can of salmon and plop it in a pan and put milk in it and she'd chop up some potatoes and some green onion and she'd make this wonderful "end of the month soup."

2

Orders

When I was a child my parents would take our family on long vacations. Our pace was never hurried. We posed for photographs at tourist attractions, bought postcards for our friends at curio shops, and stopped for the night at motels with parking lots filled with cars like ours, cars from other states.

When we left on those trips, we didn't have to worry about having our newspaper stopped or our lawn watered because our vacations began when we left one empty house to travel to the next. We had no home to return to, and no idea of what our next home would be like. We saw enormous stretches of the United States from the backseat of the car, free and unfettered.

My parents taught us a four-letter word when we were very young: *move*. I was surprised when I went to school and learned that the Pilgrims had sailed on a ship called the *Mayflower*. I thought that the *Mayflower* was a moving van.

There was something exciting about the preparation for a move. Inevitably we found some misplaced treasure behind the

26

furniture or in the back of a closet. My parents had been moving all of their lives, but they were of different schools of thought. My mother believed in traveling light; my father had an extensive library of books that always tipped the scales against us, for we had to pay the difference if we exceeded our weight allowance. Before every move, my mother went on ruthless missions to purge our extraneous possessions. Things mysteriously disappeared in my family for years, and we always blamed the movers.

It never took long for us to move out. Our bed frames were disassembled and leaned up against the walls, the bookshelves were emptied, the piano was sold, and cartons were sealed with a rip as the brown tape came off the roll.

The exhilarating prospect of going on to something new was complicated by the wrenching finality of leaving. There is something desolate and forlorn about a house that has been stripped of all signs of its inhabitants, like a theater stage after the show has closed and the set has been struck. And that's what the houses that we lived in were: stage sets, scenic backdrops.

When we arrived in an empty house we transformed it, created a home with our belongings. The pictures were hung on the wall above the couch in the same predictable arrangement in every house that we lived in. The dining room table was anchored safely on our familiar dark blue rug. The sets changed frequently, but our props, carefully packed and unpacked, never varied.

In much the same way that migrant workers follow the crops, Navy families followed the fleet, Air Force families followed squadrons, and Army families followed the whims of the personnel system. Physical moves generally paralleled career moves, a promotion or demotion, an opportunity for additional training, or a nudge to put in retirement papers. There were good moves, escapes from miserable climates, from apartments into houses, and there were times when orders were met with tears and protests.

I learned to ask military brats about their moves before I met with them, because it was rare for people to remember all the places they had lived without making a telephone call to enlist the aid of their parents. When they inquired, some people learned for the first time that they had lived in places that they

27

couldn't even remember, short stays, six months spent at some post along the way to another. Others referred to notes and lists that read like crazed itineraries.

One man told me that he hadn't really had the typical experiences with moving because his father had retired just before he started junior high school. He then recited a list that included three overseas tours and mentioned that his family had continued to move after his father retired, "little moves" from one house to another within the same state.

I also spoke to people who, for one reason or another, had not experienced the usual pattern of moves. It was possible for families to avoid moving, but such stability often meant they remained behind while their father was sent on extended tours of duty.

Moving was a fact of life, and families accepted it. "The orders came, and we went." "I wasn't even aware that there was any other way to live. I thought that everybody moved."

BILL FLYNN

They would always tell us at dinnertime. They didn't really announce anything like that until he had everything all planned out. When it was announced, it was "This is where we're going, and this is when we're going, and this is what we have to do between now and then, and when we get there, this is what we can expect." He prepared us well, as well as he possibly could. It wasn't like he got his orders and came home and threw them down and went, "Oh, God, we have to go here now."

BRENDA ROWAN

I remember at a certain point, after we moved to Maryland, I wanted to move, because I couldn't adapt very well. I wanted to move, and I would look forward to moving, and then have the same hard time come about, and then want to move. It became like a whole pattern.

My fondest memories are of Hawaii. Hawaii was the nicest place. When I was little, nine or ten years old, I felt very free there. I was kind of a tomboy, outdoors a lot. I loved everything about it at that time. We had a really open house, with screened-in lanais. We lived on base there and the school was close by. We were kind of secluded. We didn't mix with the locals that much.

I looked forward to moving, except when we left Hawaii. I remember crying when we left. My dad wanted to move because there was no baseball, no sports on television over there. He really missed that a lot. So instead of staying there for another year, which we had the option to do, he decided to move. And I was very upset. I remember throwing leis in the water as we went on the ship, because there's an old myth that if the lei goes to land, then you'll come back to Hawaii.

JOHN ROWAN

I loved moving. It was difficult adjusting once we got to a new place, but I always loved the process itself and getting ready to go. I was always ready. When we were leaving Maryland, for some reason, we spent our last night in the area, in a motel. I was terribly anxious. I couldn't stand the thought that we were out of the house and we weren't just going. Let's drive all night, but let's go. I always looked forward to it, and I remember the moves themselves as being fun, an adventure.

BRAD HOLMES

We used to play the guessing game with our friends. I'd call up one week and say, "Guess how far away I'm moving?" And they'd ask, "Is it Europe? No? Asia? No?" And I'd say, "No, it's in the United States." And they'd say, "Texas? No—California?" And I'd say, "Yeah." And then the next week he'd call me and say, "Well, I'm moving to Taiwan, so there."

PAULA HOLMES

Part of me really enjoyed moving, because I liked getting away from wherever it was that I didn't like. My dad would always put his orders in his pocket and say, "Guess where we're going?" It

29

was like a guessing game. We'd get real excited about it. I always liked getting away from wherever we were, if I didn't like it there, which is a really bad habit to get into. I was always looking forward to something new. It's hard to get that out of your system and just stay in one place all the time. If you don't like something, you have to find a way to change it; you don't just leave it.

I was real sad when we left Japan and moved to Illinois. We moved to a quaint old town, and, of course, I hated it. I had to change my dreams around, because I didn't have my boyfriend around anymore. I was mourning the loss of him.

TERRY McCULLOCH

The movers would come in and then we'd spend an entire two days cleaning the house for inspection, the white gloves. That was always fun. I used to joke, I'd think: Nobody comes in here with white gloves. Then I saw the inspector come in one day, and he wore a white glove. And that's how they inspected the houses. It was incredible. The place would be sterile. It was like a hospital. And to this day, my mom cleans like that. We were afraid of the guy.

In Arizona, we got our bunk beds from the Quartermaster. Those quarters were a joke. We had five kids in a three-bedroom house. We stayed in guest housing before our things arrived. Usually it was just like hotel accommodations, a room, maybe a little kitchenette. That was probably the hardest part for my folks, trying to stuff all these kids into these rooms for two weeks while they waited for the house to become available.

MARY CHANDLER

I always knew we were moving. That's just how things were. When we were living at Carlisle Barracks the moving assignments were posted on the same day for everyone on the post, and the next day that was all anybody talked about at the bus stop.

My father would write out a job chart outlining the entire last week that we spent in a house. All ten of us would have four days of cleaning jobs. Then the packers would come for a day, leaving the house full of boxes for a night. This was always fun because we would create tunnels and playhouses out of the boxes all evening and would even sleep in them. The next day the movers would take it all away, and we would be farmed out for the night to friends' houses, and then on day seven, we'd load up in the car and hit the road.

Settling in was like peeling an onion, with one layer of familiar objects being installed in the house at a time. One of the great deprivations, for me, was that we were never allowed to put nails or tape on the walls of any of our houses, so the walls were usually bare in the bedrooms.

NANCY KARACAND

My dad expected that every eighteen months he would have a new assignment, and so we were pretty much geared to that idea.

I used to get excited about moving. There must have been times when we'd walk into the empty house and look at the place and look in all the rooms and all the closets.

When we moved to Mississippi, we hadn't been there very long at all—it was probably during the first summer that we were there—and I asked my father, "How long do we have to stay here, Daddy?"

He said, "Oh, I don't know, maybe a couple of years," and I told him that I didn't like it there. I was looking forward to moving away from Mississippi, and it never happened. By then, I had become so adjusted to the idea of moving that it was a real blow to me to find out that we weren't going anywhere. We ended up in Mississippi. We just stayed, and stayed, and stayed.

RICARDO COTTRELL

We were lucky. We were living in Florida, and our next station was supposed to be North Dakota. There was a guy who had orders to go to Vandenberg Air Force Base in California. His wife was from North Dakota, though, so she was twisting his arm. So he approached my father about making some kind of swap. And

31

naturally my father jumped on it, so we went to California instead of North Dakota.

BARRY JENKINS

My mother was out of her mind. She wouldn't stay put even when we were in the same town. Really, she was so antsy. Once we moved to Rhode Island, we lived in five houses. She just kept moving us around. I'd say, "Goddammit, when is this going to end?" She drove me crazy.

We had to help move. We were given our own Mayflower boxes, and we'd pack all of our junk up. My mother would usually go through saying, "What's this? Get rid of this!" She'd sort of throw out half of our stuff.

Living overseas has to be like a holiday. Maybe it's rough and I don't know what I'm talking about. My mother bitched all the time: "Why can't we go to Europe, or Japan, even?"—or someplace besides Florida or Millington, Tennessee. Those places were out there, so how come we didn't get those stations? Where are those glamorous stations? San Francisco was the coolest place that we got close to. Whidbey Island, Washington, ain't no paradise. It's the dreariest place—I hated it. I got dragged from San Francisco to Whidbey Island. I can remember sitting there thinking, What am I going to do here?

BEVERLY TAYLOR

We always went across country by car, so I've been across the country thirteen times. That was done more for my benefit than for anything else, because the Marine Corps would have paid for any means of transportation that we chose. So I've seen a lot of the United States. We took a different route each time. Some of it was kind of messy. One of our cars was completely demolished in a sandstorm. I can remember outrunning a tornado and seeing it way off in the distance, spiraling. Things like that happened on our trips, inclement weather, or extreme heat. Sometimes when we would come across country back then, the car didn't even have air-conditioning and we'd hang those water coolers outside the windows.

We were in Hawaii for two years to the day, and that was the only time that we ever had a two-year tour of duty anywhere. It was really unusual that he even got that kind of tour of duty; he was stationed at Pearl Harbor. Most of them were eighteen months, because my dad had a tremendous amount of overseas duty, and those tours were always eighteen months, and we'd get transferred when he returned, so we had many eighteen-month increments.

I often wonder about what my mother did with all my things like high school annuals and 45 records and my dolls. I'm sure all of that got pitched.

HELEN PIERSON

We didn't go on vacations. Our vacations were in the car, moving from place to place. We went cross-country about five times. We had to be quiet in the car, and the only way I survived being quiet in the car was to sleep, which is unfortunate: driving across the country, and not really getting to see it.

Since we always had to be at the next station at such and such a time, we would get up at six in the morning. We didn't stop, ate breakfast on the road, and we would drive until midnight and get there as fast as we could. We would go by these historical markers and we would each read a line. My dad would slow down, but not much: can't stop, have to keep going. It wasn't very educational. I don't know how much time they actually allowed you when you got your orders, but I knew that we were always in a hurry. We hardly even had time to go to the bathroom. To this day, when I travel, I stop at every rest stop and every roadside marker.

You could have pets, but you really couldn't have pets. How could you move a pet from place to place like that, or overseas? We always had a pet, but we had to get rid of it before we moved. The worst one was our cat, Fluffy. We had to leave him behind because we were moving to Hawaii. And in Hawaii, there was a dog in the neighborhood that went from family to family.

33

The orders came and we went. I remember regretting another time, when we moved to Montgomery. I had made this beautiful papier-mâché thing and the school wanted to keep it, and I wanted to take it with me. But we couldn't pack it, so I left it. That's the one thing I remember about that move.

GAIL EMERSON

The only sad thing about moving was having to throw away stuff. I was traumatized when they threw away my rock collection, but that's the only trauma I ever suffered. It's not like they were fossils or gems; they were just rocks, but to me they were very important.

I can remember going on an ocean liner called the *Lurline* to Hawaii when I was a little over three. It must have been about 1935. I can remember that very well. They used to serve bouillon and gingersnaps.

The car trips were wonderful. Those were the only vacations that I remember taking: we'd get orders and go across the country. When we had four kids, we couldn't all fit in the car, so two of us would go by train, and the other two would go with my parents in the car. When I was seven, my father and I drove to the East Coast. My mother took my brother and sister on the train, so I was all by myself with my father. In those days, we didn't have air-conditioning. We got up very early in the morning, and drove while it was cool, and slept during the heat of the day. We went to Salt Lake City and I remember buying a bathing suit by myself; my father took me in and introduced me to the saleslady, but I picked it out and bought it, and then we went to Salt Lake. And we went to the Black Hills, and I remember going to Cedar Rapids, Iowa, and drinking two bottles of Orange Crush and throwing up all over his shirt.

DEBBIE WEST

We didn't move enough when I was a kid. I'd heard about the other military kids who got to move everywhere in the world, and oh, how I wanted that. I always resented the fact that my father could go overseas and we couldn't.

It seems to me that I got the worst aspects of being in the service all the way around. I never got any of the excitement of seeing the outside world. I thought it was so unfair that he got to go and we didn't.

SHARON GILMORE

Mom would just tell me, "We have to move." And then we'd have to clean up the whole apartment spotless, spick and span.

She'd have to quit her job as a cocktail waitress at the Acey Deucey Club or wherever she worked and make all new friends. It must have been terrible for her. We didn't have any money, so we'd always drive cross-country in the station wagon. Four days in the station wagon with four kids, and me getting carsick. I hated those trips: the Dramamine, and crayons in the back window melting all over, and sleeping bags in the back. My dad was always stopping off to drink, and we'd just sit in the hot car. We'd be fighting, and my dad would get mad.

We had learned about strip farming in school, and it didn't mean anything to me, but then we'd see it, coming across the country, actually see the strip farming.

BRUCE HUTSON

I can remember coming up over the Rockies, when I was a kid, in the snow, in a 1954 Ford. This must have been about '54 or '55. It was just freezing. Sitting in the backseat, and the windows were kind of frosted up, because the heater just blew out up in front, and we were huddled under these blankets. I can remember looking out from my blankets, out the back window, and just seeing what was going by outside. So much of our lives was just moving.

JULIE MEDINA

Going cross-country, my mom would always make us sit up and look at everything. We never were allowed to sleep in the car. It was always "When are we going to get there?" I remember

35

driving to Washington, D.C., because it seemed like we had been driving forever. Dad said, "First we are going to drive right up into the sky and then we are going to be there." I kept waiting for it. It was a real gray day and the clouds there were so thick and humid. We went up this long hill and we were actually driving into the sky. It was dark, and traffic was bumper to bumper with all the lights on, and we came down out of the clouds and there was Washington, D.C. It was so big, white and sparkling, and the monuments looked so white and pointed. I was just three then. My parents took us to every museum and every monument. I remember my mom being big and pregnant climbing every step to get to the top of the Washington Monument.

Once we were supposed to be going to go to the Philippines. We were very excited. One night my older sister was talking in her sleep, and I remember hearing her saying, "My family is moving to the Philippines and I bought a new pair of stretch pants." They were the hottest things in the world, those stretch pants.

But we got sent to New Mexico. We didn't know where that was; we thought there was only a Mexico. We learned how to spell it—*Albuquerque*. It took me about three months to learn it. We got out the dictionary and looked in encyclopedias about the critters that were there. I was totally prepared to be scared when we moved down there.

I thought I had seen all the bugs that ever lived in the world until we moved to New Mexico. If the bugs would have moved out, the house would have fallen down. They invaded at night; you never let the blankets touch the floor. You learned these things as you went around the country. In the East, you could let the blankets drag the floor, and you could hang your arm down, but in New Mexico you could never let your arm hang, never let your blankets touch the ground. In the morning, you got your shoes, shook them out, put your foot in, and then touched the ground.

RHONDA HEALEY

I had to do my homework to figure it out, and the best I can come up with is seventeen moves for me. I think we made about five major moves from the time I was born until the first grade: major moves, not including apartment changes in the same city.

Vacations, if we weren't on just a weekend camping trip, were always involved with moving. They would pile the five kids, and the gear, and sometimes a dog or whatever pets we had into the car. Eventually they bought a camping trailer. We looked like *The Grapes of Wrath* everywhere we went, with the stuff tied on the car and kids everywhere. We would make a game of it as we were going down the freeway, because we could see people driving past our station wagon, trying to count the kids, and we would all start moving around so they could never get a good count.

We left someone at a gas station a couple of times. We left one of my sisters in Oregon. We had two cars at that time and it was one of those situations where Dad loaded everyone in one car, and Mom loaded everyone else in another, and we were going down the road, counting back and forth in the two cars, and figured out that we had left one, so we turned around and went back and there was poor little Becky, about four years old at the time, sitting on the curb in front of this gas station, just pitiful. She was fairly well traumatized by that, and she still reminds us that we left her in the gas station. They had walkie-talkies in the cars, too, so I am surprised that happened.

We had to put our stuff in storage in Florida. By the time we got it again in California, we were opening boxes full of mildew. Everything had mildewed in that hot weather, and we had to throw away boxes of books, and anything leather, like shoes and belts. I remember my mother opening a box of handbags and belts and just weeping because it was all ruined; there was nothing she could do about it. That was pretty horrible; that was a terrible experience, to have all that stuff in soggy boxes and not know if it could even be salvaged.

The packing up and that kind of thing always went pretty smoothly because the military paid for professional moving companies to come in. So we weren't too involved in that level, although I can pack up a case of dishes, still, in record time. We always laughed about the movers that would pack up full garbage cans and sugar bowls, taped shut carefully. They had taken the

37

garbage cans out of our bedroom and just wrapped them up. We couldn't believe it.

Mostly I remember the tags on the boxes, yellow or whatever colored stickers they put on everything. I remember one time we moved and this guy just stood there scratching his head as he tried to figure out which was his label, amongst all of this collage of moving labels on the back of the furniture. In fact, the hutch that's in my dining room belonged to my parents, and it's been all over the country. The back of it is still covered with all these stickers. I thought about taking them off once, but I thought, no, I just love that, because they remind me of all those crazy moves.

Mother was always real organized: she had her clipboard, and had all the numbers because she had too many things lost or damaged. Damage was always a real struggle.

Because we moved so frequently, it became very simple, and we were all real good and efficient at it. I can remember one move; we literally moved across town or something like that. And we were moved in, had the drapes up, pictures hung, and she served dinner to friends that night. That was almost scary to me, to think you can do that. We used to joke about having an inflatable household: just add water and there it goes.

The worst place was Pensacola, Florida. No, Memphis, Tennessee. Maybe there is a tie there. Those two would go hand in hand for armpit of the earth. The climates were miserable, and the people were ridiculous, and I don't recall any redeeming qualities of either of those places. That northern Florida area is swampy, muggy—it makes you feel like you're in something out of *Deliverance*. That kind of atmosphere with the local people. It was real scary at that time.

We did the majority of our moving on the West Coast, up and down the coast. We had one threat of being moved to Maryland. I can't remember exactly what happened, but it was so real it was a month away or something and the orders were changed at the last minute. We didn't know where it was, what we would do there, or even how to spell it. I couldn't even imagine what the weather or the people would be like there. That would have been a real trauma.

JACK LEMONT

I remember our move to Arizona. My memory of Arizona is houses and no grass, no front yards, just dirt and rocks and tarantulas and scorpions. We had a cat that would catch them and bring them in the house and play with them. And we heard stories of big rattlesnakes out in the desert: "Don't go past this fence because there are sidewinder rattlesnakes out there."

Then when we moved from Arizona the moving truck overturned. It was in a wreck, and I remember my mom was devastated; she just couldn't believe it. We could picture our stuff all over the highway. It really came out fairly well; there was minimal damage. But they lost some handmade furniture: a miniature hutch and a little sink basin my uncle had made for my sister mysteriously disappeared. They paid the claim, but there are some things you can't replace.

ELIZABETH SPIVEY

We moved one time on my birthday. I must have been about eight. I couldn't understand why the whole world did not stop and celebrate my birthday. It was kind of rushed. We had a cake the night before, and then the moving people came the next day, on my birthday. I kept telling them, "Today's my birthday; don't you care?"

LINDA WINSLOW

There was an anecdote in *Reader's Digest* about a Marine wife who thought that her kids were just like any other two kids until she saw them playing with their trucks. They packed up all of the stuff in their trucks and moved it from one dollhouse to the other. And I thought, yeah, that's about right.

When my dad got transferred to Germany he left first. My mother and I took a train trip across the country. That's when I first learned how to play solitaire. All my schoolmates gave me a good-bye party and that amazed me. They gave me a copy of *The Bobbsey Twins on the Deep Blue Sea*. We got to New York, to the port of embarkation, and we took a ship, and I had my birthday on the ship. We spent three and a half years in Germany. And then New York, and Minnesota, and California.

I was all set. I had catalogues from UCLA and USC, I had good grades, and my father came home and said, "We're moving to Enid." And I said, "I'm here, in California; I'm a senior in high school; I'm about to graduate. Why are you doing this to me?" But, being the dutiful daughter, you pack up and go to Enid. And then, when you realize that you're eighteen, you get married.

MICHELLE SLOAN

The first move I can remember making was when I was five and we moved to Fort Benning, Georgia. We lived in these old barracks that were converted into four-family dwellings. They were really sad-looking. But we were allowed to do whatever we wanted with them, whereas usually you can't paint or anything. The people who had lived there before us had painted the walls hot pink. My dad came in and said, "I saw that, and my eyeballs popped out and rolled down the stairs." I thought that was so funny, as a five-year-old. So we painted everything with that green paint, kind of gross. We were allowed to do whatever we wanted, but I guess they provided that green paint for free.

We never had pets when I was little, and we finally got cats. On one trip, my older sister had two little kittens and they were in the Ford, and there was no way those cats were going to get in that car. So they put them in a cardboard box on the roof, and about the time they hit Chicago, the cats popped their heads out of the little air holes. My dad said he couldn't figure out why people were driving by him on the expressway staring.

MARK DENTON

We lived in Quarters 52 at Fort Douglas, Utah, for six and a half years. Everyone called us homesteaders. People thought we were Mormon. They were sandstone houses; we were in the first house on sergeant's row.

We were on the waiting list for one of the four post pianos, and during our second year, we got a piano. You had the use of the piano for as long as you lived there, so we had that piano for years, and when we left, it was like, oh, we can't take it with us. Darn.

CAROLINE BAKER

I had lived in Kansas and Oklahoma so much, and those places all had basements. We had been in that area of the country for so much of my life that it seemed strange that they don't have basements out here, in the Southwest. Every house I'd been in had a basement. All the kids would always go down there and play when we were at the relatives' houses. We had a lot of fun in basements.

DEREK LOWE

Clearing quarters was always a job. I was painting my apartment this weekend, and my landlord said, "Do you know how to paint?" I told him that I've painted many places since I was a little kid. I've done lots of painting.

SHEILA WRIGHT

I hated the moves. I hated it when those men came in, the moving people, and packed up all of our stuff. They would go in our bedrooms and just take everything and put it in boxes, and every time we moved, we lost stuff. I would feel like "Am I ever going to see my dolly again?"

We couldn't pound nails in the walls, because then you had to fill in the holes. We used cotton, because you could fill a hole with it and never tell. My mom always wanted a house all those years where she could pound in nails wherever she wanted to.

We always lived in cul-de-sacs, and the kids all hung out together, and we'd run in and out of all the houses, because you knew everybody and it was free and open. Every house looked the same. I thought it was so cool to go to my grandma's because my grandfather had built their house out of logs, and it was full of nooks and crannies. There were no nooks and crannies in base housing. You'd go to someone else's house and you knew exactly what it would look like inside.

3

Overseas

My mother has a photograph of herself as a young girl in Nicaragua, sitting casually in the living room with her pet deer. That photograph was, to me, the epitome of adventures that were only possible overseas. I had only heard about international life; I spent the majority of my childhood chasing prairie dogs in Kansas.

My family lived in Germany and Japan before I was born, and exotic places like Kumamoto and Oberammergau were mentioned only in the past tense. My oldest brother was born in Japan. Everyone had maids there, and my mother was no exception. The maid washed the diapers in a brand-new Japanese-made wringer washing machine and helped my mother cope with life in a house with primitive heat and a nonexistent hot water supply. My mother tells stories about lying awake at night listening to rats galloping in the space between their ceiling and the floor overhead; she insists that the rats did not run or scurry: they ran the daily double at a full gallop.

German stereos, Oriental wood carvings, and rattan furniture were visible souvenirs of an overseas stint in many of my friends' houses. They would not openly brag, but the fact that they had practically been around the world set them apart from the rest of us. We were jealous of them, in spite of the fact that going overseas meant that you had to get a series of shots.

Military families can be divided into two camps: those who lived overseas and those who never left the United States. For those who lived overseas, the experience was usually the highlight of their childhood. For the others, the chance to be able to tell people that you had come from France or Japan or Germany was something to dream about.

The logistics involved in moving overseas made a cross-country move look like a picnic. Shots and passports and paperwork had to be in order, furniture had to be stored, and the family had to travel to the port of embarkation. Frequently, the fathers were sent ahead, and the mothers brought up the rear alone.

The way that military brats perceived their overseas experiences depended, to a large degree, on the way that their parents reacted. For some families, an overseas tour was an ordeal, a hardship tour, and they preferred to stay within the boundaries of the post, where everyone spoke English. For the majority, though, the time spent overseas was like an extended vacation; they were disdainful of families who never ventured outside the post. They traveled and saw as much of the country as they could, struggled with the language, sampled exotic foods, and relished the cultural differences. They returned to the States as part of the elite international set.

RICARDO COTTRELL

Our first real move was right away. We went to Japan in this ancient aircraft with a propeller.

We lived the majority of the time off the base, among the natives. Our Japanese landlord owned a little piece of land, and he had put up four or five Western-style houses and rented them

44

out to the American families. He was a pretty industrious guy. He put heat in our houses; they used wingtips from jets to store the fuel oil. He had a traditional Japanese-style house without heat. The only time you got warm was at the table where the hibachi was, sitting down on the floor.

My sister and I robbed a little shrine once when we were kids. They would put real small denominations of coins, smaller than pennies, in this little container. We never knew what this thing was: it was just a little open-air building, with a little roof and an altar. I still don't know to this day what was going on there. We went in to take the money out one day. The altar was like a little box, and it had slats, gaps in the box. I reached my fingers through the slats and grabbed something and pulled, and all this black hair came out. We set world records getting home that day. Needless to say, we never went back there.

PETER VARGAS

Moving to Germany was a big transition. We had to get like twelve or thirteen different inoculations over several months. There was a ritual among military children, because everybody was always getting inoculations, and everybody always knew about it. It's not like in civilian life, where your life is private. In the military community, everybody knows. "Oh, Peter's going to get his shots today." So you'd get to school and you have the little cup over your arm from the shot, and that arm was target. The pain from getting the shot was bad enough, but the ridicule and torture from the other kids were even worse. I used to take the cup off the arm where I got the shot, and tape it on my other arm, and then go through the motions every time they hit that arm. It hurt, but it wasn't as bad as getting the other arm hit.

When we got to Germany, my father was waiting there for us. He had already selected a place for us to live, which was something I think my mother would have liked to have had a hand in, but she took it in stride, because this was the way it was done. We were not allowed to live on post at that time, because they just didn't have any housing available, so we lived in a town about twenty klicks away, and that was interesting. It was a

German town that was predominantly American military, even though it was way out in the middle of nowhere.

I got into all kinds of trouble getting used to a new culture. It was "Don't swim in the pool!" Their pools were just dug-out holes with a pipe coming in from a stream, and you could get tetanus. Eating the ice cream—there were a lot of different things we couldn't do.

We were allowed to take our furniture with us, and that was something, because it arrived quite a while later. We'd been there without any furniture at all, kind of camping out on the floor. We had to go out and buy blankets and pillows.

We got settled in pretty well, but that was probably the worst move we made. Taking a bath was a nightmare because there wasn't enough hot water even to really do a couple of people's baths. You had to turn the water on hot all the way and let it drip until it filled the tub. You'd fill it with just pure hot water, no cold water at all, and by the time it filled up, it was cool enough to get into. We fell into the German way of taking baths once a week, and I can remember my father stinking, and my mother, which was just—I just wasn't used to that. She'd been Elizabeth Taylor all my life.

Getting into that completely new culture was really a transition to make. I think it was almost as difficult as going into civilian life from the military.

BRUCE HUTSON

My dad came home one day and said, "Okay, family meeting. I've got two options here: we can move to Washington, D.C., and I'll get this big jump in pay and everything else, or we can move to— *Germany!!!*" He wanted to go back because of the time he had spent over there during and after the war, I think. In fact, we went back to Augsburg, where he had worked as an MP. Of course, as a kid, I didn't really relate to it. He was getting back into something that had happened to him eighteen years before.

I can remember walking through Brooklyn with my dad, because we were at the Brooklyn Navy Yard, trying to find Dramamine. We were from the South, with accents, and we couldn't understand a word this guy was saying to us in Brooklyn. We were going over on the SS *Rhodes,* which had been a troop carrier during the war, so it wasn't a big boat. It was snowing when we left New York. We got on the boat, and the first day was like a big holiday. Everyone came to dinner. The second day, fewer people came to dinner. The third day there were even fewer people. I never missed a meal.

It was a ten-day trip. We were crossing the Atlantic, during the middle of the winter. It got so rough that you'd look out the porthole, and you'd see sky, and then just water. You'd almost swear that the water was going to come right through the porthole. The olives would just roll across the floor; the silverware would be falling. The waiters were great, man; they could handle it. They'd come by and wet down the tablecloths so that nothing could slide. The chairs were bolted to the floor, so we'd lean back in our chairs, and it would catch and keep us from falling over backward. And they put ropes across the big open areas, so that people could hold on to them, because the ship was rocking so much. The propeller would come out of the water, and you could feel the whole boat moving up and down, and back and forth.

We had a GI die on board down in the hold. I pitied those guys, just stacked down there. They were eighteen-, nineteen-year-old guys. This guy who died had apparently been in the hospital with pneumonia, and he had his orders cut to go to Europe. The doctors finally released him and okayed him to travel, and he just died on this boat. He couldn't keep any fluids down, and he dehydrated and just flat died. It happened when we were about halfway over. And we all got real morbid about it: "Oooh, what do they do with the body? It's in the freezer, along with the food." I'm sure that's probably what they did. I doubt that this boat had a morgue on board. So they probably put him in a body bag and put him in a freezer someplace.

We got to Germany, and it was dark, and I can remember coming into the channel. By the time we got to Bremerhaven, it was after midnight. The MPs came on board, and they were checking everyone's orders. My dad had a gun, and he had a license for it because he was a part-time cop in Alabama, so he had this .357 Magnum and a case of bullets. Since he had the license for the gun, that was okay, but they wouldn't let him bring the bullets in. The MPs said, "We're going to have to confiscate the bullets," and my dad said, "Why, so you can use them? No, if I can't have them, you can't have them either." And the MP said, "What are you going to do, throw them out the window?" And my dad said, "Yeah, good idea," and he opened the box and threw them out the window. I thought that was the neatest thing. Yeah, Dad, stuff it in his face. That's the way to do it.

We went to the train station and got on a troop train, headed south. It was one of those snake trains, all sleepers, and the aisles were zigzagged, so that each section was a compartment instead of straight aisles, so you couldn't see all the way through the cars.

When we first arrived, we were in temporary quarters, up on the fourth floor. I think they make you walk up four flights of stairs just to keep you in line. My parents were always so excited about things that we did, so when we moved to this duplex, their attitude was "All right! We're going to move into this duplex, and we're not going to have people up above us, stomping on our ceilings." Since my dad's early days in the Air Force, we hadn't had to live in apartments; we had always had houses. There we were, back in an apartment, with noisy stairwells, and doors slamming, and these little snot-nosed brats around. We just adjusted to it.

We stored a lot of our furniture and things before we went over, because everything was supplied over there, Quartermaster stuff, and it was wonderful. Big old clunky stuff. Great cooking utensils. So we had this whole set of dishes and silverware and everything was from the Quartermaster.

I can remember coming home for lunch. Mom would have soup and sandwiches ready, and the radio would be playing. The first thing my dad did was buy one of those nice Grundig German radios that had shortwave on it. So we'd listen to AFN during lunch and they'd be playing music. I can remember hearing "You've Lost That Loving Feeling" by the Righteous Brothers. I can remember coming into this apartment, and sitting at the table, and eating this soup out of these flat-bottomed bowls, and looking out this huge window onto the back courtyard.

And of course, all I saw were more apartments, but I was in Germany!

Everything was so new: all the different languages we heard and around us this industrialized country. Coming from the South, you don't see a lot of the smokestacks and stuff. All of a sudden, we were in a German town, smelling the diesel. That's still with me. If I'm downtown or somewhere, and a diesel goes by, I take a whiff and just flash back to Europe immediately. A couple of weeks ago I was downtown with a guy who also lived in Germany, and he said the same thing about the smell of diesel. It was interesting, to find someone else with that shared sensory memory.

We went on trips. We never really considered them vacations. We were living in Europe: every time you go out your front door, it's a vacation. On weekends we'd go skiing in the Alps. Our cousin William had come over to visit, so there were three boys in the backseat of this Volkswagen fastback and my parents. We traveled all the way through Germany, down through Italy, to Monaco, and down the coast of Spain.

Our cousin was from Ohio, and he had this closed-mind attitude, and we were just totally different. We were just out on the coast enjoying ourselves, eating dinner at nine o'clock every night. It was wonderful. We ate calamari and squid and we just loved it. My parents were saying, "Isn't this great?" And we were saying, "Yeah!" And here's William, saying, "I want a hamburger. I don't like this food; it's weird; it's too foreign." And we felt like, no, you're the foreigner, William. He wanted to go to the air base in the worst way. So we drove out to the air base. So my cousin got a hamburger and french fries and a milk shake. And we liked it, but to William, it was heaven. I never felt like that.

CATHY ATCHISON

In Japan, we lived in Yokohama, and it was a little bit different than some of the other bases in foreign countries. There were several housing areas. They were fenced, but not guarded, so you could go into the housing areas without any identification. The PX and the theater and some of the other facilities also were not guarded. So it was a little bit more open when I was there than it was in some of the other bases, where all of the housing areas are within the confines of the base.

One of the things that they offered over there were summer classes. They had a huge selection of summer classes for kids in Japanese traditional arts, and I took origami lessons, tsumi painting, flower arranging, doll making, and tennis lessons.

I do remember that in Japan there was a lot of purchasing going on. My father bought a component stereo system—we're talking top-of-the-line Japanese products, with a hand-built cabinet for the whole thing to go into—and my mother designed furniture and had it built.

TIM BROCKWAY

I was into Elvis Presley when we went to Europe, at the same time he had just gone into the Army. When we first arrived, the GI who drove us to our quarters told us that he had driven Elvis Presley to his quarters, too.

BRAD HOLMES

It was nice to be in France as a kid. We were in a real small town in northern France, about two hundred miles away from Paris. This was before de Gaulle threw all the Air Force bases out of France, in 1958, '59, '60, around then. My dad was back there for almost a year.

We flew over there to meet him, and we had to live in this tiny little trailer. The trailers had mice in them. I had to sleep in the same bed with my brother, in bunk beds, and my sister slept in the other bed. It was kind of exciting for us.

There wasn't much at the base in France, other than the field, and some housing, and Quonset huts, and they had a few buildings. The Quonset huts were always being flooded out. I went to kindergarten in a Quonset hut.

I remember going out and seeing the civilians ride through the town. The women washed their clothes in the river; they didn't have washing machines. We would go into the barns and talk to the farmers while they milked the cows, and we would buy French bread and stuff like that. And we'd put nails in big sticks and go rat hunting. There were a lot of mice—you'd go pull boards up and see the rats and mice running around—and we'd try to stick them with our sticks. That was a lot of fun.

We'd drive around in the hills around France and find old bunkers from the war, and we'd find parts of guns, and parts of jeeps and tanks and stuff. Every once in a while we'd find bullets and some of them were live. I remember some kids at school hammered some ammunition that they found. I think one of them died, and the other two lost an eye or a hand. I never found much of anything that was dangerous, but I was always going through that stuff. The military dumped stuff, or when there were inspections, they'd hide a lot of stuff for some reason. They'd always take it in trucks and drive it out in the woods and park it. They'd never lock it. We'd go out in the woods and find all this military equipment, sonar and radar detecting things, radio stuff. We'd always twist every knob that was available, and open all the drawers, and pull everything else out. We did that a bunch of times. It was wild.

PAULA HOLMES

After Texas we moved to Taiwan. The housing wasn't even on base; it was in a compound. It looked like the Alamo. It was set somewhere in between the town of Taipei and the base, so it was kind of in the middle of nowhere. Before we moved into the housing, I think we lived in a missionary's house, as a temporary thing. To get there, we had to go down an unpaved alley, and the Chinese people lived there, in this alley, outdoors. They were very, very poor. They were always outside cooking, and the kids would be running around playing. And here we came along in this big car, and we had light hair, and everyone stared at us.

We lived in this big compound, like a big estate, all enclosed by a big fence with broken glass along the top. The first couple of months we didn't even have any of our furniture. There was a small cottage next to our house, and a Chinese family was our maid and gardener. The maid would come in and clean, but we

51

didn't have our furniture. We had base furniture, and Army blankets on our beds. I remember being sick a lot. The food didn't agree with me.

DEREK LOWE

My first ID card came when we had to go to Germany, when I was eight, in 1959. And that was when we got our first dog tags, too, because this was just before the Berlin Wall thing, before we went over to Germany. That was a real turn-on, living in Germany. We lived in Augsburg until I was twelve. We went to the military schools and learned German. We were living on the military installations, but it wasn't really separate. You could cross the street and be on the economy. That period of time is one of the most fond memories in my life. I really loved Germany.

When we first got there, because it was an emergency transfer, they moved us into these empty maid's quarters in the high-rise apartment buildings. It was really interesting to live in this eighteen-room apartment. We put the train set in one room, and we each had our own bedrooms.

When we got to Germany, all of our furniture was from the Quartermaster. You could get these pale green dishes, and in Germany that stuff was all available and very prevalent in the households; I think they wanted to minimize the shipping. You had a limit on how much you were allowed to take over there depending on your rank and the size of your family.

Once we moved into the regular housing, we'd walk through the German community to get to school. My buddies and I, Bobby and Gordon, would get on our bikes and just ride out into the German countryside. Again, it was with that sense of security, even though the Russians were literally right up the road.

Our dads were always on alert, and we were always having bomb shelter alerts, and air raid drills, and we had to keep C rations under the bed, and emergency supplies. They had all the families involved in evacuation procedures. And at the same time, there was this real sense of well-being as a child.

I hoarded the C rations. They always came in those big

brown boxes. I snuck in there and got into the cinnamon roll cans. It was the kind of can with a key, and I cut my finger. My mother wanted to know how I cut my finger, and the ultimate thing was "*Do not* get into the C rations" because those were for emergencies. But all those goodies were in there, and it was just too much to resist. It was part of the adventure.

All GIs came back from Germany with a stereo and a baby, at least, and maybe a camera. There was this routine, when you go overseas. We got china, the Dresdenware, and silverware. I also became aware of the black market economy, because that was quite prevalent in Germany. We had a maid, and we would pay her with ice cream from the commissary.

NANCY KARACAND

We lived off base in Taiwan. My dad was real definite about that. He didn't want us to live on base with all the other families, because he wanted us to know what the culture was like and be a part of it, and not separate ourselves as if we were better than other people. He always had the philosophy that we should see other people as equals, and not look down on them.

When we got to Taiwan, the first place we rented was not very well put together, and I just vaguely remember that we were kind of cramped there. The houseboy and his wife lived in the house with us, and they were sort of crammed behind some kind of sliding straw door. I just vaguely remember that, that it was weird. He and his wife were back there, somewhere, and I always wanted to see, and we weren't supposed to go back there.

We lived in an interesting house in Taiwan. It was a schoolhouse that had been converted into a family home. There was a big bamboo fence around it that you couldn't see over. We had a big yard, and we had a turkey and some other animals. It was an interesting house: the bedrooms were separated by those rice-paper sliding doors. My oldest sister got to have the only real room in the house, the only room with real walls. The servant's quarters were out behind the house.

It sounds so awful to say that we had servants, but everyone did, and I like to think that we treated ours particularly well.

Who knows if we did or not. It was slave labor, let's face it, but it probably paid as much money as, if not more than, they made anywhere else. We got so attached to one of our maids that when we left Taiwan we wanted to bring her back with us, and my dad wanted to put her through college. She was about eighteen, and she was ready to do it and then decided that she couldn't leave her family.

There was a Taiwanese family across the street who lived in a two-room shack with six kids. There was one bed for the parents, and all the kids slept on another large mat that was elevated off the floor, but it was just a mat. Their prize possession was a transistor radio. They didn't have indoor plumbing—they had the bendo ditches, which was basically just an open sewer, a ditch on the side of the road—and I remember seeing the kids urinate in the ditch. We just knew that was different, and we weren't supposed to do that.

We would play with the kids, and sometimes we would ask if they could come in the yard with us. Usually we kept within our own yard, but we could go out if one of my older sisters was out there with us. We could go and play with some of the other kids in the neighborhood, the natives. There were other, larger homes in our neighborhood, too, but I particularly remember the people across the street.

Taiwan was tropical, and they had the rainy season, and it can get really stormy. They had a lot of earthquakes, and I can remember those. I was out in the yard on my tricycle during one of them, and my mother came out on the porch. I just remember everything moving, and I was wondering what was going on, and if this was something terrible. It was kind of exciting, actually. We moved from Taiwan to Minnesota, from the tropics to three, four feet of snow in the wintertime.

MARK DENTON

The Denmark move came out of the blue. We'd been figuring that one of two things was going to happen: we were either going to stay the rest of our time in Salt Lake, or they were going to do something really strange to us. When we got the Denmark orders, it was like "Surprise! You're going to Europe!"

We flew from Seattle to London, London to Hamburg, Hamburg to Copenhagen. We got off a 707 in London and took a DC-3 to Copenhagen. There were six rows of seats on this little plane. My dad met us at the airport in Copenhagen, and we spent the night there and then left for Hjerting in the morning. We got on a train, and it was horrible—five hours, slamming back and forth—and then they loaded the railroad car onto the ferry. I was twelve years old, and, as my mom continually wants to remind me, I was old enough to know what we were doing. She's told me that a hundred times.

My dad had been there for a couple of weeks, and he was already an expert on Denmark. He was so proud of the fact that he knew some words, and he could order off a menu and know what he was getting. We stopped at a little sidewalk café and he bought us pops. It wasn't Coke; it was something weird, and it came in bottles with resealable rubber stoppers that you pried up.

We had a 1956 Chevrolet four-door when we got to Denmark, and of course, we were "rich Americans," because we had that big car. The people who told us we were rich Americans were driving Mercedeses. My dad got to be good friends with Hans, the guy who owned the service station in town, and he did all the work on the car for us, out of love for that car. He normally worked on all the Mercedeses and Volkswagens in town, and then my dad would bring in our big Chevy.

My dad went to Hans one day and said, "We're going to make a barbecue." And Hans said, "Vat's that?" My dad took him a thirty-gallon oil drum, and he split it in half and hinged it and built a rack for it. Then we had to go and find charcoal, and of course, no one knew what charcoal was. So my dad went to a small steel refinery and bought some stuff that was almost charcoal in twenty-pound bags.

This was in 1962, and the Mormons had two-man teams of missionaries all over Europe. One of the teams knocked on our door, just weeks after we arrived in Denmark from Salt Lake, so we knew the Mormon religion. These kids were just eighteen, nineteen years old, off on their missions. They started in with some speech in very broken Danish, and my mom said, "Wait a minute, are you Americans?" And they said, "Yeah!" We just said, look, we don't want to be Mormons, but come on over and we'll have a barbecue. We got to be really popular. The team who was going out would tell the new guys about our family. We had a barbecue for about thirty of them once. We put hamburgers on the grill and gave them peanut butter, which they hadn't seen in months.

We had the biggest freezer in Denmark. Everyone else in Denmark just had a little bitty icebox, and they'd go to the store every day and buy just what they needed for that night's meal. When we left we decided to sell the freezer, and the only place that wanted it was the Palazzo Hotel. It was a basic twenty-cubic-foot freezer, no big deal, but they saw it as some sort of major hotel fixture, this "huge" freezer for the whole hotel. My buddy, Kristian, came into our house one day, and saw our huge American refrigerator, just a plain old GE, and he just freaked out. He couldn't understand why we had so much food in the house all the time.

About once a month, we would get what we called a care package from Copenhagen. It would have Miracle Whip and peanut butter and lettuce—the lettuce would be wasted when we got it—and cottage cheese. The packages were boxed and shipped out of the embassy in Copenhagen. Once a month, my dad would call in and tell them what we wanted, and they'd ship as much as they could from our list and throw in whatever else sounded good. It was like part of our living allowance, kind of like pay. The closest PX and commissary were in Bremerhaven, a six-hour drive away.

They didn't have cottage cheese in Denmark. So my dad went to this dairy to see if he could put together a contract with the owner of the dairy and says, "We want you to take a huge vat full of milk, warm it up to 110 degrees, throw germs in and let it cook for about two days, slice up the curds, and add a little more milk, and package it." They thought he was absolutely crazy. Needless to say, we didn't get cottage cheese.

In 1962, when we went to Denmark, it was about the time when Kennedy went to Europe and visited Berlin, and we were sitting in Denmark figuring, man, any day the cold war's going to escalate. Then we went to Germany, sixty miles from the East German border. I was a Boy Scout patrol leader, and one time four of us went out into the woods on an overnight camp-out. We were always on post, but we didn't know where we were at times. We found a nice flat place and set up our camp.

We kept hearing this really strange humming sound, and we couldn't figure out what the heck it was. Next morning we got up and noticed that the radar for a missile site was about seventy-five yards away from our camp. We didn't know that we had camped right underneath it because we'd never been in that area before. The sound we'd been hearing was the radar dish going around. For all I know, we're all sterile. A few minutes later, this MP and his German shepherd came up to our tent, and he said, "What are you boys doing here?" We were in a clear fire area, an area that was off-limits. If the site had been attacked, we were in the position to be mowed down. We didn't know. It was just a nice flat piece of ground. I said, "Gee, sir, I'm sorry. We're the Comanche Patrol." I heard later that my dad had been told that I had camped near a missile site.

JEFFREY TAVARES

When we were coming back from Heidelberg, I got lost at JFK. I'll never forget that. I was seven. My mom went in the bathroom and I couldn't find her. I don't know if the airport is as big as I remember, but to me, it was like I was an ant in the Astrodome.

There's a dog I remember in Germany, a red dog, and his name was R.A., for "Regular Army." Every time somebody would move, R.A. would have to stay, so they would have to find another home for him because you couldn't ship the dog. So we wound up with him for a while. A big dog in Germany just doesn't work in the apartments.

ROBERT BLAKE

We went via U.S. Navy transport, the USS *Henderson*, from San Francisco to Corinto [Nicaragua] in 1929. I remember the ship coming into Corinto harbor; it was very shallow. When I read about it being mined today, I remember watching. It was so shallow they had to take soundings. It was very slow going. If you watch the Navy ships compared to commercial ships, they move very slowly into the harbor. For commercial ships, time is money. In the Navy, if the ship goes aground or hits something, the captain never gets promoted, and the guy on watch never gets promoted, and it's pretty much the end of his career.

That was my first trip through the Panama Canal. We came back up the East Coast and stopped at Port-au-Prince on the way, and then the *Henderson* went right up the Potomac River and docked at Quantico, the Marine base. I went down there for a visit about four years ago, and the dock is still there, but transports don't make their way up the Potomac anymore.

When we left San Francisco, I was alone with my mother. My father was battalion commander, and he was in charge of the debarkation. From then on he was with us the whole time. It was a really nice way to make a move, as opposed to today's method of flying, because you were on the ship long enough for a family to get reunited. In this particular case, Dad had been away for eighteen months, which doesn't sound like a terribly long time, and it isn't, compared to people being separated for years, like during World War II. But it's long enough, particularly for a kid at that age. When he left I was six and a half years old, and when we picked him up again, I was eight. In peacetime, they run the transports just like a cruise ship, although it was not quite as elegant. We had a swimming pool on the ship, a hatch with a piece of canvas put down the hatch. The troops were in their quarters, and the families were like passengers. We had outdoor movies. The dining room had two services, and the Filipino mess boy came around and rang the gong.

We did live overseas. We lived in Spain for a year, during the first year of the original Spanish Republic. In fact, we were on the ship when King Alfonso XIII abdicated, and I think, had we not been at sea, they would not have let the men go. Four years later we spent two years in Panama. We actually lived in Panama because there were no Navy quarters in the Canal Zone. The squadron, which was a little "show the flag" type operation, had a cruiser and two destroyers. It was based in Balboa. The ships themselves were switched every year, so that most of the Navy people did not bring their families. But for the admiral's staff and the Marine detachment, it was a two-year mission. The admiral did not bring his wife, but several of his Navy staff officers did, and the Marines who were married had their families. There were maybe, all told, half a dozen families and no quarters.

What we did was rent a place in town, and that worked out very well. Our neighbors were Panamanians and foreign diplomats and some Americans working down there. We were not cooped up in the little all-American enclave. The civilian employees at the Canal would just stay there, and even though it was a tiny little place, they would rarely go into Panama City. They had everything that they needed—their commissaries, their clubs, their churches—everything was right there in the Zone. They thought it was too much of a hassle to go to Panama even though, in some cases, it was right across the street.

The boundary line at that time, between Panama City and the city of Balboa, was a street, Fourth of July Avenue. One side was in Balboa and the other was in the Canal Zone. There were no border guards; it was just as simple as crossing the street.

I was in high school, and I commuted by streetcar from the residential area of Panama right through downtown Panama itself, through the red light district and into the terminal in Balboa. When the squadron was in port, I would generally ride to school with my father and take the streetcar home. About half of the student body were children of Canal employees, and another third were military kids, and they had regular school buses that brought them from the various different posts. But for people living in Panama, like we did, it was like going to school in New York. You got there your own way; they didn't send buses. So that was one year in Spain, two years in Panama.

MICHELLE SLOAN

I was four when we moved to Okinawa. I remember that because I was worried because we had to meet my dad there, and there were all the men in green uniforms. We lived on Georgia Loop. I remember the cockroaches. And we had maids there. The maids went barefoot, and they stepped on the bugs with their bare feet. They crunched. I guess if you'd lived there all your life, it was no big deal.

My mother would get her hair and nails done every week. She belonged to all these clubs, living like a really rich woman. She would go to the flower decorating clubs and the cake decorating clubs, and she was a volunteer, so we always stayed home with the maids.

Our house in Okinawa was different. Some of the housing at Fort Ord was kind of like it. They were painted pastel colors; ours was blue, and some were pink, and some were yellow or green. We had to put rags all around the doors during the typhoons, because water would always seep in.

SHEILA WRIGHT

My aunt and uncle had lived in Europe, and my cousins had told us horror stories about living overseas, so we didn't want to go to France. Stories about the kids pushing them and not being very nice. They didn't live on base; they lived off base in this little icky apartment, and nobody talked to them, because they couldn't understand a word they said. So we were like "Oh my God, no way do we want to go overseas."

LINDA WINSLOW

I think that there was table talk that we were going to be transferred. I don't remember being traumatized by it, but they didn't give me any kind of moral or intellectual support about what to expect, not even "We're going to Germany, and the people speak German."

In Germany, I had my raising of consciousness about the black market and so forth. At that point, in 1953, we were still an army of occupation. It wasn't until 1955 that we were visitors in the country. All of the officers' wives and most of the higher-ranking NCOs' wives had maids, usually single German women with kids. They lived in the basements, in these maid's quarters.

We had a woman who must have been sixty, and she sold crystal and cuckoo clocks. Everybody knew that she didn't have any pockets in her coats; the pockets were cut open, for stashing coffee and peanut butter. She was the black market lady. They had a German national, usually a female, at the gate along with the Air Policemen. Since this woman went to the officers' quarters, including the commanding general's quarters, she never got searched. Everyone knew what she was doing.

I remember the first time that I found out that my father was not the shiny-brass honest person that he was supposed to be. The officers' quarters were issued Rosenthal china, and when the packers came, my father said, "That's ours." And this airman knew what was going on, but there was a major standing in front of him. And he said, "This is yours, sir?" And my father said, "Yep, yep."

He was a model railroad freak, and he built three of these huge tables together with HO-scale model railroad with the papier-mâché. It was always shipped with us as "professional military tactical equipment." You were allowed so much weight for household goods, and you were allowed so much weight for your professional books. This model railroad was a "war scenario," and as long as you'd say it's true, and sign your name, you'd get away with it. So maybe I learned to kind of slip and slide through the system a little bit, just by watching how it was done.

Once in Erding, the next-door neighbor knocked on our door and said, "The wife and I are taking a field trip; would your daughter like to go along?" So my parents were like, sure, go along, so they could have some time alone. You know where they took me? Dachau, the concentration camp. This was a wonderful trip, for a fifth-grade kid to go see the gas chambers? I think that increased my ambivalence about German nationals.

My father had a friend who was a fighter pilot during the war, on the German side. When we got transferred to New York, Hans gave my father this silver medal with the Luftwaffe bird and the swastika on it, that he got for shooting down ten Allied planes during the war. And I'm going, "Wait a minute, this is a bad guy, and you're impressed that he gave you this?" And my father went, "You don't understand how war works."

GEORGE DEXTER

We lived in the southern Philippines when I was three, until I was six years old, so my first memories of life are of the Philippines. That was the only time that we lived overseas. We lived on a very pretty old Spanish fort that the Americans had taken over.

They didn't have anything like an officers' club, but the officers owned a launch and they used to go out to the surrounding islands for luaus and picnics. My folks really enjoyed it there. We could go swimming practically in our backyard. The house was built right next to the seawall. I can remember a big storm, with waves that came in and smashed waves up on the houses, all the way up to the tile roofs of these two-story houses.

In 1930, when I was six years old, we came back from the Philippines to go to Iowa. I don't know that I sensed that it was different when I was going through it, but when I got to Iowa, I realized that the kids there had never been outside town. I realized then that it was pretty unusual; I went, hey, this was a great experience. We had gone by ship to China and then up to Peking, and one day we went up to the Great Wall. We rode on flatcars, the open railroad cars, and then my brother and I were carried in sedan chairs.

My folks took lots and lots of pictures of us in China. My brother has the pictures now. We visited all of the temples there. That was during the time of the warlords in China and everything was going to pot, so we have these pictures of the great temples and there's grass growing through the cracks in the buildings.

4

Making Friends

Family legend has it that I was an "afterthought," coming along when my brothers were teenagers and my older sister was seven. My parents then decided to have my younger sister, less than two years later, to keep me company. People used to think my sister and I were twins because we were so close in age and my mother frequently dressed us in matching outfits.

Much to my mother's chagrin, we were shy. She literally had to drag us out of the house and tell us to "Go make friends!" We did, eventually, make friends. And as hard as it had been to get out there and make those initial overtures, it was worse to leave: we'd have to do it all over again as soon as we got to the next place.

My sister and I always cried when we drove through the gates of a post for the last time. My mother would turn around from the front seat and try to cheer us up, but her assurances that we would make new friends and could write to our old ones only made us feel worse. We were inconsolable for the first few hours, but as the miles passed, our tears would stop. At least we had each other. My parents' scheme to provide me with a companion worked. I shudder to think of what it would have been like to be an only child, for when I think back about my childhood friends, my sister is the first person to appear in my memories.

I always exchanged solemn vows with my friends to stay in touch forever. I never made a conscious decision to stop corresponding with any of my friends, but it was difficult to keep track of them when we were moving every year. Last fall, after talking to several military brats and hearing that they had not kept in touch with friends either, I went to the public library and found Becky, one of my old friends, in the first telephone book that I opened. Becky and I were in the same class in third grade, and we knew each other for only a year, but for whatever reason, she was, in my mind, the best friend I ever had. I don't remember who moved away first, but we exchanged letters for several years before we lost track of each other. It was sheer luck that I found her again. We talked on the telephone and worked our way forward through the years that have elapsed since third grade and promised, again, to stay in touch.

One woman told me, "My family was my support system instead of my friends, because my so-called friends were here one day and gone the next." With or without siblings to ease the transition into a new life in a new place, military brats went out and made friends. Despite the knowledge that a move would eventually sever the pleasures of a "best friend," military brats did not give up. The legendary camaraderie among soldiers on the battlefields extended to military families. Their friendships were forged quickly, often before the moving van was unloaded.

"It seemed like any time you moved into a place, there was always a group of kids looking to see if there were any kids in the new family. It always seemed like it took a while, but that group would get together and come and talk to you and see what rank your dad was, and what your dad did, and if you had any bicycles."

But for military brats, friendships were a process and not an end in themselves, and if, years later, they cannot remember the names of their friends, they shrug and continue with the story.

Friends are often discussed with a fond detachment. Having a best friend somewhere was like having a good set of quarters, just another memory of a place where they had lived for a year or two.

TERRY McCULLOCH

Whenever we'd go to the new house, we'd go in, and it'd be a bare place, and we'd walk through, and then the folks would say, "Okay, this is it," it had been assigned to us, or whatever.

I always used to go into the rooms and play make-believe. I would sit there and act like I was already moved into this bedroom and everything, and my girlfriend was knocking on the door, and we were going to go to the pool or go play, and I'd go, "Okay, I'll be right there!" And I'd have my swimsuit all rolled up in my towel. I'd play this whole make-believe game in every room. I'd go in there by myself, and I'd act. I'd just make believe that I was already living there, and I already had my friends, because I never had a fear that I wouldn't find any friends. People on base are extremely friendly. It takes a very different kind of kid not to make friends.

I've never had a fear of meeting new friends or meeting people. It's so easy. Of course, I had the benefit of always having my sister Sandy. Sandy was my best friend. We did everything together. We had the same friends. It was just us, against them or with them. I was never really alone, because Sandy was always there, and I was there for her. Wherever we went, we always made friends right away.

MARK DENTON

When we lived in Salt Lake, it was such a mellow, laid-back small post that everybody got along with everybody, and there was no real division because of rank. They had a little two-lane bowling alley there and a pool, and we used to hang out there constantly. I hung out with Bobby, who was a sergeant's kid. His family was there for four years, during the six years that we were there. And Larry, whose dad was the post commander. And there was a kid named Tommy, whose dad was a civilian employee working on the post. It was about a mile up the canyon to Tommy's house, on our bicycles. We'd go up there and catch salamanders and frogs, and we'd bring them to school the next day.

Bobby and Tommy were my best buddies ever. There was a stream coming down from the reservoir that ran right through the post. We built rafts and dams and did the basic Tom Sawyer kind of stuff. We had a swing from a tree, and we'd swing out from it and drop into the water. And we had the raft tethered up the creek, and we'd all get on it, and the three of us would weigh too much, and it would sink. Those were some of the best times.

In Denmark, my sister was the only American kid to talk to. I did make friends with a Danish kid, and we got to be pretty good buddies. Had there been a stream there, we would have built a dam and done all that kid stuff.

ELIZABETH SPIVEY

Left to my own devices, I would have been shy. But I guess I felt the need to at least introduce myself or make the first overture to play with someone. If I saw a kid down the street, and I really wanted to go play, I'd just kind of amble down the street and take my marbles along, or my Barbie doll, and try to strike up a conversation. Probably I would have been a shy person, but I didn't have that option. It probably made me a more outgoing person than I would have been otherwise. I was outgoing enough to make new friends wherever we went, to adjust, and to find my place within the social crowd at school.

SHEILA WRIGHT

All the kids were in the same situation, and you all could feel for each other. If somebody got transferred, everybody felt bad and knew what being transferred meant. Kids in civilian life were like "You're being transferred? Well, you haven't been here long." Kids in the military were like "Oh, no! Well, where are you going? Oh, we lived there; that's a neat base."

I was real shy, real reserved; I kind of stood back and watched. My sister was real outgoing, and I met kids through her more than on my own. It was so hard for me, every time, to have to make new friends and see my sisters have no problems and have tons of friends while I just stayed in the house. When I was in seventh grade, I broke my ankle, so then I made lots of friends, because everybody wanted to sign my cast, and all of a sudden I had all these friends. So I did better once we had lived there for a couple of years.

If you live on base, you feel like "Let's make friends really fast, because we don't know how long we have." But off base, it was real hard. Those were the people we looked for first, the other Air Force families: "Oh, good, I saw her dad leaving for work in his uniform. Oh, good, somebody to go to the base with!" I remember my friend Tammy. Both of our families lived off base, and we met at school, and we were so excited that her dad was in the Air Force, too, because then we had something in common right there. Her dad worked with my dad, so my parents became friends with her parents.

We had another friend who lived next door to us in the duplexes at Williams. Our bedrooms were across from each other, and the walls were so thin we could do Morse code to each other. She didn't have any brothers and sisters, so we were all friends with her. I remember she had long hair and I just loved her hair. She cried when we told her that we had been transferred. We were all upset, but she was really upset, because they were going to be there for another year or so. She didn't want some weirdos moving in next to her that she couldn't play with or do Morse code with at two o'clock in the morning.

GAIL EMERSON

I can remember faces now, but not names. But you know, when you're growing up in it, you don't know it's different. It's the way things are. I have extremely vivid memories going way back of specific places and things happening. I can remember playing marbles with other kids in Virginia; I can remember things we did when we played in the vacant lots and the woods and stuff.

We lived in the quarters in Annapolis, and we got together with other kids who lived in our big brick apartment building, and we'd go down to the basement. It was dark down there, and we would tell ghost stories. I can remember skating on the pond there. There was a railroad that ran through Annapolis, and we'd go out with the kids and put rocks on the railroad track and come back and see them squashed to powder. And of course we would filch money from our parents and hike through the woods to this little store where they sold penny candy and stuff. I can remember all kinds of stuff that far back, and forward, if I think about it.

But the memories are not of one place: they're just flashes, and the place is isolated. You don't see the land around it. You just see the little scene that encloses where you were at the time it was going on.

RICARDO COTTRELL

You got tired of being the new kid all the time. There's a place where personality and conditioning—there's a line there, and I don't know what it is, where you look people over or whatever. People have always thought that I'm aloof or something, because I check out who's who and decide where my place is going to be, and who I'm going to run with or whatever. You always have to find your niche. You have to be kind of a half-assed good judge of character. You don't always make the right choices, but you learn. I didn't make a lot of friends. I always had a few friends. Sometimes they were good, and sometimes I don't know. There were people that I would have been better off not knowing, but I learned.

JACK LEMONT

I run into people and they say, "I've known this guy or girl since elementary school or junior high." I have never had that. It bothers me more now, the last few years, than it did then. My friends are few, and they're scattered all over the United States. I do have some friends I have met over the last few years who I keep in contact with.

I remember writing a couple of letters. You try for a while. I remember the whole classroom wrote me a letter from Missouri when I moved to Texas. I got a whole package of letters, and that was pretty neat. But that was the only communication I have had. You don't know what happened to them, but you wonder sometimes where they are, what they are doing.

JEFFREY TAVARES

One thing I do know about is that military kids don't make a lot of friends. Me, I stuck to maybe one. Because if you don't make a lot of friends, you don't have to break it off when you move. You always knew that was going to happen. So I really either stuck to myself or I had just one friend.

The only time I ever felt like a normal kid was when my dad went to Vietnam and we stayed in Michigan when I was in third grade. I was treated like a civilian there: I was in a civilian school, and I was living with my grandparents. I could see the bond with the other children; I could really see myself just looking in. I can remember thinking: Poor me. I knew my dad was coming home and we were going somewhere.

I remember one girl from third grade. We got to be good friends and kind of had the third grade crush. Then when we moved back when my dad retired, I wound up meeting her again. It was still different, because I still knew that I wasn't going to stay. Even though my parents were retired and said, "This is where we're going to live," I knew better, so I still wouldn't let people get real close.

I still have a girl who I pen pal with. We met in sixth grade. We've kept track of each other over all these years. We probably communicate maybe four times a year. It's kind of fun. I enjoy hearing from her. It makes you feel good to go back and find a little bit of your past, especially when it's as mixed up as the military can make it.

MICHELLE SLOAN

My mom always had to go to Hail and Farewells. I didn't know, until I got older, that it was three different words. I always thought it was one word: Hailandfarewell. It was the Officers'

Wives Club thing to welcome the new people and say good-bye to the ones who were leaving. They were always coming and going. My mom was always pretty social and involved with a lot of things like that, especially in Germany, because my dad was a battalion CO, and she had his officers' wives over for coffees and teas and all kinds of stuff.

The whole neighborhood, all the kids, had welcoming committees just like our parents had. We'd all go over and sit around and watch when new people moved in.

It was always sad, but it was fun to go, too. Especially when you got older, you would think things like, I was just this quiet-little-mouse person here, but I'm going to be really cool at the new school and start all over. It never worked. You're always the same person, but you always have these grand ideas.

TIM BROCKWAY

My father has friends that he basically grew up with, and I don't have any. There are really no lasting friends. My friend Mark and I had pretty good times for a year in Fort Bliss. We had our paper routes, and we alternated days with our older brothers. We had hot chocolate and our little lanterns.

As a kid, moving was an issue. Perhaps it prevented you from opening up to people, because you knew that you were just going to move real soon, no reason to get friendly. And if you had a problem, you didn't have to deal with it, because you were going to get transferred anyway, so that was going to solve it. So you never had to resolve it. Personal problems, dilemmas with other people—you never had to say you were sorry or learn from it, because by virtue of being transferred, it ceased to be an issue. It's silly, but that was the mentality of a child who was moving all the time.

The people I met after we moved off base, when I started playing in a rock-and-roll band, had some friends they had grown up with all along. I envied that a little bit. They had grown up together and played together and gone to each other's birthday parties when they were kids. You definitely couldn't compete with friends based on that alone. There were times when I'd have liked to be closer with a particular person, but there was no way, because they went back so far with other people. If there was any competition in friendship, you were going to lose out to some-body who had been around. I envied that. You work all these things out, so it's not a big issue now.

JOHN ROWAN

I remember having the fantasy when things weren't working out: we'll move, and I'll think up a nickname; I'll go out for the football team, and if they don't like me, I'll change my personality; I'll be funnier and more outgoing; I'll be six inches taller and have blond hair. It never worked. Never worked.

When we moved from Florida, when I was in my junior year of high school, it was difficult. But by that time, I'd gotten so accustomed to that happening, and so prepared for it, it never really occurred to me to try to maintain contact or to expect that a relationship was going to continue. I think I was more concerned about where we were going, rather than about leaving my friends. In that sense, if we had been moving to someplace exciting, I don't think I would have cared much at all.

The actual leaving was never that traumatic, except after my junior year of high school, when I had a premonition that it was going to be difficult. During the time we were in Florida, I started feeling more self-confident and having a lot of friends, being accepted, having girlfriends. So as I was getting ready to leave there, that's the first time that I looked back and was able to see that I had changed a lot, in a positive way. I had some pretty close friends there.

BRAD HOLMES

In eighth grade, we moved to California and it was a real dramatic difference. I was just in awe of all the surfer kids. They all had tans, and everybody seemed to be quite a bit advanced, compared to what we had been in New York, socially. They were just a lot cooler. They were riding around on real neat Sting Ray bikes, and I had just an old clunker. The kids were wearing their hair a little bit longer, and I had my short hair, and I couldn't stand that. And the clothes. Coming from New York, you kind of wear dark clothes, and everyone in California was wearing loafers and light-colored shirts and T-shirts, and peg pants and stuff. I couldn't fit in that way for quite a while, plus I had the New York accent.

That's when I started getting into trouble. I went to junior high and high school there. We were only there for two years, but it was a real hard transition, going to California from New York, especially around the ninth grade. You have a period where you want to do whatever is not expected from you, so I did a lot of that, and I got into trouble a number of times, and learned to drink, and was hanging around with hoods.

I was looking forward to the move a lot. I liked it. I liked being there, rather than in New York. I missed my friends, but not that much. I got new ones. They weren't very good ones, but they were new ones.

BEVERLY TAYLOR

My best friends were always boys or men, and I was always going steady with somebody. I had a lot of boyfriends, and of course they all had to be preapproved, and the whole bit. I never really dated guys for very long. I was always going steady, but never for very long with the same one. I never dated guys for any length of time. I would get bored and move on to someone else. A lot of it was just the age: kids don't go steady for very long.

PAULA HOLMES

I had this mad crush on a guy who was twenty-two when I was about fifteen. I worked in a department store in Taiwan, just a seasonal thing, for Christmas. We were supposed to help the service people find things when they came into the store. I met this guy, Eric, who came in one night, and it was like instantly I was drawn to him. Once I met Eric, I had something to live for. I was in this dream world all the time; I couldn't concentrate on anything. No wonder my schoolwork suffered.

72

All I could think about was Eric. He was a GI and he worked in the chapel with my dad. He gave me kind of mixed messages, because he liked my dad, and identified with my dad, and was a friend of the family. He seemed to like me, but I think since he was so close with my dad, and I was so much younger, that he was afraid to make a move. When we left Taiwan, my biggest sadness was leaving him.

We lived in Galveston until after I graduated. I had this boyfriend, Mike, that I really liked, and he was my age for a change, but he had graduated early, so he was in college, and he was in ROTC. So that gave me a new object to fantasize about. I was so bad because I was always doing that. School was always secondary to me.

I met another guy I fell head over heels for, Mark. He was just a doll. He was a military kid. I went with him for about a year. So there I was head over heels for Mark, and suddenly Eric, the guy I was crazy about when we lived in Taiwan, came to visit. I really wanted to like Eric again, but I couldn't feel the same way, because I was older and things had changed.

We had dinner, and I was excited that Eric was there. Then we went to the beach with my dad—it was always with my dad. My dad finally got smart and took off, so I was alone with Eric for a little bit, at last. And all of a sudden I had the opportunity and I didn't want it. He was so serious, and I wasn't ready for serious. I didn't really ever know this guy was like that. He was always so happy, Mom's apple pie, sending me little cards. I got scared, I guess.

He came to visit me at work, and I watched him walk away, and that was the last I ever saw of him. He walked away, and I thought to myself, I'll see him again, I'll see him again. And some of the girls in the office looked at me and said, "You're going to get married early." I remember thinking, why did they say that? I was still in high school. They just noticed that Eric was older and so mature and serious. But I never saw the guy again. As it turned out, I didn't get married young. I was twenty-six when I got married.

Then we moved, and the guy that I really liked, Mark, followed us out as we drove off, and he didn't seem sad at all. I was crying. I know he wasn't sad. It was just a temporary, fun thing for him. I cried for I don't know how many miles. I tried writing to him, and he never wrote back. That was it, when I left. After I left, it was out of sight, out of mind.

RHONDA HEALEY

I never had a lot of friends. I always had one or two friends. It would typically be the other person in the class who was a loner or outcast and would kind of pair up with me. I can remember defending that person to the death, whoever it was, because that was my friend.

It was really hard for me to break into what I perceived as cliques everywhere. I was real sensitive about being different. I would come from one school and my clothes would be just a little different. You can't quite even put a finger on it, but I would wear knee socks because everybody at the last school would wear them, and in this school everybody would wear pantyhose, or vice versa.

I kept everything very much at arm's length. I would excel academically or artistically. I was real arty in school, so I would draw attention to myself that way and a lot of times would make friends that way. But I was really poor about meeting people. My husband laughs about that now, because if we go to a party I know everybody's story in twenty minutes, and I can visit really easily. But I think that's because I've become more confident about myself as an adult. He can't imagine me being a shy, skinny little kid.

Then there were the military kids who would go the opposite way: would be loud and boisterous, and almost obnoxious, just kind of the life-of-the-party types. Maybe that was a front. There seemed to be that end of the spectrum, too.

SHARON GILMORE

When I was in kindergarten, I had a friend named Larry, and his dad was in the Army, so our dads weren't supposed to associate. His mom was having a baby, and while she was in the hospital, he

74

slept over on the top bunk, and he had a bad dream that night. When we moved away I never saw him again. Last year, all these years later, I was shopping, and there he was, the store manager. His dad used to take us down to the hangar while he worked, and we'd get to row on the rowing machine. He had a picture taken of me and then colored it in with colored pencil. I still have that picture.

We used to go down to the movies, for fifteen cents, and we'd decide who we were going to sit with. It was always boy, girl, boy, girl. We were really young. It didn't matter who you sat with, just so you were with some guy. Sometimes you'd get Billy; other times you'd get Ron.

I never went to the barracks. In fact, a girlfriend and I were the only ones who made it off the base without ever having intercourse, and we prided ourselves on it. Very few girls that I knew ever made it off a Navy base without some kind of sexual experience. It was too easy. The guys were right there, at the movies, the gym, the swimming pool. The cafeteria was the big spot where they all hung out.

We moved when I was in the middle of my junior year. I met a girl named Louisa. I picked her out of my homeroom class. I immediately liked her because she had on an old blue homespun dress and knee socks that went halfway up her leg because they were too small. I invited her over to spend the night, and she said yes. I had never had a girlfriend from off base spend the night, never. And I got to thinking, oh, my God, I invited her to spend the night at my house. And our house was a mess. You can't imagine what it was like; it was really bad. We had one piece of new furniture in my life. Everything else was from St. Vincent's or whatever. And then there was my dad, being drunk. For a whole week I sweated it and tried to figure out how I could get out of it.

She came over and she never said anything. It was just like she was at home, you know. I couldn't believe it. I worried for nothing. The next week she invited me over to her house. Her mom was an alcoholic, and her parents were divorced and her dad had taken over the six kids. They not only didn't have nice furniture; they didn't have any furniture. They had lawn chairs. We became best friends. We're still friends now.

LINDA WINSLOW

When I lived on the base, most of my friends were brats, but we also lived in civilian atmospheres. The brats that I've met are either very gregarious and outgoing or incredible introverts. There doesn't seem to be a real medium ground, because of being the new kid in town. But I never ran with a group. I don't think it was because I was a loner; it was because I would vacillate. If I was into theater, I'd hang out with the theater people. If I was into sports, I would be with the sports people. I always felt like I could be friends with everybody.

Or maybe, maybe it's that I wanted everybody to like me, and I couldn't just put my foot down and say, "Me." I had to fit, and never with one particular group, but I always would kind of hedge my bets and live on the periphery.

JULIE MEDINA

Melinda Wasserman was my first best friend, in the early hippie days. I was fourteen then, and that was the first time I had ever had a best friend for a whole year. Her father was a college professor and her mother was a secretary, and that, to me, put them in a whole different world. They had real lives. She invited me to her house, so I found my nicest pair of jeans and her mom and dad made steak, baked potatoes, and salad. That was the first time I had ever seen that combination. My mom bought round steaks and fried the hell out of them. These were rare in the middle.

That night her parents had a glass of wine with dinner, and nobody got into a fight; nobody got drunk. Her sister had come home from Berkeley and had brought a tape of Arlo Guthrie's "Alice's Restaurant." We laughed ourselves half sick listening to this tape.

Melinda had allergies so bad she couldn't even be in the house when they were cleaning. Not only did she not have to do anything but she could not even be in the house because the dust from cleaning sent her into spasms. I couldn't believe how lucky she was.

I remember another girl. We had the two end houses in the base, and our backyards faced each other. Lucy Stilowitz, and her father was an MP. You were always on your toes at her house. One of his favorite jokes was if you bent over to pick something up, he would come up behind you and hit you on the ass as hard as he could and make you fall over, and he would say, "Girls are supposed to stoop, like this." The fights over at their place were incredible. He was a big man. For some reason MPs like to throw their weight around. It was always real exciting to be around there. Her mom was nice. She was a seamstress and made really neat things for her with little labels that said HAND SEWN BY BETTY STILOWITZ.

GEORGE DEXTER

It is rather remarkable that a West Point classmate is a friend for life, whether you like it or not, the way that we can get together after umpteen years apart, and it's just like you've known him forever. When we travel around the country, we can always stop and see people. I dated a girl in high school who married a classmate of mine and we see them once in a while.

I was reading something recently that focused on the differences between our generations. When I was growing up, dating was something you did very broadly; in other words, you dated a lot of people. We would have these parties, dances at Pope Hall in Leavenworth, once a month. These were events where the gals all dressed up in formals, and we had hop cards, and you danced with all these different girls. We got to know just about everybody in the crowd. Then after World War II, the idea of going steady became the thing, and so they say that these big parties where everybody got to know everybody stopped being so popular.

PETER VARGAS

The most difficult part of moving was making friends. I learned to make friends very easily, but there were also negative factors, in that I was a liar for most of my life. I think I needed to make up stories to make people like me, to make friends easier. They didn't know anything about me, so I could come in and create the life-style that I wanted to put myself into whatever clique I wanted to be in.

That carried through after the military for many, many years, and I lost friends because of it. That was probably one of the worst things that the military taught me to do, was to lie, and it was one of the most difficult things to get rid of. And you also lied because if you got in trouble for something, your father got in trouble, so you learned to lie to get out of trouble.

I also learned to pick up accents. I don't care where I go, I pick up accents. If I'm in New York for a couple of days, you'd never know I hadn't lived there all my life. Even the different boroughs of New York, Jewish neighborhoods, or German. Any accent from any language, I pick it up extremely fast. So learning other languages has been easy. I'm like a chameleon.

First thing I wanted to do was get out and explore the neighborhood and find out what was going on. And I made friends on that first initial exploration. You were the new guy, and you had that status, no matter what your father was. You were low on the totem pole until you got used to what was going on in that little society or that little community right there. Then you assumed your rightful spot, depending on whatever your father's rank was.

That was the first thing that you wanted to do: fit in. No one wants to be an outsider, so that was part of the making up stories about where I'm from and what I am. You made it up according to the environment that you were moving into, so that you fit in very nicely. Because if you stuck out, military kids were, I think, the cruelest of all, because they took advantage of any edge that they had. If their father was an officer, they used that rank to get what they wanted. I'm sorry to say that as my father was a major and then a lieutenant colonel, I used rank to make people like me, to become part of the clique.

Dating was very tough. I think I was a geek all my life, mostly. A lot of the other kids that I knew were allowed to have haircuts that were predominantly something that looked good for them. And me, well, my father got crew cuts; I got crew cuts.

And I can remember having crew cuts and wearing those stupid military glasses all my life, and in a sense that separated me.

But it was easy to make friends, and it was easy to give them up. And that carries over. You moved away, and there's a protective wall that separates you from that past part of your life. You can't worry about it or be sorrowful, because there's nothing you can do about it. You moved, you got transferred—that other word that all military people are aware of. So I put that out of my life. There's a wall that's built there, and then you start the new one. And then there's another wall, so your life is a constant series of building these walls. And that has carried over to today. Even now, I still have that habit.

There's someone who quit working for us a couple of months ago, and I am constantly walking around trying to remember her name. People have to remind me. It's embarrassing. When somebody leaves, you're used to closing the door and not having to reopen that door, so that part of life is over.

I don't carry a lot of old friends from the old places; neither does my sister. My parents are completely the opposite. Military contacts are definitely a boon to one's career, knowing who's doing what: Colonel So-and-So, and Captain So-and-So, and their wives. They're constantly in touch with these people. They always know where this clique of friends are, the people that were there when you got out of basic training and were going through the initial schooling as officers. They're all officers. They've kept in touch with them. And why that didn't get instilled in myself and my sister, I don't know.

We always had a wall full of Christmas cards, no matter where we were. It was a big deal—my parents would go out and buy hundreds of cards, with pictures of us on them—that was important. "Here's what we look like now."

5

The New Kid

Back to school. We went to the PX to get our new shoes and fall outfits and to the post bookstore for our school supplies, just like everyone else. On the post even the Big Chief tablets and number two pencils were government issue. The supplies for each student were put into brown commissary bags that were stapled shut and labeled to indicate grade level. First graders got paste and third graders got glue. There were no arguments and no substitutions. Everything we needed was in the brown bag, and our back-to-school shopping was done.

I was a reluctant student, emotionally, not academically. I'm surprised that I learned anything in elementary school, since I spent the majority of my time in tears or in the nurse's office. I was an expert at real and imaginary illnesses, the little girl who cried wolf. I used to lie on the cot in the nurse's office and will the mercury to rise in the thermometer so that my mother would have to come and take me home.

I can remember the boredom of repeating subjects that I had

already learned at my last school, and the panic I felt when I faced something that the teachers assumed I knew. It was only after years of frustration and guessing at basic calculations that I learned fractions. Common denominators and "invert and multiply" were lost in the shuffle when I was transferred from one school to the other, lost in the black hole of interstate curriculums that failed to overlap.

I outgrew my problems with school just as my father retired, and I was able to attend junior and senior high school, without crying, in one city. When the time came to send away for college catalogues, I tried to summon up some enthusiasm, tried to believe that it would be exciting and fun to go away to college in a new place and meet new people. But I had spent more than half of my first twelve years in school trying to believe that. I *knew* what it was like. I went to the local university.

When military brats talk about school, their stories traverse state lines and international boundaries. They count on their fingers to add up the number of schools that they attended. They bring out their class pictures and annuals, and if they had been enrolled in the school when the pictures were taken, they were surrounded by a different group of classmates every year.

Military families with school-age children were transferred during the summer whenever possible. But when it had not been possible, military brats described those midyear moves in terms of being yanked or pulled out of schools. Part of the routine after a move involved finding the school, going to the office, and enrolling. Military brats were given new books and, if they were lucky, were assigned to a teacher who was accustomed to dealing with military students, and then they were led down the hallway to the classroom to resume their education.

I was surprised to find so many military brats who had attended parochial schools; there is something comical about the image of little military children in immaculate uniforms lining up for school.

All but the smallest, most remote military installations had schools within their gates. Although people referred to them as "military" and "post" schools, they were simply schools that were located on military posts, not military schools, with a military curriculum. I encountered only one example of any distinctly "military" connection, from a man who had attended a school on a military base only once, during kindergarten. "My memory with regard to differences (between civilian and military schools) is one of marching around the kindergarten playroom to the 'Marine Corps Hymn.' You don't do that at normal schools."

"Normal" schools were civilian schools. Military brats had frequently felt more conspicuous as "the new kid," both in the classroom and on the playground, when they attended schools off post in more permanent civilian neighborhoods.

Although not all military brats reacted to changing schools as dramatically and emotionally as I did, I couldn't wait to tell my mother that I was not the only person who hated being "the new kid." Moving was disruptive to both the social and the academic aspects of school. It was possible to compensate academically, and most military brats felt that they received a good education.

But the social aspects of school, especially high school, were a different story. Military brats who had been moving and adapting all their lives suddenly balked at the prospect of another move once they reached high school. Instead of graduating with a familiar group of classmates, military brats moved away from them, and the "golden years" of high school were indelibly altered.

"I guess I have the kind of face that people think they know. People are always coming up to me and asking, 'Did you go to Redwood High?' And I go, 'No.' I don't go into it, either, because it's too complicated."

"What is the plural of alma mater?"

RHONDA HEALEY

The worst move I remember was starting school on Valentine's Day in a new school. I was in sixth grade. I was mortified and begged my mother to please let us start the next day. We had already missed a week or whatever, so one more day was not going to make a difference. I said, "Don't make us start school on Valentine's Day! Everybody else will have their Valentines and nobody will know us. Just don't put us through that!" But we had to start. I had a wonderful teacher. I was only in her class for about three months before we had to move again. It was a very difficult period.

That year was a real bomb. We moved three times. That same year in northern Florida, we had this old teacher who was a very proper kind of southern lady and she would not allow us to vote for a black kid who was running for class president. I remember my mother raising hell about that. That was in the early sixties, so that kind of attitude still prevailed at that time. Even coming from Tennessee, I was too young to have picked up some of those attitudes. This same teacher divided the class into boys and girls and had the boys doing science projects and the girls doing embroidery and sewing. Had my mother known we were going to be in that area much longer, she would have taken me out of the class, but we were only going to be there for three months, so I bit the bullet.

I repeated some basic history about seven times, and then every state that we went to required their own state history as part of the curriculum, so I picked up a lot of interesting information. In one school, I would be in an accelerated class, and then at the next school, I'd be almost remedial, depending on their curriculum. I never knew where I was at. In some ways, it was great being able to leave a school if I was having a hard time in a particular subject, which was usually math.

HELEN PIERSON

It's hard being different. At the time, that was life. You just moved, went from place to place. Each school district and state had its own curriculum, so you had to learn the state flowers and birds in each state. I didn't learn to sound out words phonetically, so for years I had a hard time with spelling. I missed a lot along the way. I compensated on my own for a lot of the gaps in my education.

I never found that it was hard to meet people. You went to a new school and you would meet people. It was a given. I think that the teachers on base were always good about that. We all stood up and said where we had come from. It was no big deal. The only time I ever really noticed that it was hard was when we got out of the service. That year, I had to get up in front of the class and tell everyone where I was from and all the places that I had lived, and that time was the worst. Those people had been in school together since first grade. It was traumatic.

BRENDA ROWAN

My horror story was our move from Hawaii, when I started sixth grade in Maryland. At that time, Hawaii was kind of rustic and the people were outdoorsy, and Maryland was more so-phisticated. I don't know whether it was that, or if I was just so tired of moving that I couldn't adapt. I had a horrible time adjusting. I was still climbing trees and playing outside, and these kids in Maryland were starting to date. I just couldn't adapt. It really has influenced me up to this time.

I was quite outgoing until that year; I had been the leader of my class and all that. I think that move really jolted me. I became shy and withdrawn and nonassertive.

I remember wanting to change classes; I was in an advanced class, and I didn't like it. I thought the kids were snotty. My parents thought I should stick it out. I don't think they knew what to do. They were upset, especially my mother; I remember her being upset that I was having such a hard time. I think they probably would have taken me to a psychologist or something, but that wasn't done in those days, and I don't think they had any idea of what to do with me.

JULIE MEDINA

We moved to Georgia, and in that three years, we moved seven times in the same area. They didn't have many schools around there, but we went to all of them. After Washington, D.C., my mom stopped going with us on the first day. We knew the routine, and when my sister and brother started school, I took them, because I knew what to do. I was always the new kid in class.

BARRY JENKINS

I hated the moves. I hated being the new kid in school; I just despised it. Moving always pissed us off, and the older I got, the more it pissed me off. I never went to a base school, never once. I was always a real shy kid. When I was thrust into a classroom, I'd just be sweating bullets. "Now, say what your name is and where you came from." You always had some asshole teacher who put you on the spot. I don't know if they thought they were doing you a favor, to make you break the ice or what, because you always felt like a dip. I wanted to just not be noticed until a couple of weeks later, when maybe the guy next to you goes, "Hey, what's your name?" That would've suited me just fine.

We moved four times in one school year, during fifth grade. I started in Los Angeles, went to Georgia, went to Oakland, and finished the year in Whidbey Island. I didn't know if I was coming or going. Every school system was different. One school didn't want to give me any credit because I hadn't taken the same classes, and they were talking about keeping me back a year. My mother can raise bloody hell when she wants to, which she did, so they didn't hold me back.

I started the next school year on Whidbey Island, and then we moved in the middle of that year to the Bay Area, and then in the middle of that semester, we moved from the suburbs into Oakland. One more little move. That was a rough one, in sixth grade. My dad was getting ready to go to Vietnam. That was the age when guys start to be tough guys and everybody has to go around testing the limits of everybody else. The Bay Area, man, everyone thinks of the late sixties as being flower power and all of that. My experience was that it was violent and tense. I got in a lot of street fights, a lot of schoolyard fights, because that's when I realized that guys would pick on you just to see what you would do. When we got to Oakland, it was really bad because it was more urban, and the school was a kind of down-and-outer school that got all the lower-class neighborhoods. My mother wasn't thrilled about it. She transferred us to another school the next year, which didn't break my heart. I fought my way out of that first school there.

JOHN ROWAN

I started the fourth grade at one school, and then my parents decided that they were going to live in a different neighborhood after all, so after about two weeks, I got started in another school. That was hard. I'd gotten through the difficulty of doing it once, and thought it was done with, and then had to do it again, just a few weeks later.

When I started fourth grade, I was especially behind in penmanship and reading. That was my first experience of being behind. I was generally within the top of the class, so it was traumatic to find myself not being able to do what most of the other kids could do.

Florida was my father's last duty station. I went through my junior year of high school there, and then he was going to retire to this small town in Missouri before my senior year started. I had some misgivings about that. I liked Florida, and I had a bit of an idea that it was going to be strange, going to school in a small town with a bunch of people who had never been any farther away from home than Kansas City and who had never seen an ocean. I had a small idea of what that was going to be like, but I wasn't prepared for the crashing reality of how different it was going to be.

SHEILA WRIGHT

In third grade, I went to three different schools. I was just traumatized. I thought: Oh, I'm never going to make it. I'm going to die this year; I just know it. I think that made me real shy. I was at my wit's end about making friends, because I'd make one, and then we'd go somewhere else, and I'd have to go through it all over again. I finally went to the third school for four months. I was behind when I got to that school. I got straight As once that year was over with, which probably shocked my parents, because I hadn't done very well in school before that time. But third grade was pretty much a write-off.

I had a speech problem, a lisp. In third grade, the speech

teacher came and called me out of class three days after I started school there, and so, of course, I was the laughingstock because I had to go to speech class to learn how to talk. It was terrible, all these things happening at once. Third grade was the worst year.

My sisters and I would always be "sick." My mom was a nurse, and she made us go to school unless we had a fever, because she knew we were faking. It was real hard to fake, but we'd do anything to get out of school. We'd forget our lunches, so we'd have to go home and get them.

I really felt sorry for my brother because we moved to Nebraska when he was in eleventh grade. It was hard for him, and it was hard for me and my sister, because we didn't go to junior high school; we went right into a high school that had grades seven through twelve. We had been going to a Catholic school, so going into public school, we felt like "Oh, my God, we're going to die here!"

My parents lived near a reservation, and there were a lot of Indian kids. It was during a real bad time for the Indian movement, and they were beating up anybody they could find. I got beat up all the time. Here's this little girl from Catholic school, trying to make it in the world of Indians versus whites, and everything else. It was shocking. I got beat up about once a month from eighth through tenth grade. Six girls would catch you by yourself and beat the crap out of you. My parents took me and my sister out of school at one point for two weeks because my dad pressed charges against one family whose daughter beat me up so badly that my whole chest was bruised. It was bad.

LINDA WINSLOW

I had been going to a military school in Germany, on base with other brats, and all of a sudden we got transferred to New York. I had never even heard the word *fuck,* didn't know what it meant, and here I am in an Italian Jewish neighborhood.

I skipped the sixth grade. We got to New York, and I spent two weeks in sixth grade and suddenly was promoted to the seventh grade. That was really traumatic. At that point, in junior high, your peers resent that. There's a certain amount of hostility.

And there was a double signal there, because it was achieve, get the awards, get the grades, but, at the same time, you're a girl, so you're just going to get married, anyway.

I had taken German from German nationals for three years while we were living in Germany, and I was my mother's translator. Then I got to Brooklyn, and the German teacher had never been out of the state.

And then, in about 1958, we moved to Minnesota, and here I was, this sophisticated New York girl, stuck in Duluth. I went in to see the guidance counselor and she said, "What language do you want to take?" I had already taken two years of German, and I figured the third year would be really fun, when you get the literature and stuff, so I said I wanted to take German. And she said, "Oh, dear, we haven't taught German here since the war!"

BRAD HOLMES

My position in the class was always changing dramatically. When I was in Europe, I was in the middle of my class. When we were in southern California for a while, I was very advanced, because I spoke two languages, and I could read, and the kids there were hardly reading. I was terribly bored, and they were going to have me skip a grade, but I was sick all the time, so they had a halfway class that was in between second and third grades, and I was in that class whenever I went to school. In New York, they had a real strict academic system, and I was well behind most of the kids, because they were doing phonics, and I had somehow missed that. The following year, I started at a new school just for military kids. Robert Kennedy came to dedicate the school when it opened.

Leaving New York to move back to California was difficult, but it was also real exciting, too. You felt you would be able to start fresh and get rid of your mistakes. I left before the yearbook had come out. I had already paid for it, so I got it in the mail a few months later, and everyone in my class had written notes in it— "Have fun in California!"—and it was so nice to get that.

TIM BROCKWAY

Junior high school in Texas was the first time I went to school off base. The first day I went there, I ended up getting in a fight with a Chicano. I'd never seen anyone with a ducktail, and I was looking at this Chicano guy's hair. I wasn't trying to start anything. And he said, "What are you looking at, man?" And I said, "I'm just looking at your hair." And he said, "Well, you want to fight?" And I said, "Well, I guess so." So he said meet me after school, and I said okay.

He didn't fight like the military guys. I'd been in athletic camps in the military and learned how to box, and I'd been fighting since I was a little boy. I went out there and the first thing I noticed was that there was a whole ring of his friends. I was so naïve it didn't even scare me, right? In two seconds, I'm knocked on the ground. This guy jumped on me, and all of his friends are going, "Kill him!" And he gave me one backhand in the face, and I just refused to fight him. I said, "Well, I'm not going to fight you if you don't fight fair," which completely blew his mind. They were all going, "Hey, he's not fighting."

That first day at junior high, it was a situation where you're used to being in the majority, and then all of the sudden you go into a place where you're not the majority anymore. It was almost like being an adult and moving out and going into the real world by yourself. It wasn't like "Hey, don't you guys know this is Tim, Colonel Brockway's boy?"

ROBERT BLAKE

I made fifteen moves, from my birth until my college graduation. Six times before I started school, five times during elementary school, twice in junior high school, and two different high schools. In all that time, I only moved in the middle of the school year twice, and that was during the same school year. We moved from Quantico to Washington, D.C., to Spain in the same school year, which happened to be fifth grade. All the other times we moved were either in the summer or between terms.

MARK DENTON

We got to Denmark, and we realized that there were no American schools. They put us in the Danish schools, despite the fact that we didn't speak the language. My sister and I thought that my parents were going to get a divorce over all of this. After about the first week, my mom realized that something was wrong, and she asked my dad, "What haven't we been told?" So my dad finally got on the phone to headquarters, and they said, "Oh, didn't anyone tell you?"

So they sent us the Calvert correspondence courses. Mom was really upset, because by the time the Calvert arrived, it had been two months, and she was worried that we were way behind, and when we got back to the United States, we'd be stupid.

We went to the Danish school every day for gym, and my sister took sewing class, and I got to take wood shop and physics. Home schooling worked out pretty well. We didn't take a lot of the superfluous junk. When we took our trip to Italy, we had just studied about all the art, and there we were, right in the middle of it.

The Danish that we learned was fairly intensive. When we were put in the Danish school, at first we were like celebrities because we already knew English. They were teaching British English, and they spelled *color* as *colour*, and I would correct the teacher. He thought I was terrible; you didn't correct those instructors. I went home from school, and my mom said, "Well, it is spelled that way." That was news to me. I was from Wasatch Elementary School in Salt Lake City and that was Americana, right there.

By the time we got to Germany and went to the American school, we were six months ahead of them. In Germany, you took German, period, and I just never got it. When I came back to the States, they put me in German II, and I barely made it. I got Ds all the way through. I still didn't get it.

GAIL EMERSON

I had a fair amount of trouble in school with being a behavior problem, mostly attention-seeking behaviors. I was a bright student, but for some reason, I wasn't very socially adept, and I'd do weird and kind of bizarre things, probably in order to get attention. I never knew why I did it; I just did it. And my parents would be sending notes to school every week for the teacher to sign, so that they could check on my behavior at school. My brother was the same way. I got over it. When I got into eighth grade, I was into achieving, rather than being the class clown, and from then on, I was able to do well.

PAULA HOLMES

I went to kindergarten in Kansas. For whatever reason, my teacher "didn't like the military"—at least that's what my parents tell me. Needless to say, I had a real bad start in school, with this teacher. I don't remember exactly what it was. My dad visited the school one day and sat in the back of the classroom, and I knew something was unusual. Nobody else's dad was there.

And first grade was bad. I had three different teachers during that year, at the same school. With that record, it's no wonder that I had to repeat first grade. There was one incident that I'll always remember. This kid, a big kid, who had probably had to repeat a grade himself, used to tease me and would tell everybody that I had flunked. I told my parents, and my dad got mad, but he never did anything about it. I couldn't muster up the courage to do anything but just shy away. I just remember it being a very bad time in my life. As a parent, I would never let that happen to my child. I'm probably overprotective now, as a mother, because of this, and I almost resent the way that my parents would not step in and do something.

I hated school. I hated it. I remember moving and getting lost, trying to find my house when I was walking home, because they all looked alike. I was just a scared little kid.

We lived off base for a while in Kansas because we couldn't get housing. I went to school off base for a while, and I loved that school. Then my parents moved on base and I had to change schools. I cried, because I wanted to stay at that school, and I had dreams that I was back there. My parents didn't care. If they wanted to move on base, because it was more convenient, then they did. It didn't matter about me; they just dragged me along.

91

They didn't even consider the possibility of driving me to that school: that would be too inconvenient. My mom was very quiet and reserved and was not one to ever speak out on anything. Her attitude was "This is what life has dealt us."

Then we moved to San Antonio, Texas. I hated that place. They divided the school up into groups according to ability. It started with 7-1 and went all the way up to 7-13, and I think 13 was the highest level. I was in 7-7, so I was pretty average. I had this friend who was in 7-13. She was the kind who always wanted to see your report card, and my report card was never very good, never anything to shout about. I would always get big speeches from my dad. "You've got to do better!" It seemed like he would have me in a room forever, torturing me about my grades.

I went through seventh grade and didn't like the school, hated gym class. For being so shy, I really started having my little inner angers and resentments building up inside. The next year, I got moved down to 8-5, and that was so traumatic to me. I cried and cried. It was a very cruel system. My parents would never do anything about it. I cried and cried, and then I finally resigned myself to a "You're just dumb" kind of attitude.

Then, in Taiwan, we went to a missionary school. The missionary kids resented the military kids because we could just be there for two years, and then we'd leave. The military kids had better clothes; the missionary kids just wore whatever they could get. They were kind of different, not with it. I never got really close to any of them. I had already decided that I wasn't going to get close to anybody, because we always left and what good did it do?

The high school in Illinois was huge, and they had a drug problem there, which was a real change from the tiny missionary school. I was very intimidated, as usual, by the other kids. I didn't like school again. I was just bored to tears with school, and I developed a habit of tuning out. I would just sit there and daydream all the time. I left high school and I haven't gone back to a class reunion or anything. I haven't gone back, period.

TERRY McCULLOCH

My first school was Catholic school, and that didn't last very long because my sister Margaret didn't want to go to school one day, so she told the Mother Superior that my grandfather died. So they took us to the office and said, "Oh, we're so sorry to hear about this. Go on home."

Well, the Mother Superior called my mom and said, "I'm sorry to hear about your father's death." And my mom told her, "He's not dead!" The Mother Superior called us all back into the office, slapped us, and kicked us out of the school. I had loved that school because I loved my uniform. I had a really mean teacher, Sister Ann Theresa, but I loved going to that Catholic school. I loved the uniform, the saddle oxfords, and everything.

School was easy. I benefited from the moves. For some reason I always did better when I moved. I fell right into it, maybe because I was going to military schools, on bases: the curriculum was pretty much the same all over. I never had any problems adjusting.

MARY CHANDLER

I went to thirteen schools from kindergarten through twelfth grade. On the first day of school, I got horrible stomachaches that would usually last for a week. I had mild versions of these stomachaches right up until my sophomore year in high school. In fourth grade, the one and only year I went to Catholic school, I had an especially bad stomachache because the class had fifty-two kids and the nun was a terror.

JEFFREY TAVARES

We moved all the time. I remember registering at the schools, and I remember that I didn't want to let my parents leave me for a long time, mainly because I was afraid of getting lost trying to get back home. That went on until I was in the sixth grade.

My junior year in high school, my mom wanted me to get the senior class ring. I didn't want to get it; I didn't want to have anything to do with it. She finally decided that she was going to get me the ring, and I got it, and then we moved. I asked my mom, "What's the big deal?" I got a senior class ring from a place where I didn't even go for my senior year. They said, "At least you got one."

RICARDO COTTRELL

When I was in high school in Spain, the Spanish teacher wore this cologne you could smell from the next building. He was so spiffed out and stiff it was pathetic. He was teaching Spanish to embassy kids who had been speaking it all their lives and knew it as well as he did. These guys in the class were ornery. They would say something about his mother when his back was turned, and he would get livid. Then we'd get sneezing powder and go sharpen our pencils and blow it on him. We really ragged on the guy. He was so uptight.

BEVERLY TAYLOR

I never had to start school midterm anywhere. I don't know how we escaped moving in the middle of the school year, but we did. I went through my last year of junior high school and the first two years of high school in the same place. So in my senior year, we were transferred. I was ready to move, that time.

I didn't care when we moved. I was tired of San Diego. I had met all the people; I had dated all the guys. I was ready for a change. I had that attitude about things, anyway. I'd met everybody I wanted to meet. I was ready to go.

We went to Virginia and I had a ball. It didn't help things that I got there and found out right off the bat that I had enough units to graduate right then, without even going through my senior year. I had two homerooms, and then I had to take whatever their requirements were, Virginia Government, or something like that. My parents always had me programmed for college. I had my language and math out of the way, but my dad threw in all of the things that I hadn't wanted to take. My parents always picked out my programs for me. I never had anything to say about it.

It was such a party school that I practically flunked out my last year, although I really couldn't, since I had all the credits. I was making a C in biology, which I hated with a passion, and in another class. And boy, my parents were down at the school so fast it made my head spin. I didn't care. I was going to graduate anyway.

CATHY ATCHISON

The one that kills me is when you apply for a job and they want you to list all the schools you've ever gone to in your entire life. There's no way I can do that: I've got no idea. I did graduate, honest!

Between my junior and senior years, we were transferred from the West Coast to New Jersey. It was very difficult. At that point, I'd been with the same people for three years—my peer group, my friends—at an age when peers are incredibly important.

Going out to New Jersey was a totally different mind-set for me. The people were weird. I remember my perception at the time was that I was going to have to cut my arm off to like everybody else, and that I was never going to be accepted. I couldn't fit the mold. The people were so concerned with the brand of clothes that you had on. That had never been a concern of mine. You dressed the way you dressed, and that was it. All of a sudden to be thrown into an environment where the girls looked at what kind of shoes you wore, what kind of clothes you wore, what kind of purse you carried—I was not equipped to deal with that. It was a very cliquey school, and if you didn't wear the right clothes, you didn't run with the right crowd. So I finally resigned myself to the fact that I wasn't going to run with the right crowd, and then I was able to move past it, but initially it was quite a shock.

I broke my date to the senior prom three days before the prom. And a friend of ours was in town, temporarily, from one of the military academies, a cadet from Annapolis or West Point or something. He heard that I'd broken my date. Well, this was delightful. He took me to the prom in his military dress uniform. That was swell.

I did, over the course of the year, make some friends and, actually, probably ended up having a relatively good time at it. I even cried when the day of graduation came. I thought, this is definitely the end of an era. I'm not going to go through this again.

PETER VARGAS

I went through the first, second, and third grades in parochial school. My stepfather was Catholic, on top of being military.

I went through three years of senior high in one place and moved twice during my senior year, so that was kind of messy. It made it real difficult to finish school. I moved to a new school, started senior high, and then moved again right in the middle of it. I watch movies, or see shows on TV or whatever, and a lot of them are high school–oriented, and I don't really relate to the concept, the idea at all. I'm jealous, envious of that whole high school scenario, because I missed out on it. I can't even remember but two or three people who were in my actual senior year, the last part of my senior year. My reunions were garbage. I feel kind of left out, in that respect.

Moving back and forth had some effect on my academics, in that you get a short-timer's attitude before you get ready to leave. Nothing's important anymore; it doesn't matter what I do here, because I'm going to leave this school, and I never have to deal with it again because now I've got to go to a new place. The thought that those grades and the paperwork from the old school carried over to the new place never entered my mind, so there was a negative impact when I got to the new school, because of the way I had acted in the last one. I was never aware of that until many, many years after school. I was burning bridges, and I didn't really realize that had an effect on me in the next place.

96

DEREK LOWE

After we left Germany, we went to upstate New York. It was a really super place. We lived in a predominantly Italian civilian community, in a housing project that was a lot like an Army post, lots of kids who were the same ages. We had a super time. Then we moved to Long Island and I went to ninth grade at a predominantly Jewish junior high school. That was a completely different experience, but it was a comfortable experience. They were very receptive to military people, Army kids, I guess because the housing and the base were nearby. You weren't too much of an oddball, and there was a lot of acceptance and involvement.

My dad went to Vietnam that summer, between ninth and tenth grade, and we moved to Louisiana again. This was in 1966. That was at the height of the civil rights movement and the racial tension in the Southeast. Having lived in a predominantly integrated environment, I don't have an accent. I have an Army accent. People ask me, "Why don't you have an accent?" Or "Where did you get that accent?" After going to these schools with all the different ethnic groups in New York, and having the Army tribalism that I was real involved in, I went to high school in Augusta at the same school my parents had gone to, which was an all-black high school. There was no integration in Louisiana at that time. That was a real culture shock. That was probably the most intense cultural change that I had to face over the whole period of change in my life. That was probably one of the worst parts of my growing up.

The schools were so poor in Louisiana that the textbooks were passed down from the white schools, so the literature was old. I was way ahead of my class, because I had come from this elite and relatively affluent, good school system in Long Island and moved into a poverty-stricken school system. That was very disruptive to my educational process. It was a depressing situation, to suddenly be injected into this.

So in eleventh grade, I was sent to a military school that had just been integrated. That was a very strange experience, too, having been familiar with living in an integrated environment,

BRATS

and suddenly being subjected to a lot of really intense racial hostility. We had to wear uniforms to school. Those years were very turbulent, and for me it was a personally related turbulence.

I look back on my high school years as the worst years of my life. I was neither fish nor fowl, because I didn't have the local community affiliations, except for my family. I hadn't grown up with the kids that I was riding the bus with. And then there was the conflict, the tension in the community in general.

And then, at the time when boys and girls are supposed to be developing social relationships: well, that had been happening in the Army, with some real limits, but then I went to this military school, which had girls, but in separate classes. So of course in a school of two thousand kids there were maybe twenty black kids, and most of them were boys, of course. On one level, your peer group at school was very small, and there was no social contact with girls. And at home, back in the community, I was sort of identified as an elitist or out of the mainstream. I was even further removed, because I didn't have the same accent, the same talk, and the background, the associations. So that was really isolating, and it was psychological isolation.

My family was my only support group, except for one or two oddball kids from the Army who were just as out of water as I was, whether they were black or white. There was a "misfit" group. And that was the first and only time that I ever associated with or was perceived as a misfit, and that's because I literally was one.

NANCY KARACAND

My twentieth high school reunion will be in two more years, in Mississippi, and I would consider going. It would be interesting. There were only thirty-two girls in my class. They had a ten-year reunion, and my mother got word of it, but there was no way that I was going to go back at that time. I had sort of a rotten attitude about the girls in my class. Most of them were town girls, so it was probably a combination of feeling inferior, or unaccepted, and feeling disdainful at the same time. I saw them as very small-minded southerners, and I hated the South. I hated the South at age nine, when we moved there, and that feeling continued. The people are small-minded, don't know anything about the world, and they think that they're at the center of the universe, and I know better. There's no big desire on my part to reconnect with people from that time in my life. It wasn't a real pleasant time.

SHARON GILMORE

When I was a senior, I had a choice, and I terminated. The school systems back in Chicago were hard, and I had enough credits to terminate, and I did. Somebody said, "Shoot, that's the best part of your high school years, your last half a year. You get to do this and that." I could have cared less.

MICHELLE SLOAN

Changing schools got worse. I worried more about what to wear. My first day in junior high, after we got back from Germany, was really disappointing, because I had this new dress that looked like denim, and it had suspenders. I had an orange top and orange knee socks that matched perfectly and these little shoes. I went to this school and everyone was wearing these cool jeans and I was totally wearing the wrong thing. That was bad. I had planned to wear this really neat outfit and it turned out to be just stupid.

My father retired in Connecticut, and that was where I graduated. I'll probably never go back to any reunions. Maybe in ten years, I'll feel differently about it. I moved there in the beginning of my junior year, and that spring I got a car, and *then* I got friends. It sounds really cold, but that's probably what it was. They used me for my car, and I used them.

My dad was looking for work, and he finally got a job down in Trenton. I remember being told about that. That was the only time I was ever upset. I had been there for a whole year, and finally I was getting into things. I had my car, I had a position on the school paper, and I was going to be in the color guard. And then my mom said, "Guess what? Your dad got a job in Trenton. You can go to four high schools. Won't that be neat?"

I just had a heart attack. I stormed off to my bedroom; I'd never done anything like that. It worked: we didn't go. My dad commuted for a year.

BRUCE HUTSON

I was in Florida during the spring of 1979, and the notices were showing up in the newspaper for ten-year class reunions. It was frustrating that I couldn't contact anyone about my class reunion. I called my high school in Germany; it took about three tries to get through. They couldn't believe that I was calling them, and they tried to claim that they had never had anyone contact them about a reunion. We're talking about hundreds of people, over a span of twenty years, who had graduated from this school. I left my name with them in kind of a futile gesture. That's the way it was in 1979. It was very frustrating; these reunions were going on, and I was thinking, "Where is mine?"

Then in 1984, I was listening to the American Top 40 on the car radio. And they went, "Coming up next, our long-distance dedication from a woman who hasn't seen her sister in ten years," or something. I thought: Oh, that's so hokey. And some synapse just blipped in my mind at that point, and I thought: Hey, I could do a long-distance dedication. Maybe that would be kind of a neat way to try and track down some of those people from my high school. Millions of people listen to that show; there's got to be someone out there. I went home and wrote a letter.

I got a letter back, telling me that they were going to air my dedication, so I found out that the local station broadcast the show on Sunday. I was in bed on Saturday morning, and the phone rang, and this woman asked, "Is this the Bruce Hutson who went to K-Town High School in Germany?" The last thing on my mind was that it was a call about the dedication, that it had aired on Saturday, but the fog started clearing. It turned out that this woman, Patty, and I had gone out a few times in high school, and she lived in Omaha, and her husband had heard the dedication and told her about it. She had just called directory assistance and got my number, which is what I had hoped that people would do.

So I said, "Patty, we've got to try to get something going, a reunion or something." Shortly after we talked, a friend of Patty's in Illinois mentioned something about the whole long-distance dedication to her hairdresser, and the hairdresser said, "K-Town? I cut someone's hair who mentioned that to me." Patty called me, and she was just hysterical that through this third and fourth party, she was able to find this guy in Dallas who was trying to get something organized for the class of 1970.

I called the guy and asked him what they had done, and how they had organized things. They had gone through the Department of Defense and were able to beg, borrow, and steal their way into the files. DOD wouldn't give out addresses for people, so what they did and what we ended up doing, was send them envelopes with the father's name at the top, and they would put an address sticker on it with the last known address for the father. There was no way for us to get in touch with any of the civilian kids, because they were part of that big, nebulous Civil Service, and that was sad, because almost a third of the class were civilians.

We had our reunion in Dallas. The class of 1970 was having theirs, so we said, "Hey, let's combine them." We had an incredible blowout, and the hotel people didn't think that we would be putting away as much beer as we did, but we said, "Hey, remember, we learned to drink beer in Germany, so this American beer's not going to do anything."

I just sat back and observed what was going on and saw people talking and those faces lighting up, and I thought: Yeah, this is nice. This is what I wanted out of my high school experience. And I was satisfied.

I guess I was just obsessed—and I've never been obsessed with anything in my life—about pulling off that reunion. I can remember the nights that I spent looking in the yearbook, looking at these seventeen-year-old faces of people, and not having an adult face to combine it with—these goofy friends of mine, and the girls I had crushes on, and the jocks I used to butt heads with.

I really haven't heard from anyone about doing anything for our class this year, but I don't feel the need to put this big effort into it again. It's great that I was able to reestablish some contact with these kids that I went to high school with, but it's funny; I've talked to people from the class, and now that we got that initial reunion out of the way, a lot of the people are just feeling sated. They don't feel this great need to do it again. I saw these people, and they're no longer seventeen in my mind.

6

Holding Down the Fort: Discipline

My parents ran a tight outfit and they outranked us kids. As long as we lived in their house we were expected to abide by their rules. Disobeying or challenging those rules was flirting with disaster; evading a question was out of the question. We were to answer questions directly, without quibbling, and when we were told to do something, we did it, "no ifs, ands, or buts about it." Talking back was tantamount to mutiny. "Don't give me any lip!" We had to look at my father when he was talking to us. It was impossible to be sullen and insubordinate when he barked, "Look at me when I am talking to you!" He frequently punctuated that command with a sharp rap to the clavicle with his index finger. I watched and learned that it was suicidal to attempt to buck my father's authority.

My older siblings have been telling me for years how easy I had it. According to them, my father used to be a real martinet. They told me tales just like those that soldiers tell, descriptions of the horrors of battle that I could never fully understand because I hadn't been there. I had it easy. It could have been worse, but I certainly got my share of lectures from my father, the master of psychological intimidation. I used to tell my sister, in the heat of many adolescent dramas, that I wished he would just hit me and get it over with. Those lectures were torture.

It was my father whose wrath, whose disfavor I feared, but my mother was the central authority figure in our household simply by default: she was there. I knew the limits with her, and she frequently drew upon my father's repertoire when I pushed those limits. "Don't you talk to me like that!" And that old parental standby, "Because I said so, that's why."

I often wonder whether there was a military regulation, some military code that specified "All military families will convene in their dining rooms at 1800 hours for meals." We had dinner at the same hour every night, and we had to be home before dinner was served for what we laughingly referred to as "togetherness time." Dinnertime was sacred and we were not late. Other kids got to play right up until the food was on the table, but we didn't.

The kitchen was a scene of controlled chaos as seven people prepared to eat. "Let's dish up!" "Go wash up!" Subtle variations in tone of voice meant the difference between a reminder and an order.

At the dinner table, my father reigned from his seat at the head of the table. We quaked in our boots when his attention came to rest on us for real or imagined offenses. He had a captive audience when we were gathered at the table, and he used that time to exert his influence. "Sit up straight!" "Don't play with your food." "Get your elbows off the table!"

Every minute detail of the design on our china and every swirl of our silverware pattern is etched into my mind, for when someone was in trouble at the table, I kept my eyes on my plate. "MYOB." Mind your own business. Acting too interested in someone else's misbehavior was an offense in itself.

My father's word was law at work and at home. I knew that in the Army soldiers could be court-martialed for things like failing to obey an order or for going AWOL. Repercussions when I committed the same offenses were swift and predictable, and my father never had to lift a finger to me or shout to make his point.

He had a way of saying, "Get with the program, young lady!" without raising his voice, that made me flinch.

Even our dog was a model of obedience. He was not allowed on the furniture. The dining room was off-limits to him at meal-time, so he kept his nose just on the safe side of the threshold and he was trained not to beg or whine. There were times when having a dog must have been my parents' salvation, because he actually did what he was told to do without giving them any lip. He obeyed.

When we left the house, other men in uniform were in charge: the post commander, who had the authority to establish rules of his own for the entire community, and the MPs, who enforced post rules and regulations.

My mother used to tell me, "Don't be ugly," which meant don't act up, don't stick out your tongue at GIs, don't fight with your sister or with other kids. It was ugly to get in trouble, and, in the process, get your father in trouble. The unspoken consensus among kids was "Don't get caught." We once lived near a wooded area that was periodically guarded by GIs, probably an ammunition cache of some kind, and the neighborhood craze was to sneak up, as close as we could, to the GIs on guard duty. We would be discovered and they would chase us off, and as soon as our hearts stopped pounding we would creep through the woods again, troops on a covert operation, always careful not to push our luck too far, never getting close enough to be captured.

The risks that we dared each other to take were hardly acts of juvenile delinquency, but there was always that guilty thrill, the threat of being caught and having to give your name, the danger that your father would be called on the carpet because of you.

I picked up everything I knew about authority in the world outside the post from cartoons, Nancy Drew mysteries, and school lessons about the presidents. Inside our house, my father was the ultimate authority. On the streets outside our house, there were MPs, who were nothing like "real" police; they were just lowly GIs who gave out speeding tickets and would get you if you didn't stop in your tracks at five o'clock when the flag was lowered.

The MPs and my father were ruled by the post commander,

who, as far as I knew, reported directly to the president of the United States. My father was in the United States Army, and I knew that the United States was the land of the free. I never perceived anything contradictory in that: everyone knew that kids and GIs were excluded from participatory democracy. We weren't to question orders; we obeyed them, "no ifs, ands, or buts about it."

There are plenty of military brats who endured eighteen years of military discipline without appearing on the military payroll. There were, indeed, martinets, the military fathers who used tried-and-true boot camp principles with their children. When the subject of discipline came up in interviews, it was not at all unusual for military brats to slip into another persona, complete with a strident, stentorian drill sergeant's voice, when they described their fathers.

One man described his father with a single sentence: "These guys knew how to make grown men quiver." The boot camp principles that were so effective in training grown men were equally effective at home. But the military brats who resisted being treated like "little troops" often engaged in a futile battle, one-to-one combat with fathers for whom the military had truly become a way of life. In such households, military brats were never "at ease." Boot camp, the rite of initiation for GIs, lasted for thirteen weeks, but it was daily life for some military brats.

Like so much of military life, the military brat's lot in life depended, to a large degree, on his CO, his commanding officer. Not all fathers were martinets, and not all military brats had to bounce coins on their bedspreads or stand at attention against the doorjamb for punishment. But the regular dads and lenient parents were characterized by the ways in which they differed from the regimes of the martinets.

"We were not a yes, sir, no, sir, family."

"I didn't even know what being grounded was."

Disciplinary tactics that are now considered abusive were a matter of parental prerogative for many years in both military and civilian families. Family discipline was a personal matter, to be handled behind the closed doors of the neat rows of houses on military posts, but the implication that fathers who fit into the orderly world of the military should be able to control small children was clear.

Rumors spread quickly on post, but it was only the most indiscreet behavior that provoked whispers. Inevitably, the post grapevine—which no one would admit was gossip—was abuzz whenever there was a neighborhood child, usually a teenager, or even worse, an entire family who was out of line, whose behavior attracted negative attention. Neighbors weren't just people who lived next door; they were superiors and co-workers.

Military brats were aware that their behavior or misbehavior was a direct reflection on their parents, and specifically on their fathers. Fathers were held accountable for the behavior of their children, just as senior officers were held accountable for the men in their command.

GAIL EMERSON

One of the guiding lights of my childhood, one of the things that my parents used to tell us about and hold up as something for us to hear about and emulate, was this story about my cousin and my uncle. My uncle was in the service, too. Apparently instant obedience was the rule: no questions. You never asked questions, you just instantly obeyed.

And the virtue of this was born out by this story. My cousin Betty was sitting at the end of pier, fishing, and my uncle said, "Betty, don't move." And being a good girl, she didn't move. There was a snake behind her and he kicked it off the dock. This was really pointed out to us. This was why we had to obey instantly.

JACK LEMONT

When Dad came back, we had to get used to the "iron hand." I say "iron hand," but I don't remember him being that strict. He'd let things slide once in a while, depending on his mood, but for the most part, it was "I'll tell you once; you do it." He was used to telling these young knotheads what to do and they did it, and he expected that at home, too.

BILL FLYNN

Discipline is a big thing. I don't mean to imply that discipline was shoved down our throats in a military fashion, but we had a regiment in our family. We had job boards on our refrigerator. Everybody had to pitch in and carry their load. If we went on a picnic, nobody left until we policed the area. I'm sure that came from some squad that my dad was in when he was a soldier, policing the area. I think that was definitely good, in the formative years, to have had that kind of structure, that kind of discipline as a good example.

RHONDA HEALEY

My parents' own curfews and behavior standards and discipline were usually more imposing than anything the Navy could have demanded from us. You didn't walk in five minutes late in our house. If you did you'd better be half-dead, because if you weren't, then you would die anyway. We were expected to keep our curfews.

I can remember having a little trouble with that, calling my dad one time from the pizza place in town where I had gone on a date and telling him, "I don't think I can get home," and my dad was there in two minutes. It goes without saying that I never went out with that guy again.

The family-imposed rules were very strict. I had to "do" my hair every day. And that was in the days when everybody had straight hair. Forget it. I had to put it in a little pony tail or roll it up in rollers. No straight hair for me.

BRENDA ROWAN

We were kind of afraid of my dad, in a way. We never called him "sir," so in that way it wasn't real rigid or strict, in fact, we always called him "Poppy," which was a very affectionate name. There was affection there; it was just that he had his rules, and there were no transgressions beyond those rules, or else.

All the fathers of the kids I knew were all the same. They were all kind of strict, authoritarian fathers. I don't know how much of it was my dad and how much of it was the system, the Navy. It was kind of intermingled.

JOHN ROWAN

I never called my father "sir." He didn't bring the military structure home with him at all. But I don't feel like I was spoiled: there were certainly rules and expectations; they just weren't real strict. Especially in high school, I could see that my friends who were also officers' kids would be put on restriction for getting bad grades and things like that, and they had strict schedules for doing homework and chores. I never had anything like that. My friends whose fathers were enlisted would get restricted for other things, for misbehaving. But I didn't have that happen, either. I don't think that there's any way that anyone would have known that we were a military family.

DEREK LOWE

My parents were fairly strict, and I don't think that was different from what was going on with the other kids in my neighborhood. Corporal punishment was not unusual. In retrospect, you become aware of the stresses of the job, whether it was long hours, or being away, or circumstances as a squad leader or platoon sergeant being responsible for other people. There were stresses in the household that people now would be more aware of. That was fairly typical: the corporal punishment, the discipline and rigidity toward children, a mentality that was kind of modeled after behavior at work.

The one thing that we had the most conflict about was school: grades, performance, and homework. Oh, God, the ordeal of homework. I think that came from his own need to be self-disciplined and his intolerance for anything less than self-discipline. And perhaps that came from guys who he was responsible for at work who weren't doing what they were supposed to be doing. I think that kind of spilled over to home.

We were a "yes, sir, no, sir," family. That was reinforced not only by the Army, but in my family outside our household: the southern black family view, with a real respect for elders and a sense of family hierarchy. And, of course, the Army supported that, too.

Boys did a lot of wild and crazy things. In Germany, I remember going over the fences and breaking into the supply depots that were kind of out in the open, exposed. There wasn't anything for us to get into, just cans of oil, or insect repellent. It wasn't vandalism, just the curiosity and the challenge of doing something sneaky. But we realized that if we got caught we'd have to deal with our fathers, and there would be repercussions. The first thing they asked you was who was your father, and where did he work. I was always conscious of that. I made it a point not to create problems, because that pressure was out there. The rules were very apparent. I think you learn that in the Army. All those big fields gave you lots of running room. We'd heard of people getting busted in rank for things that their kids had done. That was probably a myth, but nonetheless we knew about it.

TERRY McCULLOCH

My parents were very much in unison when it came to discipline. My dad was the disciplinarian, the one who handled it. There was never any argument between my parents about how these kids were going to be raised. My mother deferred to him in everything, and when he was gone, she just took up his role and knew exactly how to handle it.

We had rules. You could not go anywhere on a school night. We definitely had to be home for dinner, and we stayed home after that. We could use the phone, but we could not leave the house. And then on weekends, we could only go out one night. We had to choose whether we went out on Friday or Saturday night. In Arizona, Sandy and I were riding the bus home from school one day, and there was a girl I hated, named Ellen. We ended up fighting, and the whole time, I was thinking in the back of my mind, Why am I doing this? I was crying. Sandy and all of my friends were yelling, "Beat her up; beat her up!"

The MPs came and everything, and the base commander found out about it and wrote a letter to my dad that said, "Control your daughter." It was this horrible thing. My dad—well, it's the first time I had ever done anything bad, and my dad did absolutely nothing to punish me. He just looked at me and said, "Should you have done this? Did you have a reason to do this?" And I said something like, yes, she provoked me, like it was her fault. And he said, "Okay, that's all I wanted to know."

He didn't restrict me, didn't beat me, didn't do anything. He wasn't even mad at me. And he got into worse trouble with that than he'd ever gotten into, for anything. "Control your daughter." I was thirteen or so. It was the first and last time that I got into a fight.

HELEN PIERSON

We were definitely raised by the rod. Both of my parents were very strict. Mom wasn't easy, and Dad was worse. We were raised very military, with a little southern heritage thrown in. I'm not sure how much of it actually had to do with being in the military, or if it was because of the way that my dad had been raised. I also wonder how much frustration had to do with it, too—all the moving, or whatever.

People would always remark on how well behaved we were when we were kids. When you had to drive across the country with four kids in the backseat, they had better be well behaved. We knew how to be quiet.

My dad was a mess sergeant at one time. He was just like the drill instructors in the movies. He would relate stories about some GI asking him to pass the butter without saying "please," so he would smash the butter in the GI's face, stories like that.

Once when I was about eight years old, I was riding my bike. There was a big rock in the road, and I accidentally swerved and was almost hit by a car. It just happened to be the base commander's car, and his driver got out of the car and started yelling at me and asked me for my last name. My dad heard about that incident. There was always that underlying fear: the fathers could get called on the carpet for the things that their kids were doing.

I ran away once, and the state police caught me. I will never forget that. They put me in the back of the car and took me to the main gate of the post and turned me over to the MPs. The MPs called my dad out of a meeting to come and pick me up. I don't know if anyone talked to him about that particular incident, but that was always a concern of his. We couldn't mess up, because he could get in trouble.

BRAD HOLMES

When we moved to Georgia, that was where I started drinking. I didn't have any idea that we were going to get into that. The last thing on my mind was drinking, but then I got these friends who were real nice kids. One of them was a general's son, and another guy was the son of a full colonel who was in charge of the whole command.

We'd always go over to their houses, and their dads had huge bars. Military guys are pretty heavy drinkers, most of them. So the kids would start daring you to drink some, and pretty soon you'd get bombed. Next thing you know, it happens a couple of times, and then soon you're asking airmen to buy beer for you. The airmen didn't have any friends. They were young guys. They'd like to have anybody pay attention to them and be their friends, so they'd buy us beer.

We had some friends who were getting into more trouble than we were. Some of them got sent to juvenile hall. I had friends who missed school on Monday because they were in "juvie." I always wanted to go to "juvie," but I never did anything that warranted that. I never got into too much trouble.

We had friends whose parents had real problems with alcohol. I had a good friend whose dad would get real violent and chase his mom. He'd beat her up a couple of times. She'd run down by our house and hide out behind our house, and he'd come down and find her.

The other time that I knew about that kind of thing was when some of my friends' dads would take us for the day and all they would do was go from bar to bar to bar. They'd drop us off at a play area, and they'd say, "Okay, why don't you guys play here in this parking lot? I'm going to be in that building over there," which was a bar.

So we'd play there for a while, and we'd be like, let's go somewhere else. So we'd go into the bar, and we'd go over to the dad, and we'd say, Can you please take us somewhere else? And so they'd say, Okay, and they'd take us to another place, and they'd say, "Here's a new place for you to play. I'm going to be in that building right across the street there." And it would be another bar. That happened a couple of times. I think my parents knew about it later.

When we were kids, our favorite thing to do was have the MPs chase us. They just weren't scary at all. All you had to do if you saw an MP drive by in his blue truck was just stop in your tracks and then start running. They'd stop their truck and they'd chase you, just because you were running, but they could never catch you.

MIKE NEWCOMB

I would get in trouble with the MPs because they can't touch dependents. I learned that, well, they have power, but they only have so much, and the only power they have, really, is against your dad, and that's only if they catch you and get your name. Nobody was robbing people or breaking into apartments or anything.

We would throw snowballs at cars, and the MPs would stop in their jeep, and we'd be standing there, holding these snow-balls. They'd say, "All right, you kids, drop the snowballs."

And we'd go, "What snowballs?" We'd throw the snowballs at them and just run like hell through the housing area. They'd try to catch us, but we knew the area, and we'd run down into the basements of the big apartment buildings, and we'd never get caught.

I knew a kid whose dad did get in trouble, so we learned stuff like that. The kid was caught trashing one of the snack bars, not real badly, but he had ketchup and was slinging it around on the curtains and stuff, and his dad got written up for it.

When I was a senior, my dad was sent to some kind of training school. I don't even remember how long he was gone, at least one semester. I was too busy raising hell, going out drinking with my buddies and coming in at all hours of the night, and just driving my mom nuts, I guess. When my dad finally got back, I went out and just got really bad one night. My friend took me home and just left me on the porch. I can remember leaning against the wall, going, "Hi, Dad!"

And of course, my mom was raising hell. She was screaming, "Did anyone see you?" She was more worried about whether or not anyone saw me like that. My dad was saying, "Now, honey, let him sleep it off and we'll talk to him in the morning. He's not comprehending anything we're saying right now." I almost fell over; he had to carry me to my bedroom.

And boy, did I get shit for that. I had the worst headache the next day. I just couldn't even function. When I saw my friend I could've pummeled him. He could have done anything, kept me out later, got me in trouble for staying out too late, but he could have helped me sober up a little. It was just a disaster. I was on restriction forever.

Sometimes I wish my parents had been more strict. I'm not saying they didn't punish me. I heard "Wait until your father gets home!" enough times. That was worse than the punishment, because I'd be nauseous, and by the time my dad got home, I'd be sick. He'd have his own problems, coming in from work, and my mom would be ranting about this offense I had committed. I'd be thinking: Oh, my God, what's going to happen? And my poor dad was like "Well, I guess I have to punish you." He used to wield a great belt.

LINDA WINSLOW

By the time I was a teenager, we were at Paine Field and we had this tight-ass commanding officer. You could not wear your hair in rollers, and you could not wear shorts to the BX [Base Exchange]. Just little, picky things. It's like, wait a minute, whose

114

life is this? It was a whole series of restrictions. And I think that causes a lot of ambivalence and schizophrenia. You're not told what to do; you're told what not to do.

If my father had been a corporate executive and I had been running loose through the neighborhood, nobody would care. But if my father is a lieutenant colonel, and everybody knows me because we're living in this contained environment—I think it's a real burden of responsibility.

TIM BROCKWAY

My mom was the house mom. She took care of us kids, and if we needed any parental help, we went to her. And on the weekends, Dad was definitely the authoritative, scary guy. I remember him saying, "Post to your quarters," and doing all this military ordering around. I remember how his voice thundered when he issued his commands around the house. That's my dad.

My brother and I ran away from home in Germany because one of the general's sons was having a birthday party and we were not going to be allowed to go. They had all the military police and German police looking for us. My father must have felt real good. He was a major at the time and couldn't even hang on to his own family and had to involve not only the military but the foreign police as well.

I was a great embarrassment to my father. One time in North Dakota, we were being wild and crazy on the way to school, and they had military police directing traffic, and we thought, Let's try to spit on this guy as we go past him. There was no thought of being malicious or disrespectful; it was just kid stuff, like "Let's see if we can break this window." The cops stopped the bus and yanked me and another Army brat off the bus, and my dad had to go talk to the base commander. Oh, God, I really got in trouble for that. That was his worst embarrassment. Here was a career military officer's kid spitting on military policemen.

PETER VARGAS

There were regulations, restrictions, and rules. I was brought up surrounded by them. You left the base, and it felt like you were

115

relieved of a burden of having to follow rules. There was a curfew on base; you weren't allowed out after ten. You had to show IDs to get in and out of the base, and there were specific driving regulations you had to follow, one thing after another. We were surrounded by rules.

I don't have the image of my father that I think most civilian kids have of their fathers, because we were different. My mother raised us pretty much, and when my father was home, he did his best to get his two cents' worth in. He came home with edicts, rather than my mother's assignments for chores and things like that. He had edicts, and we didn't argue. That's carried over, all my life. I "sir" people to death, regardless of who they are.

My father tried to instill in us that military way of life, that there is a lot of discipline and that there are rules and regulations to govern everything, and those rules and regulations are not violated, period. He really forced that on me and my sister, so whenever we had the opportunity to get away from that, to rebel, we took it.

MARSHA KATZ

My dad treated us kids like he treated his troops. And it worked really well with my brothers, but then I came along, and that's when the trouble began. He expected us to be like soldiers and take any discipline that was dished out to us, and my brothers could do that. But I was too emotional, and I'd just burst into tears. My dad just did not know how to deal with me at all, so I spent the better part of my childhood trying to control myself and my emotions, trying to be a good soldier like my brothers. We just had the constant struggle; he was trying to fit me into his military mold, and I just couldn't do it, whether it was because I was a girl or just because I was me. His tactics worked with his men, and with my brothers, and it really seemed to bother him that those tactics didn't work with me. I think he was harsher on me because his normal tactics didn't work; I was a disciplinary problem because I couldn't just stand there and take it, like my brothers could.

116

My dad is not a big man, physically, but he scared everyone in the neighborhood with his booming voice and the way he used to act. The double standard that he had really showed up when I started getting interested in boys. My brothers could pretty much do as they pleased, as long as they were home on time, but everything I did came under his scrutiny. My dates had to be marched in for inspection, and he gave them the third degree. "What's your name? Where do you live? Who is your father and what does he do? What are your plans for the future?" So I finally figured out that it was easier to just sneak around, and I stopped bringing my boyfriends home. I would arrange to meet them at the movies, or wherever, just to avoid the scenes with my dad. It was like the Inquisition. It made a date seem like a really serious commitment. It made it impossible for me to just be friends with boys, because my dad wanted to know what their intentions were. Even as an adult I felt really uncomfortable about going on typical dates where someone comes to your house to pick you up, and I know it's because of all the trauma that I went through back then.

BEVERLY TAYLOR

Once when I was in my senior year of high school, I was riding in the car with my parents. I was relating a story to them. I said, "Oh, and she said this, and boy, was he ever PO'd at her."

My father pulled the car over to the side of the road and stopped and said, "What did you say?"

I said, "He was 'put out.' " I literally believed that's what it meant; at that age, I was not a con artist. I was so naïve, I cannot believe it. I can't speak for every military child, but I was so protected and my environment was so strict that I had no idea what was going on in the real world.

And my father said, "If you're going to use that kind of language, young lady, then you can clean the cat's litter box for a month." And I did. That was my punishment. That was the way that he thought. If I was going to use that language, then I could be around it. But I literally didn't know any better.

DEBBIE WEST

My father was different. Everybody else seemed normal to me. Everybody else's life-style seemed to be the goal to which I aspired. Actually, my family, I guess, seemed fairly normal. It was my father who was different. Nobody had a father like mine. He's a very stern person; he never really had a good word to say. He was belittling and condescending, but condescending with a vicious edge to it. Everybody was afraid of my father; my mother, too, for that matter. As kids, we were just very distant and respectful. I liked everybody else's parents better than I did my own.

Makeup wasn't allowed. I'd put on makeup when I got to school and wash it off before I went home. My mother has a very conservative sense of style, and she always sewed, so I always wore what she made me and what she made me make. And of course I hated everything I wore. I'd roll up my skirts when I left the house, because short skirts were in and my mother just thought that was terrible.

I had curfews, very strictly applied curfews. I wasn't allowed to date until I was seventeen. When I finally did start dating, I had to be in at eleven-thirty. It was ridiculous. And this was when I wasn't grounded, by the way.

Being grounded meant that I couldn't be off the family property. The only time I could leave home was to go to school and come home. My father never called it being grounded; that was a popular term among my friends. It was "You're on restriction." Sometimes I'd get off restriction and get back on the same day. It seemed like I spent all of my high school years going from one restriction to another, for long periods of time.

I remember my father saying, "Dinner is at 1800 hours." The Navy permeated our life, in that respect. He *was* the Navy, to me. But I'd throw it back at him. He'd say, "Well, it's Saturday morning; you can swab the deck," and I'd say, "You mean mop the floor?" I refused, I dug my heels in all the way, and it was a constant battle between the two of us.

I've asked my mother several times, why did you stay with him? He was very brutal. He used to beat my sister and me badly, but my mother couldn't do anything about it. He'd start in on one

118

of his tantrums, his rages, and he'd be completely out of control, and she'd just leave for a couple of hours, because there was nothing that she could do, and she couldn't stand to watch it.

I've never blamed her or faulted her for that. I can understand. When somebody's out of control, they're out of control. I think my mother's become a little bit more independent. I think she is more willing to say that maybe it was not as it should have been; maybe she should have stepped in more; maybe she should have realized that my father had really deep-seated problems.

I used to resent my friends who were so close with their dads. It always seemed so neat. I felt like the little match girl, on the outside, looking in. Any time I had to go somewhere with my dad, he'd be driving, and I'd be the only other person in the car, and I'd sit in the backseat, because I couldn't stand being that close to him. He gave me the creeps. There was something about him. After a while, I finally made my peace with that. Okay, it was good for other people, and I could see it on TV, and get all misty-eyed over it, and it might have been a good thing, but it wouldn't have worked with us. When it came right down to brass tacks, I didn't want it. I didn't want to be close to him.

CAROLINE BAKER

My dad was real strict. He ran his household just like he ran his company: very demanding, very controlling. But then, he was fun, too. He had his times. He would do things that would drive my mom crazy; like at the dinner table, he would act real funny and just drive my mom crazy.

But when he said jump, we jumped right now, and we didn't ever ask, "How high?" I don't remember him ever using it, but we were threatened with the belt. I still can't figure out how he could have controlled four kids so easily. He would snap his fingers and we would run.

He was real strict about curfews. We always knew when dinner was, and we had better be there five minutes before.

He was still strict even when he got out of the service. It was kind of embarrassing for me because I felt so different from the other kids in civilian life. All these other kids could do whatever they wanted. I thought it would be neat if we could be like that for a week.

My dad started giving my boyfriends the third degree when I was in high school. I would have to bring them home, and he would have to know where we were going, what we were going to be doing, and what time we were going to be home. The guy knew he'd better stay in line after that. They didn't want to mess with my dad. He would usually be waiting up for me when I got home. Sometimes he would just be lying back in his easy chair with one eye open. Our curfew was never later than midnight. That meant we had to be home at ten minutes to midnight. We always were.

There was one family on the base in Illinois who had these wild kids who were totally out of control. There always had to be one of those families. My dad knew about them, too, and he would use them as an example of how you get a reputation on such a small little base, of how rumors go around. We knew we definitely better not screw up because it would reflect on my dad and we would really be in deep trouble.

SHEILA WRIGHT

Standing in the corner was our punishment, and there were so many minutes depending on what you had done, for example, fifteen minutes for slapping your sister. That was the worst punishment I could think of. I would rather be spanked and get it over with than stand in the corner for fifteen minutes. You just knew Dad was watching you with that eagle eye, just waiting for you to move so he could yell at you, "Get that nose in the corner!"

My brother swore once in front of my mom. We were sitting at the dinner table, and he said "hell" or something; it wasn't even that bad. He sat on my dad's right-hand side, and my dad is left-handed, so he didn't even break stride; he just went "wham" and kept eating. And he said, just as natural as can be, "Don't ever swear in front of your mother again."

My sister was the rebellious one. She screwed up and ran away from home, the whole bit. My dad and I used to get in real horrible fights. I was sabotaging anything I wanted to do by picking times when my dad had been drinking or was upset about something. We'd get into these fights, and I would storm off and my dad would complain about me. That's what my role in the family was.

We spent three months with my uncle one summer. He was in the Air Force, too, but he was an officer. He was totally into manners. You eat with one hand and keep the other in your lap. He showed us how to eat potato chips the right way: put it in your mouth, put your lips over it, then bite it, so you don't make any noise. Even those little Jell-O squares had to be eaten with a fork. Every night there would be an incident at the table: somebody would knock something over, and he would go, "I can't eat with these people at the table." And we would be laughing, "Let's see how we can get Uncle Larry tonight."

SHERRY RUTLEDGE

My father was really almost sick about discipline. By today's standards, we would call him an abusive parent. He prided himself on having the ultimate control; we were going to listen to him. He ruled with an iron fist, and he liked to think that he didn't use physical punishment, because he used other means of punishment that were better. But I sure remember lots of spankings.

I spent many, many nights in the corner for giggling at the supper table. To this day, I remember those nights. I still have this tendency to laugh inappropriately, when things are tense and serious. I would have to go and stand in the corner, and then he'd call me back, and say, "Now are you going to sit here and not giggle?"

And I would say, "Yes, Daddy," and I'd sit down and look at my sister, and there I'd be, all over again.

We had to eat anything that he would eat, and we didn't have to eat anything that he wouldn't eat. My dad's background was Armenian, so there were some pretty exotic things. He liked fried calf brains, so we had to eat them. And his policy was that if we didn't eat our food at that meal, then we got it for the next

121

meal. And we didn't get anything else until we finished it, by golly. There's a classic story about my sister eating Cheerios that were twenty-four hours old, that had been sitting there through three different meals. I can remember sitting there in agony, because I knew that I didn't want to eat the food in front of me, and I knew that he wasn't going to give an inch. The family dog helped us out, many times. We could always pass the dog something under the table.

We always had to say, "Yes, Mommy," "No, Mommy," or "Yes, Daddy," "No, Daddy." In fact, before I came along, my older sisters had to say, "Yes, Mommy, dear," and "No, Mommy, dear," and "Thank you, Mommy, dear," and he was very rigid about it.

SHARON GILMORE

My mom was very lenient, with me especially, because she'd leave for work at five o'clock, and I'd do all the cooking and the laundry and take care of the kids. I was always afraid to get into trouble because I didn't want her to think less of me.

My dad, on the other hand, because he was always drunk, would come home and say, "Why isn't the goddamn house cleaned up? I want my goddamn dinner." I'd fix him dinner, and by that time, you give him ten minutes, he'd pass out on the couch. One time I fixed him dinner, and I waited for him to pass out, and he woke up a half an hour later. "Where's my dinner?" I said, "I already fixed it for you and you passed out." And he said, "Don't get smart with me."

Never once did he carry through with a promise, or a fishing trip, ever, because we'd never make it. He'd stop at a tavern, and he'd go in and buy us a bag of potato chips and a Nesbitt's orange pop, and we'd sit in the car for over an hour, and then he'd drive us home drunk. My mother had fits.

He would go on four-day blackouts where he'd be doing things and wouldn't know it. He came home one night and passed out in front of the house, so while he was passed out, my mom painted his toenails red and put his socks back on. He went off to duty the next night and was in the barracks and took his socks off, and there were these red toenails.

122

I can remember one time my dad came home and was checking, "Is your bedroom clean?" If he'd had a bad day, and if he'd been chewed out by his superiors, he'd come home and rank on us. "I'm going to check your bedspreads." And he never would, of course.

He carried the loud voice and stuff home with him. If you smarted off to him, he'd backhand you. One time he hit me, and my mom told him if he ever laid a hand on me again that was it. All he had to do was yell, and I'd cry. My mom gave me one spanking in my whole life that I can remember, with a zori, one of those sandals, and we ended up laughing about it.

BARRY JENKINS

My little sisters didn't take half the shit my older sister and I took, and that's a fact. They took their share, but my parents were so much more tense with us than they were with my little sisters. My older sister and I, for different reasons, got special treatment that neither of us wanted. Me, because I was the only son. I think if I had had a brother, it would have been a different story; it would have been spread out a little bit. I got all of that macho bullshit on my head. It had its advantages to be the only son: I got my own room, while my sisters were walled on top of each other in a little room. But that was one of the few advantages. I would have traded that for less bullshit.

Dinner was a formal thing; they made us sit there, and then they tortured us to death. I had friends who got to eat TV dinners in front of the television, but in our house, it was mess call, and you didn't miss it or the shit would fly.

He was a bastard about manners. He sat at the head of the table with me on his right, and he'd be on me the whole time. I got thunked on the knuckles and on the head with the handle of the knife. He was great with a backhand to the forehead. To this day, I wolf down my food. Sometimes he'd say, "Well, you're staying here until everybody else is done." I just liked to get away from the table just so I could get away from him.

My dad was kind of schizo: on the one hand, he'd be this sort of gnarly cussing old sailor, and then the other side of him was the officer and the gentleman. And he would say, "That's not proper English; don't speak that way." And then the next sentence he'd go, "I ain't gonna do that, goddammit," and I'd go, "Oh, yeah, that's proper English." There were two sides of him.

I was rebellious, but it was a subtle rebellion. I wasn't allowed to talk back, or sass, or openly do anything that was out of line. My old man would smack me down the hallway. My dad had the attitude that if you're told to do something, "because I said so" was a good enough answer. It never was good enough for me, and it never will be. And still, that kind of authority can just kiss my ass. I just don't buy that stuff. I wasn't in the Navy, and I didn't want to be, you know?

I got booted down a flight of stairs once. Boom. I'll never forget that staircase. My mother was telling me something, and I was standing there saying, "I don't agree with you," and he came up to me yelling, "Goddammit, I told you to get downstairs." And I turned to go downstairs and boom, he just booted me, let me have it. There were two flights of stairs and the front door was right there at the bottom, and I went flying down the stairs into the front door.

My parents didn't always get along, so if my mother ever sided with me, he hit the roof. Shit, I was in the middle of it, and you throw in all that military stuff on top of it and his whole attitude of "I demand respect," and it gets real ugly.

I was having another disagreement with my mother shortly after he gave me a boot down the stairs. I was asking why, and he grabbed me by the shirt and he had his fist right in my face and he was going, "Goddammit, you don't disagree; you just do what you're told!" And I just didn't even react, I was getting so used to it. I turned to my mother and I said, "You know, I hope I don't turn out like this."

And he just went *pfft*. I swear it was like someone popped him with a pin and all the wind blew right out of him and he shrunk down to about this tall. I'd never had such an effective weapon against him in my life. It was unbelievable, the reaction.

I never really got into trouble. I was not out shoplifting; I wasn't doing drugs. But I was always treated like "Unless I ride your ass, you're going to fuck up." That was his attitude. Thanks for the faith. Glad you feel so confident.

He was a brilliant mathematician, because he had never finished high school, and he had fought like hell to get into that college program, and he had taken all this math, and he really valued it. He kept saying, "You gotta take math; you're going to need it." For what? I'm not going to be an engineer. But he had this tunnel vision: if I wasn't doing good in algebra, he flipped out. He'd ignore the fact that I was doing well in music and foreign languages, you know. But algebra was a big thing.

"I'll help you. If you're having problems, just ask, and I'll give you help." That was like asking for a nail in the head. "Dad, will you help me with my algebra?" That was masochism. He'd yell and bite my head off, because I'd say, "I don't get it," and he'd say, "Goddammit, bullshit!"

I didn't go to college. That was another big issue. That was the first time I had the old man dead to rights. I was sixteen, and he was asking, "Well, what college are you going to?" We were at dinner—he loved to bitch at me at dinner—and this college thing came up. I was going to play in a rock-and-roll band. I had known that since I was ten years old. That's what I was going to do, and they could kiss my ass. Of course, they all thought that was a passing fad that I was going to outgrow. I still haven't outgrown it.

And I said, "I'm not going to college."

He goes, "Yes, you are, you got no choice, you're going." I said, "I'm not going, and you can't make me." And he goes, "Well, what's wrong with college?"

It turned into this plea, and my sisters are sitting there going, "How'd you pull that off?" There was nothing he could say. I told him that they couldn't teach me anything I wanted to know. He was like "Well, take music classes, for Christ's sake!" He was even consenting to that.

We were having it out one day, when I was about twenty-one, and he decided to start chirping on me. I didn't want to hear it. I didn't live there; I had been paying my own way since I was eighteen, which is always a big deal with guys like that: "As long as you're under my roof!"

We got into it, and the subject of my sisters came up, and I said, "Well, they don't take half the shit I did."

And he said, "Well, maybe not." And I said, "Definitely not." Somehow I got him to admit, and for him, this was an incredible concession, "Well, I guess maybe I wasn't the best father, but goddammit. . . ."

You could have just pushed me over, and I would have fallen dead. For him to make any admission of any deficiency, any mistake, was phenomenal. From that point forward, we started getting along. We actually got along real well. He started to rethink his military situation, rethink Vietnam, and finally, toward the end, he was saying, "Yeah, it was bullshit."

By the time he died, he was so different. Finally he did start to loosen up, but it took him getting out of the military and getting a little distance, two or three years away from it, before he started to even thaw out a little bit.

7

Holding Down the Fort: When Daddy Comes Marching Home

When my father was in Vietnam, our family was allowed to remain in our quarters at Fort Riley, Kansas. We lived in a semicircle of large duplexes gathered around a parade ground, in much the same way that the pioneers pulled their covered wagons into a circle to make camp.

During our first months at Fort Riley my father, who was a lieutenant colonel at that time, was busy getting his men ready to go. He began to wear fatigues and combat boots to work, and he was gone on maneuvers with his men for days at a time. We assumed that maneuvers were like camp-outs, and my father would come home with whiskers, the beginnings of a beard. Until then the only time I had seen my father unshaven was when he was sick.

The atmosphere on the post was different during those months before my father left, as if the whole post were getting ready to go, to move out. We saw convoys of jeeps and tanks and trucks with headlights on, lumbering along the post roads every day. I always hoped to see my dad passing us in the steady stream of vehicles filled with men in green fatigues. Sometimes helicopters landed on the parade ground in front of our house and I watched the men duck to avoid the downdraft from the whirling blades. The helicopters looked too fragile to fly, and I did not want my father to ride in them. Before, when my father had worn a tie to work, the military had seemed remote. I began to realize that he was connected to all the activity, to the convoys and helicopters, long before I realized that he was leaving.

Years later, my mother told me that some of the younger wives and women were hysterical the day that the battalion left, and she felt obligated to remain calm and set a good example, as a "senior" wife. I try to imagine what it must have been like for my mother to kiss my father good-bye and get us back in the car and go home while he was rolling across Kansas, bound for Vietnam. She wore her sunglasses even though it was overcast, and I had my first introduction to a funny feeling that things were not the same. My father and his battalion of nine hundred men departed, and it seemed he had taken all of the men on post with him, except a few MPs and the guards at the gate. We were alone.

There were just three of us at home for my mother to deal with, since my brothers had gone off to college. I'm sure that his tour in Korea, when there had been five kids at home, had been much more difficult for her.

But a lot of strange things, things that seemed more alarming because my father was gone, happened during that year in Fort Riley. Escaped prisoners from the post stockade seemed to head straight for our neighborhood, and the MPs would call and warn everyone to lock all the ground-floor doors and windows. One of our neighbors was vacuuming her living room one day and looked up to see a prisoner run through her house, followed by MPs with search dogs. The Richard Speck murders were in the news that year, and my teenage sister was particularly obsessed with the story. One night she and a friend were babysitting me, and they heard a noise downstairs and immediately hid under the bed. My mother returned home to find us all hysterical.

Tornadoes were an inevitable part of life in Kansas. Our

basement in those old quarters was dark and damp and medieval, and even under normal circumstances, we hated to go down there. I can remember my mother saying, "Okay, girls, come on; we're going to the basement to put the clothes in the dryer." Later, she admitted that she didn't like going down there alone. But during the tornado alerts, she was organized and calm while we waited for the all-clear signal.

The mothers on our street were all counting the days until their husbands returned, and we had friends whose mothers were having trouble coping with children who could sense the tension. The post engineers had to be called when the girls down the street jumped on their bed with such wild abandon that the legs of the bed went through the floor and appeared in the middle of the living room ceiling below. This incident raised a few eyebrows among my mother and her friends. There was no jumping on the bed in our house. The rules were still in force.

We referred to the master bedroom as "Mom's room," as if my father had never been there, as if it had never been "their room." Mom's room was our haven, and not just because she had our only air conditioner in there. My sister and I felt my father's absence most acutely when the house was dark. Every night she tucked us into our own beds, but it was never long before my sister and I would race down the hall to her room.

My mother was busy that year, busy with projects and fifteen-hundred-piece puzzles that she worked on a card table in the living room, and fat novels that she left on her nightstand. She knitted obsessively on a sequined sweater that took her forever to complete. She had skeins of gold yarn and a long string of gold sequins that she caught on each stitch, creating dazzling rows. Her needles sounded like a ticking clock.

My father had been gone a lot during my life. He had been in Korea when I was four years old, and I vaguely remembered that year. We had moved off post while he was gone. My brothers were alternately bossy, taking their role as the men around the house very seriously, or in trouble, no doubt making the most of the respite from my father. My mother went to Hawaii to meet my father for R and R and hired a neighbor to take care of us, which was more traumatic for me than my father's absence. I have absolutely no memories of my father's leaving for Korea or coming home, but I can distinctly remember sitting at the table with my breakfast in front of me when my mother left for her week of R and R in Hawaii.

After Korea, my father spent two years at the Pentagon, years in which I rarely saw him because he was gone before I got up and came home after dinner was over. His departures and returns were a part of the routine.

It never occurred to me that he might be in danger in Vietnam, that there was the possibility that he could be wounded or killed there. All my life I had seen the soldiers, the GIs, marching around, and I knew that my father wasn't a GI, so there was never any connection, in my mind, between my father and the news footage of combat, although I always looked for him on television whenever I heard Vietnam mentioned.

I thought that he had gone to work at a desk, in a regular office, in a building in some faraway jungle. My sister and I played with our baby dolls and pretended that the dolls' daddies were in Vietnam, too.

Military families were geared to accept a father's absence as an occupational reality. There were cruises, hardship tours, basic business trips—although the business might have been delivering jets—and a variety of duty assignments that meant long hours away from home.

Sons and daughters alike were given the "man around the house" speech, with varying degrees of comprehension. The impact of emotional departure scenes was often lost on younger children, who tended to be oblivious to the facts about where their fathers were going, what they were doing, and when they would return. Parents were often deliberately vague about such details, and when war or military action took fathers away from home, the families protected themselves with a "Nothing will happen to my dad" mantra, an almost superstitious belief that if they did not acknowledge the potential dangers of war, their fathers would be safe.

The effects of a father's extended absences from a family accrued, over time, during the long days and nights that elapsed between his departure and his homecoming. The reality was often tempered with a guilty sense of relief—"Oh, good, Dad's gone. Now we can relax!"—and later, with a feeling of remorse. When military brats subtracted the total number of years that their fathers had been gone during their childhoods, they spoke in terms of loss.

Military mothers kept the home fires burning and the children gathered around, hoping that their mothers would forget the misbehavior that had provoked the cry "Just wait until your father gets home!" They were all waiting for their fathers to get home.

MARSHA KATZ

My dad never really said anything about where he was going or what he was going to do, he'd just say, "Be good for your mother while I'm gone."

When he was gone, my mother was in charge of everything and she was always really tired and overworked. Of course she had five kids, ranging in age from teenagers to babies, and was basically a single mother during that time. She was always about an inch away from tears. When something would happen with us, if we were misbehaving or whatever, she'd go into her bedroom and slam the door and hide out in there. Then we'd all be really good and tiptoe around and take her cookies because we knew that we had driven her to her room in tears.

There was always a lot of chaos at the dinner table when my dad was gone. We'd be laughing and fighting and spilling things. It seemed like every night at dinner I'd get into a fight with my brothers and sister, and I'd run into my room, which was conveniently located next to the dining room, in tears. The baby was in the high chair, and then she would spill her milk, and then my mother would run into *her* bedroom.

I can remember the tapes we sent to my dad; my mom would be in the bedroom talking into the tape recorder for what seemed like hours and hours, and we knew that we shouldn't disturb her while she was making her portion of the tape. Then she'd call us

131

in, one by one, to say something, and we'd stand there and get all nervous and try to think of something to say.

We made this tape one Christmas morning when he was in Korea. My mother turned the tape recorder on before she let us come running downstairs to see our presents, and she recorded us all morning long. You can just imagine, the typical "Christmas morning with the kids" stuff. She sent it to Dad, and the guys in his squadron came and sat with him and they all listened to it and got teary-eyed. They all missed their families.

I guess that's the difference between the military and other jobs—the business about "duty" and all of that. Sure, other people have to work on Christmas and be separated from their families. But even as a child, I knew that there was just something really sad about all of us having our Christmas in front of a microphone so that my dad could feel like he was a part of it. There's no way that you can really recapture those times. Once they're over, they're gone for good.

BILL FLYNN

The first time my dad went over to Vietnam, I was thirteen. That was his first tour. That was the tour when he was wounded about eight months after he left, so he was pretty short [a short time before his tour was over] when he got hit. My mom found out about it when someone from the Air Force base, I guess, brought her a letter that my dad had signed. He was obviously pretty doped up, because his signature was pretty erratic. I think someone came out to our house, because I came home from school, and they had just been there, maybe an hour before school let out. My mom was pretty choked up.

I remember I was having some trouble with school at the time. Actually, without my dad around to keep me in line, my mom was doing a creditable job. But I remember feeling awful, because after he was shot, she went to see him at the hospital in California, and a couple of days after she left, I got suspended from school. There was my dad in a hospital bed, and all I could do was get thrown out of school. I was only on suspension for a couple of days, but I felt terrible about that.

BARRY JENKINS

He was in Vietnam for two years, two tours. He was a Navy flyer. Before Nam, there was a period when he kept getting sent to schools, when they were training him to be an officer and go over and do that bit in Vietnam, so he was gone a lot. My mother ruled with a firm hand. She had a tough gig, with five kids and the old man gone all the time. It was my mother and us, pretty much. When he'd come back and start bitching and throwing his orders around, we felt like "Where do you come from? Who the hell is this guy?" It was weird.

On the other hand, my mother would get on our nerves, being the only disciplinarian. During his second tour in Vietnam I thought, I can't wait until my dad gets back. You started to distort your image of what he was like.

I was ten when he first went to Vietnam. We were living in California and they flew to Hawaii, where they met the ship. They brought all the wives and kids into this room and showed a movie called *Flight Deck*. I'll never forget this. They showed the movie, and it's all these planes flying off the carriers and doing all this stuff, with *Star Wars*–like music in the background. This movie's going along and everything's hunky-dory, and then all of the sudden the narrator goes, "And then, one of them didn't come back."

And about twenty little girls went "Wahhh!" all at once. I was just sitting there going, whoa. My mother was pissed, because all of my sisters were freaking. She dragged us out of that theater just huffing and puffing. And my dad said, "What? What?" And she goes, "What the hell are they doing?"

I don't know who came up with that idea, and I still don't know if that was a great idea or not. How do you prepare somebody, little kids, for the fact that their dad might die, you know? I don't know how I'd do it. The Navy's got their little tap dances that they do. I know them only too well.

This was right before his departure. We saw the movie, and then we could walk up and see the airplanes, and then they all climbed in them and off they went.

He gave me the man-around-the-house speech before he left.

133

"I want you to take care of things." What does that mean to a ten-year-old kid? Not a hell of a lot. You still feel like you're a kid, and you want to be a kid. And that's all I was going to be anyway, no matter what he said. I remember thinking it was pretty weird.

My old man never touched me. But he put his arm around me that night and said, "You're the man around the house." I don't remember ever feeling like he was in danger. Maybe subconsciously I did, but it was never in the front of my mind, that he could get blown away. Vietnam was on the news every night. You didn't know if your old man got shot out of the sky that day or what.

My parents lied to us, outright, about what he was doing over there. I have a feeling it was my mother who instigated it. "Oh, he's not fighting; he's just flying radar planes." Which he was, so it was half the truth, they were planes stuffed with radar-jamming gear and really involved electronics gear, but they were also low-range bombers. I didn't know it until I was twenty-five years old.

One day he was talking about doing a bombing run, and he said, "Yeah, if I didn't get the target the first time, I'd get the hell out. Some guys would come around again, do the same thing again, and if they missed, they'd get shot right out of the sky, because they'd figured out what you did the first time."

And I went, "You were bombing?" And he said, "Oh, yeah." And he looked at me like "I thought you knew." And I'm sitting there thinking, what? That was pretty strange. I don't know why they didn't tell us in the first place.

BEVERLY TAYLOR

He was never around. He was always gone at the crack of dawn, and he'd be home late. It seemed like he and I used to do a lot together, but looking back on it now, I really wonder if we did, or if that's just a little girl's memory of what my father was.

All I knew was that he was a pilot and he flew. Even now, if someone asks me what he flew, I have no idea. He never told me. When he was overseas, I never knew what he was doing.

His departures were traumatic. It was really tough when he left, and I'm sure a lot of it stemmed from the fact that he and my mother were fighting so much. I can still remember, in my mind, certain scenes of him leaving. Certain airports . . . I can visualize the airport, and the plane, and my father getting on the plane.

But it was part of the ballgame. Part of it was realizing that he would be gone for so long, and he was the one person I got along with. Typical of being an only child, I spent a lot of time with my father, and I had absolute adoration from him. My mother was the disciplinarian. I think this happens with girls, anyway; I really swore that I hated her. She and I have become close just in this past year.

So he would leave, and I'd be stuck there with my mother. And now I think of how awful it had to have been for her, because I didn't understand what was going on. All I knew was that my daddy was leaving me. And my poor mother was there all by herself with this kid. We used to fight, just horribly, particularly as I got into my teenage years. I ran away from home a couple of times when my father was overseas. I would take off for a girlfriend's house and not tell her and not come home. And of course then she'd send out the search party.

In the earlier years, my mother would put in these calls to him. I can remember the phone ringing at two or three in the morning when he returned her call. She was doing the typical thing that I hear now that so many military wives did. They would invent excuses to have the husband come back home. I can remember hearing her once. She put in this panic call to my father and finally got through to him, overseas, who knew where, and she told him that she had a suspicion that I was pregnant. She had run out of excuses, and now she was using me, and that made me really hostile toward her.

What I didn't realize then was that about twelve years before he and Mother divorced, he had met the woman that he later married. At that point in time, if he had divorced my mother and she had contested it, it would go on his fitness report, and the whole bit. She wouldn't give him a divorce, and that's why he requested so much overseas duty, and when he got it, a real

135

blowout would occur. I knew that fighting was going on, but I didn't know what about, or what was happening.

When he requested overseas duty, he would see this woman, and I guess my mother knew about this. It was a real strain, a lot of tension. There are certain scenes, like I say, that stick in my mind. And I think how hard it must have been on my mother, because I didn't understand at all what was going on. I think as I got older, she really grew to resent me. I think that's why she ended up using me as a tool. He promised her that he would stay married to her until I got engaged.

DEBBIE WEST

All of my life, I knew that he was in the Navy, and the Navy took him away for a while. I don't recall that it ever broke my heart. Daddy was gone, but in some ways, it was good for me, because as the oldest, I assumed a better status in the family. He went overseas a lot when I was a kid. His first real war experience must have been in the early sixties in Vietnam. He did three tours of duty.

He always left in uniform, and the bags would be packed and sitting at the door, and he'd say good-bye, and he'd leave. For me it was like "Sigh, good-bye."

I was my mother's helper. I think it's a position that's always been relegated to the oldest son, but since oldest son wasn't old enough, I got it. I always felt like it was doomsday when he came back. The day would approach, and my heart would sink. I resented it when he came home. I was displaced; I really did not feel like a member of that family when he came home. It wasn't a time of joy for me; although my brothers and sisters would be bouncing up and down, I'd go, "Oh brother, here we go again." There were lots of preparations. We'd clean the house and my grandma would come and stay with us, so he and my mother could take off for a while. I don't think it struck me like it struck my brothers.

He always brought a bunch of stuff home with him. There was always that excitement, because his Navy chest always had the smells from the Orient and stuff like that, and boy, didn't I love the smell of sandalwood. My mother always got bolts of silk and pearls and other things. So he would bring nice things, sewing machines, and bikes, and stuff. He really made use of his buying power over there. We got beggar's beads and jewelry boxes, and I still have all that stuff.

We never talked about it, about Vietnam. I don't know if I ever even asked my mom if Dad was there, or what he was doing. The war didn't touch us. I don't think that I had any doubt that he would come back. I secretly thought every now and then, boy it would be nice if he didn't come back, but I never had a doubt, really, that he'd be back.

My mother wrote to him a lot and he'd correct her grammar and send the letters back to her. That's just the way he was. I caught a glimpse of one of those letters that he had corrected in her room. I don't even know what I was doing in there; her room was fairly off-limits. I asked her about it later, and she said, "Well, I was going to school at the time, and this was his way of helping me."

PETER VARGAS

My father went on TDY [temporary duty] a lot. I'm not even sure what TDY stands for. I think it's something that every military brat in the world knows about. If you asked them about one word in the military that they remember over anything else, it's probably those initials: *TDY*. Conceptually, it's a trip, away from home. He was gone for a minimum of a week, almost invariably for two weeks. What he did was never an interest of ours. "I'm going to deliver a plane to wherever. . . ." None of that ever came into it. It was just there's that word, TDY, and Dad's gone. We were used to dealing with things by ourselves, and my mother was very much in control. So there was no issue about that. I don't even remember his homecomings as any big deal.

We got used to doing things as a smaller family: my mother, my sister, and me. We'd have nut nights. We'd go out and do stupid things. Progressive dinners—we'd start at one place, and have salad, and move on to the next place, and have something else. We'd keep a list, and see who could eat the most in one night. Or we'd visit haunted houses. My mother was intrigued by the occult, so we'd go to strange neighborhoods and look at these haunted houses. All the neighbors would be standing across the street, wondering why we were there and what we were doing.

GEORGE DEXTER

In 1939, we went to Leavenworth, Kansas, so that my father could go through the course there, and the war broke out in Europe. In fact, the war broke out the day before we arrived in Leavenworth. They announced that the course would be curtailed; it would only last until January, and then they would be sent on maneuvers. They let the families stay there for the full school year, and my father went to Germany. My brother, at that time, was also in the Army. I was a junior in high school, so with my brother gone and my father gone, I had a great time. Leavenworth was a wonderful place to live.

I never lived with my father again, after he left, except for a brief period of time. That summer, my mother and I went to Fort Meade. And just about the time that we arrived, during the summer of 1940, my father was given command of a tank battalion. At that time the tanks were part of the Infantry. During that summer, my father's battalion got sent to Fort Benning, Georgia, when they decided to form the Second Armored Divisions at Benning. Patton was in command of that.

Of course, now the buildup was starting, and there were no quarters available, so my parents got a place off post and decided that I'd better go off to school somewhere. From 1939 on, things were hectic. I was coming up on my senior year of high school, and they sent me off to Georgia Military Academy. And really, I say that's when I left home, at the beginning of my senior year. I never lived with my father again.

TERRY McCULLOCH

He volunteered to go to Vietnam when I was thirteen. He was gone for about eighteen months, during 1969 and 1970. I was very aware of what Vietnam was. It was a constant quiet

138

awareness in our house, that Dad was in Vietnam, but it was not anything that we really discussed.

I was at the age where I really couldn't hide from it. I was thirteen; I knew exactly what was going on. I was seeing it on TV. It was like this bombardment of war every night, in detail. I guess my dad was just so invincible to me, he was such a definite presence, that I just didn't ever think that anything could ever happen to him there.

He was in Cam Ranh Bay. He was Medical Corps NCO-IC for the dental clinics there, so he kind of toured around with the medics, but basically he was stationed in Cam Ranh Bay, which was not really a battle zone. He definitely didn't see battle.

I don't know what my mom's feelings were. She was very subservient, always. My dad made all the decisions and she just went along with him. She was afraid, of course. He was leaving her with all these kids to take care of by herself, and she wasn't on base anymore, which was kind of scary, after you've lived a sheltered life for so long. I'm sure it was a real adjustment for her. Just being a family of five girls and a mom, living in this house all by ourselves was the hardest thing.

Once a month, we all had to sit down and write him a letter. It was like this horrible chore for us, to write those letters. "Oh, Mom, what are we going to tell him?" We had to do it.

The oddest part was that he had volunteered to go to Vietnam. Whenever I told anyone that, they said, "You've got to be kidding. He left the whole family, to go to Vietnam?" It was a real big adjustment for us when my dad came back. My mom was happy to give up control to him. She was happy that he was finally there to handle taking care of all of these kids. He seemed to be a lot lighter than he was before. For about six months I think he was relieved to be back and have his kids around. He didn't want to immediately come on as the real heavy, but then he fell back into his old role of tyrant again.

DEREK LOWE

At the same time my dad was in Vietnam this active debate was going on in society. And on top of the external things, my mother had been going through a great deal of stress, in our own household, with us five kids. She had been living on her own, and then we went back home to Louisiana while Dad was gone, and her family was there, and they wanted to tell her what to do. The house we lived in was very small, so I lived in the dining room. It was a real drastic time. We were dealing with a lot of losses, a lot of stress, at that time. I was a horrible person to be around.

What I recall is that I did my job. And my father would write to me and remind me of his expectations and my responsibility. That was always a conflict. As a teenager, I could hardly stand my mother, and yet at the same time I had to be there for her and with her.

I was fifteen when he left the first time, and I was angry about having to live in Louisiana. I was really aware of being a misfit, and I was a little more intimidated by civilian life. It wasn't the controlled atmosphere of an Army post. I always wanted to live on post at that time, but there was no way to do that, I guess because the Army was so full. It was during the height of the Vietnam War.

That was a lousy time. I was aware that he was in Vietnam, and I was a little angry about it, and at the same time I was worried about him. He wrote pretty regularly and sent tapes to us, and we would make tapes and send them to him. This was in 1966, 1967. And the news was on every night, every single night. News about everything. That was an intense time. It was crazy.

I was aware of what he was doing in Vietnam, because I was aware of the Infantry. And once I started attending the military school, it was very obvious. It was basically ROTC, so we had military class, and we'd see movies of sucking chest wounds and all kinds of stuff like that.

He was a first sergeant when he was in Vietnam the first time. When he came back, we could see the stress, that post-traumatic stress phenomenon. He didn't sleep well at night, and he was irritable. His patience was really short.

And then he came back and became first sergeant of what's called a special training company. It was the misfits who were draftees who really needed a firm hand; it was a disciplinary unit, mostly rebellious teenagers. He did that for thirteen months. He was very conscientious about his work. That was a very difficult time, between his two tours of duty. Then he went back to Vietnam and was there during the Tet offensive.

The worst conflict I had with my dad when he came back was about the car issue. I had gotten my license while he was gone. Shortly after he came back from Vietnam, he wanted me to run an errand, and I, in a typical seventeen-year-old-boy way, said, "Well, I don't want to go."

He was in utter shock. "What are you talking about, you don't want to go?" And I said, "Well, you know, if you don't want me to use the car when I want to use it, then why should I use the car when you want me to use it to do something for you? I don't understand what the difference is."

I have never seen my father come unglued like that. He was eating, and he threw his sandwich at me, and just really lost it. At that point, I realized the stress that he was under, from Vietnam and from the stress of our relationship.

Shortly after he returned from Vietnam that second time, I graduated from college, and I had gotten a job and was moving out. He wouldn't even help me load the car as I prepared to move myself out of the house and move to Virginia to start my job. He was utterly silent. I really think he had a sense of remorse—not for being in the Army, not for any of that—but I think it was because of the impact that all of that had on our relationship. He was so angry, and I think we both had a sense of loss, for his being away, and the lack of contact, and then all of the conflicts between us. He was away a lot of the time while I was growing up. It had a cumulative effect.

NANCY KARACAND

My dad was really the disciplinarian, so when he was gone, we would just raise a lot of hell. By the time he was due back, my mother would be pretty well wiped out.

In some ways, it was fun while he was gone, but it was also terrible, because my mother would just become a witch. She did not know how to deal with us, so she would just get wild and scream and yell. She resorted to ridiculous measures, and we would just laugh at her. It was really kind of sad. We gave her such a hard time. I think there was almost a sense of relief when my father would finally get home and restore some kind of order, although we also had to anticipate getting punished, because inevitably, we had done something.

RHONDA HEALEY

My father went to Vietnam when I was eleven or twelve, and he was gone pretty much until I was fourteen.

The squadrons tended to be very tight knit, and the squadron commanders' wives were very much in charge of keeping track of people and making sure that everybody was okay. They started what was called the Ombudsman Program and my mother was our squadron's Ombudsman. They did a lot of things with other families—potlucks and that kind of thing— frequently, on a weekly basis.

Departures were always a big deal. The flyers were their own little community and the fly-outs were a really big deal. I don't remember being sad when he left, but more stunned. But that was my reaction a lot. I don't remember being real emotional as a kid. But his returns were much more emotional. Again, it was the fly-in, the ready room, and the mothers had bought new outfits because it was a big deal.

It was a big transition when he returned, especially for my brother and me. They really laid the man-of-the-house thing on my brother, and then when my dad returned, he was expected to step back and be the kid again. As a result, he and my dad had a very tenuous relationship for a number of years. I was surprised that John stayed at home, because it was so hard on him. We would often hear about someone's son leaving home as soon as the dad got home.

My father never knew our names. I don't think that he ever called any of us without going from the top of the list. He had to start at the top and go down. He wouldn't know our teachers or our routine or situations that would require special rules, because he couldn't be there all the time. If he picked up on how much we had changed while he was gone, he was pretty subtle about it, didn't say very much. It is hard on families, and our family was no different.

Friends always wanted to drop in on the day he got home, not realizing that we really needed that day to be a family time. I'm sure it was very well intended; they wanted to greet him and wanted to say hello. I can remember my mother being what I thought was actually rude a couple of times, but I can now understand that she was really jealously trying to guard that time that we needed as a family.

We wrote and would make him tapes, and usually all of us kids would get involved. We would write a script and make a big deal about it. One of my sisters said she found a couple of those tapes and was replaying them, and they were just hysterical.

It would be really bad news when we would get the word that a pod had been shot down, which happened a lot, especially in Vietnam. These helicopters that transported the mail pods from the carrier were prime targets, and if one was shot down, that could mean that several weeks' worth of mail was lost forever. I suppose it was worse on their end, when they knew that they wouldn't be getting their letters from home.

We had one period when there hadn't been mail for weeks and my mother was hysterical. That was one of the worst periods of time for her. There had been some talk about planes being shot down, and they didn't know who it was. We couldn't even get communication at all. We would hear that someone had gone down in the squadron and that was it. Nobody knew.

Finally a letter came, and I was so grateful to see it. I put it up on the mirror that was by the front door so she would see it as soon as she walked in the door from work. One of my little sisters thought she was being helpful and took the letter down and put it in the mailbox at the corner. She thought it was outgoing mail. We almost killed her, the other four of us. She was real little, and she couldn't read very well. She sneaked off to mail this letter and thought she was being so helpful.

Somehow we got that letter back. My mother called up the post office, and they came out and got the letter back out of the box. That tells you just how important it was.

JACK LEMONT

I must have been in about fifth grade when my dad went to Vietnam for the first time. He would send a lot of pictures and postcards and stuff. When he took his R and R he would go to Singapore, and he sent us pictures of snake charmers and sacred cows. One time he sent me an Australian bush hat, and I wore that thing for a year, just like a cowboy hat. And we got some of the Asian woven pants, like they wear in the rice paddies, and little Chinese skullcaps, and elephant-hide wallets, and ancient money.

My dad wasn't in a fighting company; he was NCO in charge of some kind of construction base. When I was a little older, he told us stories of bodies floating down the river and he had to go out and retrieve them. He called them "floaters." I didn't think that much about it. It was just a term; you still couldn't visualize, couldn't imagine it. He would always take a story and make an adventure out of it. I guess they had jaguars over there, and some kind of jaguar ended up in the latrine one night, and a guy went in the latrine and saw it in there and came out screaming. He has always been a storyteller.

ELIZABETH SPIVEY

I was seven years old and then eight when my dad was in Vietnam. My mom cried a lot that year he was gone. She would cry in the evenings; I would hear her sometimes. I don't believe that I was fully cognizant of the potential danger or the seriousness of the situation, but something was amiss there.

My mother talked about him every day. She used to figure out what time it was in Vietnam and say, "Well, your dad must be having dinner." And she'd say, "I wonder what your dad's doing today."

Just before Christmas, my mom had taken us downtown to see Santa Claus and tell Santa Claus what we wanted for Christmas. My youngest brother, who was only about four at the time, told Santa Claus, "Well, the only thing I want for Christmas is for you to bring my daddy home from Vietnam."

And Santa Claus kind of said, "Ahem, uh, well, I'll see what I can do."

As it happened, my father's mother became seriously ill and had a series of strokes, and he was allowed to come home, and it just happened that he came home on Christmas Eve. The Red Cross had tried to call us and hadn't been able to get through.

That was the most triumphant, wonderful Christmas, because Santa Claus brought our daddy home. Somehow my mother had gotten out the presents for us that were from Santa Claus, and then my dad arrived, and we all thought, Santa Claus has come, and he brought Dad. We stayed up the whole night—he had gotten home late, and we were just so excited. It was a really wonderful time, aside from the fact that my grandmother was ill. It was incredible. He was only able to stay a short period of time, and then he had to fly to Virginia to see his mother before he had to go back.

I was eight when he came home for good. I guess I felt a little bit estranged from my dad even though I remember him being very loving to us when he got back. I would stand back and look at him and kind of stare at him.

He brought me those Vietnamese dolls. Every military kid whose dad ever went to Vietnam brought back those dolls in the traditional Vietnamese costume. Shortly afterward, I somehow heard—probably my parents were talking about it—that the Vietnamese had planted bombs in some of these dolls to destroy the American children who received them. So I was deathly afraid of the dolls after that and would have nothing to do with them. For some reason I put them in the front window, and I stayed away from them. I expected them to blow up at any time.

SHARON GILMORE

He'd go on overnight duty every two weeks, or something like that, flight cruises for two weeks at a time. We were glad to see him go. What I remember from those is that every time he came back, we'd get his little packets of silverware and PK gum. We always waited for that.

Before he left, my mom would iron his uniforms. The blue

uniforms had to be ironed inside out, because of the fabric. And she'd have his flight bag packed, and then he would get up early in the morning and leave, and that was it. No tears, believe me.

MARY CHANDLER

I remember the day we heard he'd been shot in Vietnam—I was ecstatic. To this day, I can't remember a happier moment in my life. It meant, to me, that my father was coming home. I had no idea of the extent to which he'd been injured, and that when he came home, he wouldn't be able to romp with us the way he had before. Even the fact that my mother was crying when she told me had no effect on my enthusiasm.

What did sink in was the sight of my father, four months later, when he was finally released from the hospital and shipped home. I remember being afraid to touch him for the next year, as he seemed so fragile and his balance on those braces and crutches seemed so precarious. I used to watch him do his physical therapy exercises, trying unsuccessfully to squeeze a foam rubber ball with his left hand.

My father wrote to my mother every day that he was away, on all three of his tours. The first time he went to Vietnam, when I was eight, he called us on a field telephone. When it came my turn to talk with him, I got so mixed up with saying "Over" and "Out" that I got very upset. Thereafter, every time he called, I hid in my closet. It was really hard on me to have him gone, and then to have to talk to him and juggle "Over" and "Out" was adding insult to injury.

About a year before my father went to Vietnam in 1965, a friend of ours was killed over there with one of the very first units that was sent. I was in first grade, and what I remember being told was that Vietnam was a place where "the children are so poor that they have to run around naked." For me, at age seven, I could imagine no horror greater than a place where fathers were killed and children were so poor that they ran around naked. By the time my father was sent, I had a very vivid idea of the horrible place he'd been sent to, and my friend's father was proof positive for me that daddies don't always come home from that place.

CAROLINE BAKER

Since we had been in Japan, I was able to relate to my dad going to a foreign country. I don't remember what my parents told us as to why we couldn't go, but I'm sure that was a question we had. We had been to Japan with him; why couldn't we go to Korea, too?

It just didn't occur to me that he was in any kind of danger. We had been so safe and comfortable in Japan that it didn't occur to me that being in Korea was dangerous. I think my parents tried to keep a lot of that from us kids.

By the time he got back it seemed like he had been gone forever. My parents had tried to make it sound like it was going to be over with sooner than it was. It just kept dragging on. I was in third grade, and for me, at that age, a year was a long time. We met him at the airport and saw him getting off the plane. I think I was the most excited of all the kids at that point. I was glad to have the family back together again and have my mom happy. That was a real happy time.

SHEILA WRIGHT

When we got older, my dad was gone for three weeks out of every month. When he was home, we were the little troops. Certain things had to be done certain ways, and he made us clean our rooms so we could bounce a quarter off the beds, and then he'd leave, and we'd run rampant. We'd all relax and go about our business and forget about Dad for three weeks. And then we'd go, "Oh, my God, Dad's coming home. We've got to clean this whole house."

When he came back from Vietnam, I remember that he drove up in this bright yellow taxi, and we were all standing there, just beside ourselves with excitement, and we were saying, "What did you bring us? What did you bring us?" There he was, back from Vietnam, and we were wondering what he brought us.

When he retired, we said things like "Hey, you haven't been around; why should we listen to you now?" My mom went to work and my dad stayed at home and was a farmer. So all of a sudden, Mom was gone, and Dad was at home and it was driving us crazy. We hated it, because my dad's rules were so different than my mom's. I remember telling him, "Why don't you go back in the Air Force?" And my brother one time had the nerve—I still can't believe this—to ask him, "Why don't you get a job?"

ROBERT BLAKE

From the time I was one year old, there were always periods of separation. On one of those occasions, it was long enough and I was young enough so that I really hadn't remembered my father as a person. What I remembered was the photograph that was sitting in the living room. And I have no recollection of this, but I am told that when my father came home that time and he and my mother embraced, I was outraged and I went up and kicked him in the shins. And my mother said, "Bobby, this is your father," and I said, "No, that isn't Daddy; Daddy is over there" and pointed to the picture.

We followed the fleet. The wives and kids moved up and down the coast just like sailors' girlfriends, to be where the fleet was. Sometimes it was a pain in the neck when he was gone. For example, when we went to Panama, my father had orders to report to the ship and the ship left three days later and our household effects hadn't come, and my mother had to find a house to live in. We had to get the car when it came off the ship and license it. All the commissary cards and our club cards, and all the details had to be handled, without the military person there.

My father served in World War I, and Nicaragua three times, which was kind of like Korea or Vietnam on a smaller scale, the basic guerrilla-type operation in peacetime where service people were getting killed and people at home were not interested.

When he went to Nicaragua the first time, I knew that he was up in the hills chasing Sandino at that time. In January of 1928, President Coolidge made an address to Congress to double the size of the Marine expeditionary force down there. They had pulled officers and men from ships that were stationed all over the U.S. to create another regiment. I remember one of my best

148

friends' saying to me almost gleefully—he must have gotten this at home—"Your father is going to be killed."

We had regular letters from him all the time. My parents were both very good correspondents. When he first went down to Nicaragua, there was no airmail, at least not to Central America. The mail all went by surface; it would take weeks, maybe a month, to send a letter and get any answer back.

And then one day, my mother got a letter back in five days. In the spring of 1929, Pan American Airways started airmail service from Brownsville to Panama, stopping at all the capitals. That was just a few months before the Eleventh Regiment was decommissioned and it was very convenient that it happened that way, because from then on, we were getting information on what was going to happen in a timely fashion. That gave us all a very nice feeling for Pan American Airways, and I eventually spent forty years with them.

LARRY WILLIAMS

When I was six, my father went to Vietnam as an artillery battery commander to replace the one who had been killed in a recent raid. We had just moved to Quantico and had been there for about five months when the battery was raided, and my father received his orders as the replacement. Within a week, we were moved to Raleigh, North Carolina, and my dad was gone.

I vaguely remember the night before he left. He came into my room to put me to bed. He explained that he would be going away for a while. I don't remember exactly what he gave as a reason, but he was always straight with me. He stayed there, in the dark, and talked to me for a long time about where he was going and gave me the "You're the man around the house speech." I knew he was going to Vietnam, and I knew what was happening over there, as only a six-year-old can, but I don't remember being concerned. When you are six years old, your father is immortal.

I wrote letters to him, and he always answered. Every now and then he would send me packages. I got a parachute, and a South Vietnamese fatigue uniform, and some North Vietnamese money. He explained that the money was put on the doorways to scare away spirits; today I wonder how he got ahold of that North Vietnamese money.

His return was great. We had gotten orders to Germany, and I knew that my dad was coming home, but I didn't know when. One day while I was outside at school, in gym class, he drove up in his old MG, still wearing his combat utilities, complete with his sidearm. He hadn't even been to the house yet to take it off. I just stood there, looking across the playground at him. My teacher finally asked me what I was waiting for, and I went racing over and jumped in his arms.

8

The Home Front

My father and his battalion began the first leg of their journey to Vietnam on a train, which made the entire concept of "Vietnam" that much more confusing to me, at age seven. I knew that there had been problems with my father's men going AWOL, so I watched the crowds of uniformed men carefully in case one of them tried to make a break for it. The MPs took an unwilling GI in handcuffs aboard the other side of the train that day, so that the wives and families wouldn't see what was going on. I had no idea that my father's men—young GIs, guys who looked like my brothers—were going AWOL in desperate attempts to avoid being sent to fight the war.

A little over a year after my father returned from Vietnam, one of my brothers enlisted and shipped out. My brother had gone off to college just as my father left for Vietnam. When his interest in college waned, my father told him, "You can go to college, or you can enlist in the Marines. You can go to college, or you can enlist in the Navy," and so on, through all the branches of

151

the service. I wonder if my brother, at that age, had any idea of
what he was doing when he forsook his student deferment. I
certainly didn't. One day he was my brother, and the next he was
a GI with a crew cut.

My sister went to London and sent me love beads and cards
with peace signs on them, and my brother came home for R and R
with thirty-five-millimeter slides that he snapped into cartridges
and showed us on the wall above the couch, postcard scenes from
hell. If my family had differences of opinion about the war, no
one mentioned it. To this day, there is a stiff-upper-lip reticence
about the subject of war in my family. It doesn't make polite
dinner table conversation. Any discussion about military policy,
the morality of war, or combat experiences went on among my
brothers and my father, late at night.

For every soldier on the front, there is a family at home waiting for
news, hoping for the best. Military families might have been
more accustomed to the role, but previous experience can never
allay the fears of a family who has sent someone off to a combat
zone.

Until Vietnam, families and citizens were able to contribute
to the war effort so that every possible national resource could go
toward the war. There was a patriotic sense of purpose behind the
war effort, a belief that our forces were the good guys, defending
democracy and fighting evil. During Vietnam, the war effort
became personal, as Americans struggled to believe that sending
men over to fight was worth the cost in lives.

Military fathers went off to Vietnam—not the Vietnam War,
just plain Vietnam—as if it were another overseas assignment
like a hardship tour in Taiwan. But the youth of America were
fanning the flames of the antiwar movement, and the fact that the
military was fulfilling a very real function in an increasingly
unpopular war became impossible to ignore. The cultural sym-
bols of the antiwar movement began to show up on post. We'd
furtively flash the two-fingered peace sign to the GIs on the
convoy trucks and they would grin at us and return it. Rock-and-
roll blared from the barracks and the bedrooms in quarters all
over the post.

Protesters were burning their draft cards and chanting, "Hell no, we won't go," in the familiar cadence of the troops who marched on the parade ground. The Vietnam War became a virtual civil war in America as generations squared off over the issues of the war, and military families were not spared from the controversy. Military brats were no different from any other young Americans during the turbulent sixties. Some of them served in Vietnam, and some actively protested the war in the streets and in skirmishes with their fathers. Others who were not protesting or fighting the war rode the fence, attempting to reconcile their own attitudes about the war with their knowledge that it was being waged not just by "the military," but by individual men—fathers, neighbors, brothers.

I talked with one woman in her living room on a sunny autumn afternoon. A ceramic elephant painted with decorative headdress and ceremonial fittings, one of the souvenirs that her father had brought home from Vietnam, watched over us from a corner of the room. She talked about the Vietnam era and events of twenty years ago and chose her words carefully. "Vietnam is a pivot, and I don't care who you are, or how far removed you were from the military, everything turned on Vietnam. The world took a completely different turn at that time. Everything is different. I don't care if you were a Carmelite nun—your life, somehow, has been affected by Vietnam."

BILL FLYNN

When I left to go to college, I was a young man from a rather conservative southern high school, and the next time my folks saw me, I had long hair and I had a conscience. They handled that time, I thought, really well.

It must have been really tough for my father, when I went down with my long hair and an earring to visit on this tiny little installation where he was the commanding officer. I'd go in and out of the gate, and I remember one time this MP said, "Have a nice day, ma'am," or something like that, and I stopped the car and gave him a piece of my mind.

I had friends who told me, "My dad hasn't talked to me for

153

years." If I had come home as a radical, then of course, my parents would have had to be reactionary. I wasn't going to come home and accuse my father of being a military pig, when I knew the man wasn't that way at all. I had no qualms about telling him at the time that I disapproved of the military-industrial complex in Southeast Asia. I had no problem with telling him that, but I wasn't going to extend it to him, personally.

I didn't want to ever go to Vietnam. I had too many friends who had gone over and got messed up. As far as the war protests went, it was more of a social thing for me than it was a real permanent commitment; it was kind of like a thing to do on campus, to get out there with everybody else. But my parents understood from the start. There never really was any turmoil in our house over that.

My father was a West Point graduate with five sons, and not a one of them chose a military career. I almost did, and I would have, if it weren't for the Vietnam War. I wasn't going to go to Canada or anything like that. I was ripe for getting drafted, but it just turned out that I got a lucky number in the lottery and I didn't have to go. I had taken the test to get into West Point, and I had a good chance of getting a congressional appointment. But I knew too many guys who had gotten messed up. I didn't want to do it. I didn't know what I wanted to do; I just knew that I didn't want to do that. It wasn't because I had grown up with a lot of military discipline at my father's hand; that wasn't the case. It just wasn't a good time to be in the service. And I thought my father handled it really well.

It was a real tough time for military families. So many people I know didn't speak to their parents for years. My family doesn't have any scars from that time, and I can't believe it.

RICARDO COTTRELL

When he was in Vietnam, he had an alcoholic assigned to work with him, a young guy, lower ranking. He was on Antabuse. And I guess Vietnam was such a gut-wrenching place—well, you could die from drinking and taking Antabuse, and this guy would drink on top of it anyway. So he was always a mess. My dad would tell this other guy, "Get him cleaned up; he's supposed to be at work." The guy would be out getting sick somewhere in the warehouse, and that's all he would say: "Get him cleaned up and get him in here."

A psychiatrist got me out of the draft. I don't know what he wrote—probably that I would flip out. I'm not real keen on authority. To have somebody shoving me to get in front of bullets, hey, no thank you. I was disqualified real quick. He didn't even finish looking through the first page. He was an Army physician. He said, "I'll disqualify you right now." My father and I had a little falling out. He called me a draft dodger, and I didn't see him for years after that.

I never protested the war. In conscience, I was against it. But I would never go out in the streets and do the thing. The guys who went to Vietnam were just guys, just like me. You really can't put anybody down unless you walked in their shoes. No one can imagine what it was, unless they were there. As I was growing up, I saw that servicemen were human beings.

BARRY JENKINS

We had horrible rows over Vietnam. When I was fourteen or fifteen years old, and Vietnam was still going on, he'd done two tours and he was very defensive about it. The officers who came back from there, I think, felt very responsible for a lot of it. He felt responsible, which is bullshit: he's not responsible for the Vietnam War.

He believed that he was doing the right thing, which is something I always respected. But I told him that I wasn't going to go, and if they tried to draft me, I'd leave the country. And my mom's standing there saying, "I'll buy your ticket," which of course blew the top right off the whole issue.

He'd say, "You have to fulfill your obligation to your country!" And I'd say, "Where the hell is that written?" And he'd go, "It's in the Constitution!"

It took him a couple of years after he finally retired to stop being defensive about Vietnam and turn into a human being that you could talk to. He got a job working on the base doing the same thing; he just wasn't in the Navy anymore. For a while it didn't make a difference, but eventually he relaxed.

He also realized, later, that I didn't fault him for going there, but I sure as hell wasn't going. I was not in a situation where I felt I had to go, whereas he was in the military, and for him that was the right thing to do at the time.

I remember when *Apocalypse Now* came out, because I thought, wow, it was great; it demonstrated how helpless those guys were. They were over there, they weren't told what to do, they were terrified, it wasn't organized, it wasn't well led, they didn't even have a sense of purpose. It was "Go over there; cover your ass; that's all you can do." He didn't like it at all: "It made the military look like monkeys." I didn't get that impression. In my mind, it wasn't a shot at the military, or the guys who were involved; it was broader than that. They didn't have a chance. They were stuck in a situation and they weren't given a good reason to be there, but they were there and they had to make the best of it. And making the best of that situation was no picnic.

DEBBIE WEST

My dad didn't get in on World War II and he's always bitched about that all of his life. He was just too young. He was sixteen then, and he sneaked into the Navy right at the very end of the war and got sweep-up operations. It just rankled him to no end that he never got in on this world war that was clearly black and white, because no war has ever been that clear-cut since.

I think his first trip over to Vietnam must have been in the early sixties. I have been hearing about the cold war and Laos since I can remember. I was becoming a teenager about the time that he was coming back from Vietnam. He was just sizzling angry at the world, right on the edge, and anything could throw him into a rage. In personality, my father and I are very similar, but politically, we were very polarized, so there was a lot of head butting.

During Vietnam, toward the end, while I was still in high school, I was writing to guys who were in Vietnam, who were older than I was. And my father was laying down the law: I'd better write to them regularly; our boys needed our support.

I almost felt obligated to marry one of them when they came home. It was horrible, because I felt that it was an enormous amount of responsibility. I didn't want to write to them; I didn't want to hear about that stuff. It was really horrifying to me. There were some pretty awful things going on over there, and these guys would write to me about it.

I was trying to pull away, and my father would say, "You got a letter from Tom today; you'd better write back to him!" I really resented that. For me, it was more like I wasn't in love with any of these guys. None of them were my boyfriend. One of them, as a matter of fact, was a guy I had been in high school with, and we'd just been friends. So he started writing to me and he asked for a picture, and I sent him a picture, and some of his buddies saw it and went, "Oh, God, she's cute, let's write to her."

So suddenly I was writing to three or four people, and they'd send me presents. When they came home for R and R or whatever, I had met a couple of them, and they were nice guys, you know, but nobody that I really—there was so much longing, and so much desperate intensity in these letters, and it felt really oppressive to me. It made me feel weird. It made me feel like they were asking a lot more of me than I really wanted to give.

I didn't want to know if they died. There were a lot of people dying over there, and if any of the guys I was writing to died, I didn't want to hear about it.

That was my early experience with Vietnam. Later I was involved in the antiwar rallies, and we printed a newspaper in our basement. We were really on the other side.

All the time, there were fights, and fights, and fights. My father called me "My pinko commie daughter." And that's when I decided to change my name. I said, "To hell with you. I don't want anybody to know that I was ever related to you." So I changed my name and that's it.

I think my father probably has the same emotional love for this country, and he probably wants the same kinds of things for it that I do, but he saw the military action as being the way to pull it off. We've butted heads on that throughout the years. It's been a room clearer, a couple of times; people will just get up and leave. He doesn't just argue with me; he argues with everybody, and the decibel level just climbs and climbs until everybody is *screaming* at one another.

I'm not really sure what he did over there. It seemed to me that he was commandeering these bayou boats that shot snipers out of trees. I always got the impression from watching *Apocalypse Now* that that must have been what he did. For some reason, as much as he admired war, and the chance to show off all your machismo and your patriotism and so on, he never had a lot of stories to tell.

As a matter of fact, later on, when he got drunk, he would cry and cry over his experiences there. And I never got the story about what it was that finally traumatized him so badly. It seemed to me that there were young men, his own young men, dying in his arms. Some really tragic thing happened—they blew up their own ammo dump, something—I'm not sure. I'd just get little bits and pieces; I never got the whole story. I don't think my mother even knows the whole story. He never got any counseling about it.

He was a rigid, hard man, all locked up inside himself. Whatever it was, it was bad. I think he got a real awakening. The Navy was like his second wife, and everything about it was perfect; he loved every single thing about it and everything about this country. He still feels that way, but I think his experiences shocked an awareness in him, which I think he has since managed to put down inside again. It made something inside of him really raw, and he's covered it over with a lot of layers again, because he's a very conservative man, and he goes for the most conservative knee-jerk politics that you can imagine.

I know that there were other men, other officers in similar positions, who were able to say, "There is something not right here" and were able to make that right turn and go with it. But my father just seemed to think, If there's something not right here, I don't want to know it, and went on with his life.

Do you know that none of my brothers went to Vietnam? Somehow, I suspect that my father was behind it, and he kept them out of there. One brother went in and wound up in the

Chicago area, working as a military journalist. Another brother
went into the Marines and later had an honorable discharge:
"Psychologically unsuited for military life." My other brother
didn't go into the service.

For some reason I always felt that my father had a hand
in them not having to pull any combat duty. I'm glad, because
I didn't want to see my brothers getting their butts into a sling,
but in a way, it's really unfair. But he had a lot of pull. My
brothers went in just shortly after he came back from Vietnam.
We had the ceremony at home, where he swore my brother and
his friends in.

JOHN ROWAN

What was a shock for me was that when I joined the Navy as an
enlisted, that was when I really saw the difference between the
officers and enlisted. Then I discovered that there really was a big
difference that I had never seen as an officer's dependent.

I had no concept of what I was getting into; I just knew that I
was going to be drafted if I didn't do something. At that time,
there was a small chance of being drafted into the Marines. It was
before the lottery, and at that time, they weren't getting their
quota. So I didn't know very much, but I knew that being
a drafted Marine was the worst thing that could possibly
happen.

I joined the Navy because I had heard that they had the best
food in the military, and I had this vague idea that it would be
more fun to be out floating around on a boat. I had no concept
that people in the Navy still had jobs to do, no concept of the
petty, mind-numbing, stupid busywork. I considered the Air
Force, but my eyes weren't good enough, and I couldn't be a pilot
anyway, because I hadn't been to college at that time. I thought
that if I couldn't fly, there wasn't any point in joining the Air
Force, so the Navy was what was left.

I graduated from high school with no idea of what I wanted
to do, no notion whatsoever. I hitchhiked around the country for
a while and came back and went to college. About midway
through the semester, I stopped going to classes. I was too bored

to even officially drop out. I just stopped going to class, and that was when I knew I was going to be drafted.

I joined the Navy, and I think that my parents were glad that I was doing something. They knew that I'd be taken care of, develop an interest in something. They didn't express any dissatisfaction with the fact that I was going to be enlisted. They might have had a better idea of the shock that I was in for than I did.

BRENDA ROWAN

When I was going to Indiana University, when I was about twenty-one, the student upheavals were going on, and I was in a radical organization. I remember my mother asking me, "What would they do if your father walked down the aisle of that meeting? Would they spit on him because he is an officer of the Navy?"

In other words, she didn't want me being in that organization because of the way she saw the whole scheme of things. I don't think that my father was as caught up in all that as my mother was. He's always been a kind of nonpresumptuous kind of person, a real down-to-earth kind of guy.

LINDA WINSLOW

I was kind of a fringe hippie during the Vietnam era, but I had friends who had served there. And they told me things like "Oh, yeah, Irving's really crazy; he used to get really ripped on Thai stick and go up in the helicopters and fire tracers just for the hell of it." And I was thinking, wait a minute; this person was my age, about twenty-one. I just couldn't imagine. I was going to college and I got into the theater crowd and I got into the liberals. I had a MAKE LOVE NOT WAR bumper sticker, and I was in more than one demonstration.

It was disturbing to me. Why are we doing this? People are getting killed. People my age are getting killed. And it's not our country that we're fighting for. If you want to invade Portland, I'll fight you. But the more that I read about Vietnam, and about Ho Chi Minh; and the more I read about Dien Bien Phu going on, back in the time of the Korean War the French were booted out; here was this country that had been at war for a hundred years. My belief in individual choice: who gave us the right to go over to that country?

I remember watching a newscast with my father, and it talked about rescuing some South Vietnamese infant, and the huge amount of money they spent on reconstructive surgery, and flying him to the United States, and all of this business. And I'm thinking, wait a minute; there's this imaginary line between North Vietnam and South Vietnam, and we're spending all this time and energy and money to rescue the people on this imaginary line, and we're blowing the hell out of the people above the imaginary line.

And the reason I got from my dad was "You just don't understand politics, daughter." And I don't. I don't think my father was misguided. It's just that Vietnam was happening.

I remember the first guy I knew who volunteered for Nam, a young second lieutenant, who was about twenty-two, said, "Me and my machine are trained to kill. I'm going to go over there and do it." But you figure if you train a person and spend x amount of dollars to train them, and put them in x amount of dollars' worth of equipment, they want to play with it. They want to use it. The boys and their toys. Why do boys like to play that way? I don't think any of them really like it. Do they think it's their duty? What is the whole military mentality?

In 1969, we had a loose group of hippies, about three couples, and we knew a guy who had just got back from Nam, and he had a buddy who was coming back from Nam.

I was into making beads, so I made some for this guy, with three orange, two blue, three orange. When he showed up at the house, I handed him a beer, stuck a joint in his mouth, and put the necklace on him, and he said, "My kind of woman." He had to go back—he was in the Navy. The CO said, "You can't wear beads," and he said, "I'm not going to take these beads off."

So he ends up in front of the captain. And the captain said, "Is there any chance that these beads have been blessed, or are they a religious artifact?" He was trying to let him off. And Ed

had the presence of mind to say, "Oh, yes, they've been blessed."
And he got away with it.

BRAD HOLMES

Military kids perceive war and stuff like that so differently. I
remember military kids wanting to grow up and join the military
and be in a war. They wanted to be in the war and they wanted to
kill somebody. They were looking forward to that. This was in the
mid-sixties. Kids who were in the Boy Scouts with me wanted to
be in the Army and the Air Force and be in war and kill
somebody, like their dad had done in Korea or Japan and stuff
like that. They'd always tell stories about how their dad was the
toughest guy in the military, and how he had these scars and how
many guys he'd killed.

I had a student deferment. I was twelve on the draft list and
as soon as I got that notification that I was twelve, and I said, "No
way, I'm not going to be a grunt, or be a private or something." So
I signed up for ROTC and got accepted at San Francisco State, and
then I got out of it. I was in an accident and got classified 4-F, so I
didn't have to go. I would have been a pilot.

TIM BROCKWAY

My dad didn't go to Vietnam. He was out by then. We knew
friends of his who did go and actually got killed there.

One of the happiest days of my childhood, besides when my
dad retired, was when I was given a 1-Y, so I didn't have to get
drafted. I danced and was jubilant. I was in high school when I
got the deferment so I didn't have to go to Vietnam.

PETER VARGAS

He was in Vietnam before I was, in 1971. I joined the Navy right
after I got out of high school, and went through hospital corps
school, and was a medic. He was still in Vietnam when I started
into the Navy, and I went to Nam before he got back. We were
kind of crossing oceans together. I was eighteen years old.

I know that my mom was worried to death about my father while he was over there. So many of the people in his squadron were shot down and captured, and that was one of her biggest worries. I've read a couple of his letters since then, and I know that she was really worried about that. But how she felt about me being over there, I still don't know. We haven't shared that. I'm sure she worried about me.

BRUCE HUTSON

I was in Air Force ROTC in college for one year, thank you very much. Fulfilling my dad's semidream. In fact, my brother and I were both in ROTC. My brother was in the Army. I just never would have gone into the Army, after living on those Army posts for all those years. The Air Force had so much cool. I didn't know anything about the Navy, so I never even considered it an option.

But to me, the Air Force was cooler, because it had the big bases, and the big clubs with tennis courts and big swimming pools. They had to have all that space for the airfields. The Army posts were just stuck anywhere. My God, they were just tucked away in these little bitty places, and people were living in these little hovels, and their PX was just this annex, and you had to drive to Stuttgart or someplace else to go to a big PX. But on these air bases, they had these huge new BXs. The Air Force kids came to school on rented German buses, with plush seats, just right for a little afternoon rendezvous with your girlfriend, you know, instead of the Army buses. So that's why I went into the Air Force ROTC program.

There I was. I felt, at the time, that's okay, I can go in, and spend my time as an officer in the Air Force, and get out and have the GI Bill, and do this and that.

But just dealing with some of these idiots in the ROTC program! We went to Wright Pat Air Force Base to take tests, physicals, and everything. We had already taken the Air Force officers qualifying test, and they wanted my ass really bad, like "Here's somebody who can actually think."

Immediately, as soon as they wanted me, I didn't want it. If they hadn't wanted me, I guess I would have fought to get in. So we went up to Wright Pat, and I was great in everything, except I have a bad knee. So they put their heads together and conferred and then came back and said, "Well, we need to do some more tests on your knee."

And I said, "Forget it. Is this going to keep me out of the military?" And they went, "Well, yes, but if you can come back . . ." and I went, "No, I'm fine, thank you very much, but I don't need to do this anymore." And that was it.

That was in 1969, 1970. When Kent State happened, there were demonstrations going on at our campus, and I was involved a little bit in them. I just couldn't rationalize going on with something like that.

It didn't really bother my dad that I had dropped out of the ROTC program. He said, "The only thing I ask is that you stay in school, as long as you can keep the 2-S deferment, because I don't want you drafted and sent to Vietnam."

I was just stunned. This was from my dad, who radically supported Spiro Agnew and Tricky Dick. When Agnew blew his cover, it just devastated my dad.

So there I was back in the civilian world, and it was so radically antimilitary. And yet, they just had this focus on one aspect of the military, which was this wrongful aggression, so they were pulling against Vietnam.

They didn't see the families of the guys who were over there, especially the career people. They were people, just like us. And the military wasn't just this war machine when you have kids and wives living there. So even today, there are people walking around who have absolutely no concept of the military life, of growing up, the family feeling: the human aspect.

DEREK LOWE

During his second tour I was approaching draft age; in fact, I think I received a draft notice when he was in Vietnam that second time. I became antiwar and anti–Vietnam War when I was in my sophomore year of college and Kent State happened. And during my last two years of high school, my world view began to change at that time.

I hadn't heard of Jimi Hendrix until I was in high school.

People like Janis Joplin were dead by the time I heard about them, because of the provincial nature of Louisiana and the even more provincial nature of the environment that I lived in. So that was a real interesting time to be growing up. I was waking up, in a lot of ways.

When my dad came back from Vietnam the second time, that was when my relationship with him began to break in a more positive direction. He said, "You don't need to go into the Army. I saw too many kids who were your age die there for no reason."

He had really begun to think in a different way for himself, which was so different, because he had really been gung ho. And he didn't cease to be gung ho about the Army; he was just definitely not gung ho about the war.

He had a very different experience during his second tour in Vietnam. He was in the Tet offensive, and he was up north in I-Corps. He worked with the Montagnard people quite a bit, and he became involved with an orphanage and an old Vietnamese man, as some adjunct to his activities as sergeant major. He developed a real empathy and compassion for the Vietnamese people.

During his second tour over there I was in college and was more active in the antiwar movement. We never had any conflict about that, oddly enough. Even after the first time he went over, during that interim period when I had begun questioning, we never had any conflict over that. That was when we began to develop some of our own intimacy in our relationship; up until that time, we were not atypical of military fathers and eldest sons.

JEFFREY TAVARES

We always heard about the kids whose fathers died. You'd always hear about the staff car pulling up in front of their house, to tell them that their dad wasn't coming back. That's when I really became aware of what was going on. I think I got pretty disillusioned at that point, because I realized then what my dad was doing in the service. I remember asking my dad about it after he got back, and he said, "That's what I get paid for." He didn't want to go, but his view was that it was time to pay the piper. It was time to do what he got paid for.

9

Rank Has Its Privileges

I learned to snap off a salute before I learned to ride a bike. There were plenty of role models for me to imitate; people were always saluting my father. It didn't seem unusual. Some men saluted, and others were saluted.

The military jargon that was so pervasive on the post and in our household included many rank-related qualifiers. The size and location of our houses were based on rank. We lived on "colonel's row" in stately three-story duplexes with full maid's quarters in the basement, but we had done our time in apartments before my father made colonel.

My father had "his men," the men under his command. My mother came home from the Officers' Wives Club functions and frequently told my father about the "little captain's wife" or "little major's wife" she had met. Too young to remember when my father had been a lowly major, I developed a mental image of a community of Lilliputian people, captains and majors and their families, inhabiting the smaller and, I knew, inferior housing on the other side of the post.

The ascending rank was always part of a family name. I answered the telephone with "Colonel Truscott's quarters, Mary speaking." I addressed all adults with their surname and current rank. I never knew many men who were "mister," with the exception of school principals.

We lived on post for the most part, only minutes away from my father's office, but I had no idea of what my father did at work. My dad was in the Army; other men were businessmen, doctors, lawyers, Indian chiefs. In his study at home he had a framed poster from a lecture he had given that had his picture on it and the caption THE NATION'S FOREMOST EXPERT ON RADIOACTIVE FALL-OUT. Whatever it was that my dad did at work, I felt certain that if we were bombed and fallout came raining out of the sky, my father would lead us to the designated fallout shelters on the post and we would survive, no matter how awful the blast, because he was "The Nation's Foremost Expert."

We visited my father's offices a few times, and they were remarkably devoid of any sign or indication of his work. The walls in his office were pale green, with perhaps a flag and a strictly functional map or two to break the monotony. His desk was typical Army issue, either wood or metal, and the chairs in the offices had convex seats covered with slippery green vinyl that made it impossible to sit still. The Army seemed to be a serious, boring place to work.

Rank truly had its privileges. The written and unwritten rules that established the chain of command for the men in uniform also applied to their families. Rank created a virtual caste system, and life on a military post had no uncertainties. There were stripes and insignia on uniforms, stickers on cars, and name-plates on houses. Families were segregated, by rank, in separate and not necessarily equal enclaves, and there were separate club facilities for officers and enlisted men. Post housing was the most obvious indicator of rank.

"Your rank was plastered right on your house, on your name-plate. If you're from a private to an E-5, you live in one area. If you're E-5 to E-9, you live in another area, and if you're an officer, you are over on the other side of the post in the nice buildings."

The privileges accorded by rank were highly visible, but the social taboos on post were often not apparent or even official. The officers' children tended to cross the lines of rank without compunction, but the children of enlisted men were conscious of the rules that forbade their fathers from fraternizing with officers and kept to themselves for the most part.

The military brats whom I spoke to were quite aware of the positions that their fathers held in the military hierarchy, but not many could actually tell me what their father did at work. I thought that perhaps the sons of military men would have known more about the day-to-day workings of the military, but I met several grown men who had done stints in the military themselves and still have no idea of what it was that their father's work involved. Rank was a significant part of careers and of daily life on post, but it revealed very little about the actual work that was involved in a military career.

Regardless of who the father was and what he did, rank was either a source of pride and status or an embarrassing label that put the military brat on the wrong side of the tracks. And all military brats, no matter where their father had fit in the hierarchy of rank, emphasized, over and over, that rank was pervasive and clearly defined.

RICARDO COTTRELL

Actually, my dad's rank might have saved my neck once. When we were living in Florida, my buddy and I stole some cigarettes out of a GI's car. We weren't too bright; we were in plain view of the barracks, and of course, these guys were all sitting in there, polishing their shoes and looking out the window. So we were busted. These GIs were trying to decide what to do with us, and they asked me what rank my dad was, and I said, "He's a tech sergeant," and they said, "Well, he's got enough trouble then." And they cut me loose.

When my sister was about sixteen, a guy asked her, "Who's your father?" And she told him, and he said, "That SOB! I know that guy!" I guess my father was tough on the guys who were under him. But he had it tough, too, sometimes.

HELEN PIERSON

A lot of my mom's friends were officers' wives. My dad was not an officer, although we lived in the officers' quarters. She used to go to coffees with the women, but she used to get mad because they would introduce themselves as "Mrs. Captain So-and-So." My mother hated that. She just couldn't stand it. The military women had the same attitude about rank as the men, and maybe more so, the status business. It filtered down to the kids.

I hung around with a general's son for a while, and we used to go up to the GIs and tell them they had to buy us candy bars. They would tell us to get lost, and this kid would tell them who his dad was, and that he would tell his dad if they didn't. He'd whip out his ID card and we got whatever we wanted. If our parents ever found out, we probably would have gotten a licking, but we played it for all we could.

Because my dad was a noncommissioned officer, he was really low man on the totem pole, but he had the pay scale of a lieutenant or captain, or something like that, so he wasn't that low because he was noncommissioned. He wasn't in the elite type of area, though. I think that always bothered him a bit.

TERRY McCULLOCH

You're stuck into one of two categories immediately: NCO or officer. They put the officers on one side of the base, and they put the NCOs on the other, and they did not ever mix. They each have their own club, their own pool. The only time kids ever see each other is if they're going to public schools, off base. They really don't mix.

It was always a mind-set that your dad was not an officer. And no matter how high-ranking he is as NCO, he's still enlisted. You're on the other side. That was always obvious. They always made it real clear: rank.

DEREK LOWE

My dad was in the Eighty-second Airborne, and we would go out and watch him jump, so I think that was when I became aware of his job, his function. I think at that time, too, I became aware of my mother as part of my dad's career. She would iron his clothes and sew the patches on, and when they weren't right, they'd have a big fight. I think she was more aware of her involvement by that time, too.

My dad said that the key to being a success in the Army is having a strong wife, someone who can tolerate your being away, and take care of business, and deal with all the situations that come up.

MARK DENTON

In Giessen, there was a major split. You were sergeants' kids, or you were officers' kids, and you didn't mix. All my buddies were sergeants' kids.

I was attracted to this gal who was a captain's daughter, and I was not to cross that boundary. It was an unwritten rule. And I thought Diana Miller was the greatest-looking girl in the entire world. All my buddies warned me, "You're going to pay. This is bad news. You're not supposed to be messing with her."

Every Friday night at the AYA they had a dance. At the AYA dances, all the officers' kids were over there, and all of the sergeants' kids were over here. We all danced together, us sergeants' kids, and the officers' kids all danced together, and very rarely would there be any intermixing.

Anyway, the big eighth-grade dance came up, and it was "tolo," so the girls were asking. Diana asked me to go with her, and we had a good time. The next day, two of my buddies beat me up because I'd "crossed the line."

School was interesting, because school knew no rank. You'd be mixed in school, and you'd be sitting next to anybody: I sat next to Diana in one class. The caste system wasn't tolerated at all in school, but the kids made it work.

If you met anybody or knew anybody, you knew what their

dad's rank was, period. "My dad's a sergeant." "Well, my dad's a colonel, so there!" You did your best, but all he was was a sergeant.

My dad didn't make as much as the captains and majors and lieutenants did. The military did an excellent job of keeping us well versed in exactly how important we were, by the size of our housing units. The officers definitely lived better than the enlisted men did.

When we were in Germany, which was where I got most of that ingrained in me, my dad was the ranking sergeant in our building, which gave us certain privileges. We had the keys to all the apartments and to the storage area in the basement, and that gave me just a little more prestige than all the other kids who lived in our building. I don't know that I flaunted it all that much, but it made me stand just a hair taller.

JACK LEMONT

I only saw my dad get on some people once. When we were in Texas, they had a Marine Corps training center there, and my brother and I went in there a couple of times with him when he had work to do. They had a pool table, and some guys came in—I think they were Seabees or low-ranking Navy guys—and they proceeded to take the table away from my brother and me, just kind of playing around; they weren't being mean or anything. And my dad came in, and, and, boy, he jumped their case, just really tore them up. I had never seen him get mad at other men before. I had seen him get mad at us. He had an awful temper, but he kept it inside most of the time. They were jumping through their rear ends to get out of there.

I remember the "few good men" thing, saying the Marines were tougher. They had a more extensive boot camp, and to this day, I talk about the Marine Corps with a little more pride, even though I wasn't in it. I always thought we were the best, so a little bit of that rubbed off on me. Evidently, my dad thought so too, because he wore a Marine Corps ring for years. My mom was put out because he wouldn't wear a wedding ring. He was married to the Marine Corps. The ring wore out, so he finally did start

171

to wear a wedding ring. He wore this silver Marine Corps ring for as long as I can remember. To this day, I don't know what he did.

I think as I got older, rank was a little bit of a status thing. In later years I had to explain what first sergeant was. I didn't want people to think he was demoted or anything. He wasn't a *sergeant* sergeant; he was a *first* sergeant.

SHARON GILMORE

I knew my dad was a first-class petty officer, but I didn't really know what that meant. I knew that he was not allowed to associate with the higher officers, and that it was a good idea that we didn't associate with their kids. And I knew why: it was because if an officer ever had to order him to go to war or to do something, if they were friends, it would be hard to do that, to give orders. So they didn't encourage that. We associated with officers' kids, but we weren't supposed to.

When my mom divorced him, he quit drinking, and right after he quit, he was promoted, which he had tried for all those years and never could get. So it wasn't his intelligence; it was the booze.

SHEILA WRIGHT

My dad was as high as he could go in the enlisted before he retired. He was a master sergeant. My mom said we lived in nicer places than the lower-ranking people did, the privates and corporals. I became very aware of rank when I stayed with my aunt and uncle, who was an officer, during the summer and we got to go to the Officers' Club and to the pool there. It was so much nicer, and there weren't as many people there; it wasn't crowded.

We used to go to the Enlisted Men's Club. We just called it the Club. The pool was *always* crowded, and the snack bar was crowded, and the club wasn't as nice.

All I knew was that my dad had a lot of stripes on his arms. That's how it went, by stripes. I can remember my mom saying, "Dad got another stripe today." It wasn't money; it was a stripe; and we would count his stripes.

We always had a party when my dad got promoted. And that meant that he was going to be transferred, more or less. "Oh, Dad got promoted. When are we moving?"

CAROLINE BAKER

My dad was an aviation specialist in the Air Force, and also, later on he was a senior master sergeant. I don't know if he was ever a drill sergeant. That's what *he* thought he was. That's what he acted like, even at home.

I remember my dad's last two promotions before he retired. We knew that my dad was in charge of—or over—a lot of guys on the base. My sister was in the ninth grade, and it got to the point where she was getting older. These enlisted men, the younger guys who were just in for four years, knew better than to mess around with the girls on the base, especially my dad's kids. It was a big joke that Baker would kick butt if he ever found out anyone was messing around with his daughter or even looking at her.

BARRY JENKINS

They have this thing about their rank. You respect rank, whether you know that man or not. But even when they're in the military, there are limits to that. If they don't know an officer and he's barking out orders, they'll follow to a point, but when it's a life-or-death situation, they may not: "We're going in the other direction; *you* can go get shot up."

I was always aware of rank. I always knew what he was. My dad wasn't an Annapolis graduate. He joined the Navy when he was seventeen and retired a lieutenant commander, so his attitude, his military attitude, wasn't one of a cadet graduate. They called him a *mustang*, which meant he started at the bottom and retired an officer, which never happens these days. So in a

173

sense, he had this sort of working-class pride; you know how a sergeant acts, a noncom, that attitude of "I work for a living." He had that attitude even as an officer: "I came up from the ditches, pulled myself up by my bootstraps." He was one of those guys, the working-class officer, as opposed to the real military, Annapolis, bred-to-be-an-officer types.

He was not into pomp and circumstance. He hated wearing ribbons and medals. He hated dress braids; he hated full inspections. He had a sword, the officer's sword, and he hated pulling that out. In the Navy, they put on their dress whites and have to do all that nonsense. I thought it was great; that was the hippest part about it. He didn't like the showbiz aspect. He'd just as soon do his job.

BILL FLYNN

We used to ask my dad all the time when he was going to be a general. We knew what the next rank was. We knew what all the ranks were, from private first class, all the way up to sergeant major and so forth, on up to general.

I think his assignment at the Pentagon was probably the only assignment where I wasn't sure what he was doing. I was in high school, and I don't think I really noticed. I don't think he was supposed to talk about his work; it turns out he wasn't involved in top-secret projects or anything like that. But before and after his Pentagon assignment, I was always aware of what he was doing. He was a professor of the military psychology of leadership, and after that, he was a commander in a couple of locations: Okinawa, Vietnam, also Panama. After I left home, his graveyard assignment was at Arizona State with the ROTC program.

So I knew what he was doing, except at the Pentagon. I don't know how he handled it. For the two years there, he left for work at seven in the morning. He would never eat dinner with us; he would come home at about eight at night and have to eat by himself. That was a tough assignment. I don't think he enjoyed it very much. Of course, my father never did like a desk job.

174

BEVERLY TAYLOR

I've got it all: I'm an officer's daughter, an only child, and was raised in the Marine Corps. And the Marine Corps just thought of themselves as the crème de la crème of the service. So I just sort of have an attitude, and I know it just kind of goes with it all.

I was always aware of rank, always knew about my father's promotions and his rank, and what it brought, where we were in the structuring of the scale, particularly when he became lieutenant colonel and colonel. Of course, I was older then. Not only was I aware of my father's rank, but I was aware of his seniority. That was always made very clear to me.

I never dated very many military boys, because I would have had to date all colonels' sons or generals' sons. I had to date a certain type of boy. There was a definite caste system. They'd have to come from an equal rank: *never* an enlisted man's son, my God! It would have to be someone within the same rank that my father was, so that really narrowed the field. As a result, I didn't date many military boys; I got around it by dating mostly civilian boys. I remember in California my mother always wanted me to date John—not that he wasn't a nice boy. His family owned a chain of stores, and he was hand-picked. I couldn't stand him: he was tall and freckled and had red hair. He was a nice enough guy, but . . . There was always somebody hand-selected for me, but I always managed to date someone else, but even then, they were still within my parents' realm of acceptability.

DEBBIE WEST

Rank was always a source of pride. He advanced up the ranks about as quickly as you can go, I think. I was always aware when he was a lieutenant JG, and then a lieutenant, and then lieutenant commander, and I believe he was a commander when he finally retired. We always had a lot of pictures of whatever rituals, ceremonies they went through. I've got one of my father. He's such a grim person, and yet other people found him to be such a charismatic person, but I never saw it.

I think he was always involved in intelligence and communications, and most of what he did was secret, so we never got any details. After he was home and he was no longer going overseas, he was working at a defense contractor for a while as the naval consultant to some project. No details; he always said, "Well, it's secret." We never got the details, just that he's in the Navy, whatever it is they do.

What I can remember of being "up close and personal" with the Navy was when my father would take us aboard the various ships that he was on, and he was officer of the day or something like that, and all the men would stand at attention and salute him and say, "Sir!" And we would go aboard and have dinner. I was a teenager at that time, and the sailors were falling all over themselves. My father always wanted me, of course, to marry a Navy man, so he was really exposing me to sailors and stuff. I was afraid of boys in those days, and they were very intimidating in those uniforms. Hundreds of sailors.

PETER VARGAS

You didn't screw with the colonel's kid too much, because if it was something that you could get in trouble for, your dad would get in trouble. We all had our father's rank, whatever it was. There was a pecking order that carried down from the fathers to the kids, to some degree.

"Who's this guy?" Well, he's Major Kelly's kid, he's Sergeant Thompson's kid, or whatever. And then the officers' kids were always separated from the enlisted. So what we found, also, was that the officers' kids would go pretty much anywhere to play, but the enlisted kids, the NCOs' children, would very rarely go over into the officers' quarters yards to play. I don't know if it was a taboo area, or maybe it was due to the fact that their fathers stayed away and didn't fraternize with the officers. It was a different clique. You had your NCO clique, and your officers' clique. Although, as I said, the officers' kids tended to move around a little more freely. We had the privileges of rank.

We had our own pool; they had their own pool. So you never swam with an NCO's kid. You always knew who the NCO kid was because we had blue patches on our swimming trunks, and they had red patches. So if you saw a red patch in the officers' club pool, it was always someone's guest, and we'd always go up and say, "Who are you here with?" So even we tended to create that schism.

BRAD HOLMES

When we were in California, my dad was in Strategic Air Command, the bombers, and he was a navigator. They were always a real tight cluster of friends, the six guys on the plane. They were always together, and then when they'd get off, a lot of times they stuck together, too. We'd end up going over to their houses. Those guys really kept their families close together.

My dad was always real quiet about getting a promotion, or working toward one, or how he was being perceived by his peers. He never mentioned that at all, or the fact that anything that we might do would influence him or his promotions at all.

He would take us to the base on Sundays, to the strategic headquarters, and he would show us his office and where he worked and where he slept. Other people, the airmen who worked for him, would talk about my dad. One of my baseball coaches was really afraid of my dad, because he'd have to wake him up if needed when they were on duty.

We knew where the other housing was. Of course, we always had friends whose fathers were full colonels or generals, or something like that, and they had the real nice housing, and then you had other friends whose parents were staff sergeants, master sergeants, tech sergeants, and they always lived in kind of junky houses.

I never had any direction placed on my friendships at all. Some kids had it down and were concerned about it: I guess the reflection of what their parents had instilled in them. But pretty few. The kids who went to private school, military school, were always very aware of "what my dad does" and were concerned with that.

177

PAULA HOLMES

Rank. He talked about it a lot. He used to talk to my mom and we would overhear it. He was a very verbal guy, and he would get frustrated about the whole thing and voice his opinions at home. He was a lieutenant colonel when he retired. He never did make full colonel, and it bothered him. He always attributed it to the fact that there were other guys who walked all over people to get up where they were, and he wouldn't do that. I don't know if there was a lot of truth in that or not.

My dad's being chaplain always made me stand out. And that was the bigger thing to me than his rank, the fact that he was a chaplain. I didn't want people to know, because once they knew, I was like Miss Goody Two Shoes. But that bothered me more than the rank. You didn't really know what the fathers did. I didn't know what my dad did.

GEORGE DEXTER

The difference between officers and enlisted was clearly evident to me. Generally speaking, my friends were the other officers' kids, and our fathers were all pretty much the same rank. Promotions were going very slowly at that time. My father came out of World War I and was lucky enough not to be dropped down to first lieutenant. He spent seventeen years as a captain; he might have had to spend those seventeen years as a first lieutenant.

By the late thirties, I think, all of my father's friends were majors. But we were definitely aware of the differences. His promotion to major, at Benning, in 1935, was a big event: he had been a captain for seventeen years. And then, of course, his other promotions came after World War II broke out. He was promoted to lieutenant colonel after I left home.

BRUCE HUTSON

My dad was in the Air Force and then later on worked for the Army. I know the only way that I would have gone in was as an officer. I saw too much of the shit that the GIs had to go through. I would not have done that. You see these other guys who are college grads who don't want to be officers because they want to be with the GIs where all the shit's going on. Forget it. I don't want to live in bunkhouses and be a grunt and get yelled at by everyone and be a martyr. Because you're an educated person and you're slumming, is what it amounts to. I didn't need to do that. I'm going to get the best I can out of whatever I do. You get more money, you can go to the Officers' Club, you don't have to take a lot of crap from people, and that's one reason that I don't regret not going in, because as a second lieutenant, you get all of the shit from the officers. No one respects you. The enlisted people don't respect you because you're a shavetail. You finally get to first lieutenant, and, if you're lucky, you're a captain by the time you get out. It's a long road. I just felt that I wouldn't be able to do that. I would question too much.

That's another thing that my dad taught me. You listen and you do what you're told, but if you really have a question about it, you ask a question. That's how you learn—is by asking questions in life—and the military doesn't work on that principle. You don't ask questions because they don't care if you learn. They don't admire that. I learned that in the ROTC. I didn't like the way that they treated each other. I hadn't seen that at all as a dependent. I saw that it was definitely this chain of command. No respect. I knew I would've gotten into trouble, if I had gone in, because I would have talked back to someone. "Wait a minute, excuse me, Captain," and these guys would have just bristled.

NANCY KARACAND

My dad was an officer. Although he was an officer, he never went to college, and he had a real inferiority complex about that. Most of the officers that were his rank were younger than he was, because they had college degrees, and they had gone through OCS.

He had really come up the hard way. He had started off as an enlisted man, and he was able to go through officer's training before they required a college degree. I think he had come in through the Army, and then when they established the Air Force, he went into that and then somehow worked up through the ranks. He was five or ten years older than a lot of the men who had a similar rank, and I think that was always really hard for him. Plus he had some medical problems, and he was apparently hospitalized a couple of times. I think that set him back rankwise, too, so that was sort of a family secret. Every once in a while, you heard these little tidbits about it: that Dad was upset because he didn't get the promotion that he was supposed to get.

He was a captain for the longest time, and then he finally made major, and that was such a big concern for him. We were so proud. There was some kind of ceremony, and we were so proud that he was finally a major.

My dad was getting ready to retire with twenty-six years, and he was quite proud of that. Yet it was a real sore spot for him that he had been in for twenty-six years, and his retirement rank was lieutenant colonel. He was given that rank after he died. His reserves rank had been lieutenant colonel, and his regular active duty rank was major when he died. I remember that being a really big thing. We wanted to be able to call him lieutenant colonel. We were so proud that when he died, we got to call him a lieutenant colonel. It's kind of sad.

Although I knew that he was an officer, and there was this definite distinction between officers and NCOs or enlisted men, I tended to be more comfortable around the NCO kids, because their dads, if they were career military, were as old as my dad and more of the same mentality, more from that working-class mentality. And a lot of the officers that we lived around in the base housing were either young doctors or attorneys, young professional people, and they had younger kids. It seems like we sort of ended up with that group, the NCO kids. If my father had been higher-ranking, we would have been in a higher grade of housing, around people who were more our ages.

My dad took a lot of pride in his work, and so much of my awareness came out of those later years, when we weren't moving around but it was still the military experience. In Mississippi, we went into his building occasionally. He was in one of those huge two-story buildings with no windows. It was real awesome to me, to go into the building where my father worked. I was so proud of the fact that he was in charge of all of the people in his area of this huge building.

You knew that so-and-so's dad was a lieutenant colonel, and they wore nicer clothes. There was clearly a difference, in the way that people dressed and in the way that they acted and the kind of activities they were involved in. Kids from the higher-ranking families could do the more expensive things, like horseback riding. That was very clear.

RHONDA HEALEY

In the Navy, they have traditions: when people move up in rank, they do different things. When he got one of his promotions, they had this enormous ceremony, where they took him out and I'm sure they drank until the cows came home, and put his shirt on backward and put eggs in his shoes—all these really horrible things. I can remember him coming in the morning after, and my mother didn't know whether to laugh hysterically or hit him. All of us were standing back in horror because we didn't know if he had been beaten up or what had happened. Then it was explained to us that it was a big deal. And I can remember they were looking for the names in the paper, because they'd published the promotions, and when they found his name in the list, everyone in the household was jumping up and down and it was a big deal. I was excited, but I really didn't know why. I could read just enough to read his name in the paper.

After that, he was a chief forever, it seemed. Then when he was commissioned as an officer, we knew it was a big deal because Mother made all these formals and bought long gloves and went to Providence, Rhode Island, where they have the Officer's Candidate School. And they do the big, formal, East Coast ball, and he had to wear his white uniform with gloves. My father hated it and my mother loved it. We went to stay with an aunt for that week. We kind of knew he was going to be an officer. We didn't know what an officer was, exactly, but we knew it was a big deal. After he got his commission, they bought some new

181

furniture, which we had never had. My mother would take the old junk and reupholster it and do amazing things, but we never had new furniture before that time.

He was so low-key about it, you have to understand. My dad was even embarrassed about receiving medals. When he received a commendation of some sort, I frequently didn't know it unless I came home and found the certificate, which always had a beautiful cover. I would find it lying casually on the coffee table or something.

We didn't have a keen sense of what was happening. The biggest one was his last promotion, when he made lieutenant commander, because that is where they begin to go through the process of string commander and that kind of thing. And that was a very big deal, because he was older, for one thing, and it wasn't typical of these mustangs who started out as enlisted to make command. He was more interested in the work he was doing professionally, and less interested in the military aspect of it.

Mother pushed him to some degree; I'm sure she did. I know there was a lot of discussion when he went to college. Also when he was going to take the tin can or the destroyer duty out of San Diego and instead went to flight school, there was something that went on. She was either for or against that. I think he was promoted faster as a result of the flight stuff than he would have been on a destroyer.

ROBERT BLAKE

I never went to any of the promotion ceremonies. Part of it was that for the first twelve years of my life he was a captain, so there weren't any promotions, and then when he was promoted to major he was in Nicaragua.

The last time we saw him, he was a captain, and when we saw him six months later he was a major. When he was promoted to lieutenant colonel it was shortly after, sort of simultaneous with his assignment to the special service squadron as squadron Marine officer. There was a wetting-down party that was held at one of the beer gardens, but there were no high school students allowed.

We all knew who the general's kids were. The general's kids had little extra perks. They had a driver to take them around, so they didn't have to go on the school bus if they didn't want to. And of course this business with the staff car with the red flag and two stars on it. You're bound to know who that was.

I didn't know everything he did by a long shot. It depended. When I was a little kid, I really didn't know too much about it. But he would take me to ceremonies, so I got used to the idea of formations, inspections, things of that sort.

When he was at sea, I had a rather confused idea. I thought that the *Pennsylvania* was his ship. He had a very good relationship with the actual captain, so that when the ship was in port, and we went aboard to visit, he usually managed to borrow the captain's gig, or the admiral's barge, so instead of having to go aboard the ship on one of these old gray motor sailers, there was a snappy little gig or barge, with a special flag on it and a white superstructure, and so on. I would tell my friends that "My father's ship is here, and there it goes." It *was* his ship, as far as I was concerned. Of course, later on, when I got older, I realized where people fit a little better than that.

MICHELLE SLOAN

When he was CO in Germany, we always went to his battalion parades. And they had a parade for his change of command. That was the biggest deal that I remember. There was a general present, I remember. He was turning the command over to the next guy when we were leaving Germany, and as CO, he was in charge of whatever went on, and so he planned this big deal, which nobody had done for him when he came in. When he had arrived for his change of command, it was just some dumb thing in an office somewhere: "Here you go." My dad did all this neat stuff; they had a horse-drawn carriage for the incoming guy. They had big helicopters come in, too. My older sister was in high school, and she had her hair all done up, and she had so much hair spray that it didn't move, and the helicopters were beating, and we were all saying, "Look at Leslie's hair!"

He was always gone when he was promoted, twice in

Vietnam, until he was promoted to colonel. That was the only time I ever saw the ceremony, and my mom had a big party. My little brother had just had his tonsils out, so my sister and I were going back and forth to the hospital during the party.

My other sister also was in the Army. She went into ROTC in college, so my dad swore her in and that was kind of neat. They had a little ceremony, and we all had champagne.

The neatest part was when we were in Germany, when he was battalion CO. That was fun, to go to his office there, and he had a big desk. And we got to feel important; his bumper sticker had the number one on it. Now that he has retired, he has a sticker so that he can go on base to go to the PX, and the number on it is in the thousands.

You were housed by rank, also. It really wasn't that big a deal, because your neighbors were usually the same rank. It wasn't like a thing to be snotty about, or if so, you kept it to yourself. I remember in Germany, when we were living in the temps, there were lower-ranking people in the buildings. I was in second grade, and this little girl who lived in the apartment buildings asked me where we were going to move, and I told her Dambach, and she said, "Oh, I know where that is. It means that my dad is more important than you." And I remember thinking, no, that's not true, because those are better houses at Dambach. But I didn't say anything about it. It wasn't cool to make a big deal about it.

MARY CHANDLER

"Outrank" was a pervasive system in our family, where whoever was the oldest in the room got the best seat, the best everything, as "rank" was decided by age. Our bedtimes and privileges may as well have been a "pay grade" assigned by age, with only fifteen minutes between my bedtime and that of my younger brother: merely a gesture!

I always knew who was of which rank, because not only did I hear those people referred to by rank; it was written on their houses. I always knew my father's rank, too, probably from the moment I was born. His promotions were obvious, because his uniform and insignia would change, as would the nameplate on the outside of the house. I don't recall bragging or mentioning my dad's rank to friends. However, my parents must have been afraid we might, because the night we flew to Panama, my father had a meeting with all of us kids who were still at home, making it very clear that he was going to be commander of the entire Atlantic side, and that if any of us were to take advantage of being "The Colonel's Kids" in any way, we'd be in *deep shit*. None of us were the type to do it anyway, but I appreciate that he would be concerned.

GAIL EMERSON

When we lived in military housing, I can remember very clearly—it must have been when I was in fifth grade—somebody said, "You shouldn't play with people whose parents aren't officers." I thought, What in the hell are they talking about? It seemed so absolutely ridiculous.

With civilians, it didn't matter. It seemed strange to me; it seemed unreal and not right. It was the same feeling that I had when we lived in the South, dealing with segregation, and they had the blacks and the whites separated on the buses and stuff like that.

LINDA WINSLOW

My dad was drafted and then sent to OCS. He was a ninety-day wonder. He took a series of courses throughout his military career and eventually graduated from the University of Illinois and got his master's. He didn't want to say that he admired West Point graduates, but at the same time he made it clear that he had the equivalent status; he said, "It's the same as being a ring-banger."

One of the questions was, Was your father rated or not? Meaning, does he wear wings. I had to explain that my father was in the Air Force but he was not a pilot.

Of course, I was raised to marry an officer. My sex education

185

consisted of "Well, when you marry your second lieutenant, thus and such . . ."

I took a bunch of little kids around caroling at Christmastime because I was the leader of the kindergarten choir. There was this cute bus driver and we were flirting, and when he dropped off the last kids, I said I lived on Bonn Boulevard, named after some dead hero. He took one look at the house and said, "Your dad's a major?" I went yeah, and he freaked out. There were the officers and there were enlisted people, and never the twain shall meet, not even if you were a kid. I always thought it was ridiculous, but that was the power structure.

The general's wife always got in line first at the Officers' Wives' luncheons, and you just kind of accepted that as a fact of life until you got older, and you think, I don't think this is right.

My mother was a colonel in a fund-raising drive, and she used to just beat it into my father, because at the time he was a major or a captain or something, and she would say, "I'm a colonel."

I saw, at the functions that I attended, that the wives had more of a hierarchy among themselves than the men. With the men, it was, "Okay, you're a lieutenant and I'm a captain; how you doing?" But the women were very aware of status and rank, I guess because they had nothing else to do.

I used to hang out with a general's son, which was very convenient, because if I wanted to get my baseball glove fixed or something, we'd just go out to the parachute shop and say, "Hi, I'm General So-and-So's son, and this is Major Winslow's daughter." And some corpsman, scared out of his mind, would say, "Okay, kid."

BRENDA ROWAN

My husband and I met each other's parents for the first time when everyone came over to Hawaii for our wedding. It didn't go real well. Both of the fathers wanted to have control, and they were both playing king of the mountain. It wasn't very comfortable. I'd rather see them separately. The mothers seemed to get along real well, but the fathers were constantly tangling. They're both officers, and I don't know if that had anything to do with it, but they're both kind of the same personality, serious and wanting to be in control of the situation. I was uncomfortable with it.

JOHN ROWAN

I'm still not quite sure what my dad did in the Air Force. I had only vague ideas. When I was very young, I knew that he was a navigator. I knew that basically because there was a portrait of him hanging in the living room, looking through a sextant. He must have been doing something else all that time, but I have no idea what.

I knew that some of my friends lived in duplexes, and that I lived in a house, but I didn't know the difference between officers and enlisted. But really, even in high school, I wasn't aware of how good I had it, being an officer's dependent. The swimming pool was nicer, the beach club was nicer, bingo was better. I had little concept of the difference between officers and enlisted.

When we lived on the base in Sacramento, we lived near the back gate, and I'd go down to the gate and talk to the guards, and there were a couple of them who were pretty friendly. They taught me how to salute, and I'd stand there beside them when the cars came, and salute with them. I thought for quite a long time that the most important people on the base were the guards at the gate. That was what I imagined was the top of the line, as far as influence and importance goes.

10

Civilian Life

I always knew that we were fortunate to be living in the oasis of order on post. My father described the anarchy that existed in the world outside the gates of the post with a compound word, *damncivilians*, accompanied by an exasperated shrug that implied that they didn't know any better.

We were surrounded on all sides by civilian life, an alien world that defied military logic and order. Whenever we had to go to downtown Leavenworth, Kansas, we used to beg my mother to drive past a spooky, dilapidated house so that we could hang out of the car windows and stare. It was the kind of house that inspires childhood legends and nightmares. I realized only recently that the house was so fascinating to us because there were never any empty houses with broken windows and mysterious reputations on the post; such a phenomenon was possible only in civilian life. We lived in a civilian neighborhood when my father was stationed at the Pentagon, and it was there that I was introduced to the concept of freeways, as opposed to the highways we traveled when we moved. An interminable series of beltways and bridges lay between our house and Fort Belvoir and the commissary. My father detested the commute to and from his office; civilian life was a rat race, and the freeways were the maze. We were relieved to leave Virginia and move back to the convenience of a post, where there were no mundane problems like traffic and rush hour.

When my father put in his retirement papers, my parents got out a map and by process of elimination decided where they wanted to settle. I didn't want to move again, but at last we finally had a choice, just like civilians. The East Coast winters were too harsh; we had spent enough time in the Midwest; the West Coast was too expensive. They chose New Mexico and decided to have a house built, and they unrolled blueprints and studied them as if they were battle plans. I was fascinated with the entire construction process because I had never seen a house being built; we had always lived in houses that were just there, waiting for us. We were overwhelmed by the samples of carpet and paint and the decisions we faced about such details, but our newfound sense of permanence made us giddy. Once again we settled in a new house, but this time it was ours.

As part of my father's retirement benefits we still had our privileges, and we immediately learned the route to the base. It was the best of both worlds, as far as I was concerned. We had cheap food from the commissary and our own "real" house. My mother went to work and my father stayed home and learned to cook, which was slightly unusual in our suburban neighborhood. When other fathers were home during the day there were discussions about unemployment and layoffs, but our household was, still, exempt from civilian life and its problems. We weren't in the Army anymore, but we still had our ID cards and the security of my father's government checks.

Damn-civilians lived in a confusing, chaotic world of choices and risks. They could live anywhere, yet they didn't move as we did. I had, however, been so indoctrinated with the belief that moving was an adventure that the stability of civilian life seemed boring. Civilians had supermarkets and drugstores and, it seemed, a store for everything. The array of choices in civilian stores was deceptive, though, because the prices, so much higher than those we paid at the no-frills commissary and PX, offset any temptation. My father's military career had been a virtual calling, but civilians could lose their jobs at any time, and, according to my father, they had no vested interest in performing their jobs with any pride or efficiency.

I used to cringe when my father's military mentality about the way that things should be done met with the incompetence of a damn-civilian. My father is still military. He can be imperious when he pulls rank with people who have no concept of rank, but he gets results. I know that he has to make a conscious effort to refrain from saying "superior officer" when he barks, "Give me the name of your superior and spell it," to some unlucky minion. In civilian life, there are no superior officers to hold accountable.

Hawaiians refer to the continental United States as "the mainland," prisoners refer to anything beyond the prison walls as "the outside," and soldiers in Vietnam counted the days until they returned to "the world." For military brats, anything outside the gates of the post was "civilian": civilian housing, civilian schools, civilian relatives. There were families who lived off post, sent their children to civilian schools, and willingly exchanged the security of the post for some semblance of a "normal" life, but even the military brats who consistently lived off post were aware of the distinctions that set them apart from their neighbors. Their fathers' uniform was emblematic, and no matter how civilian or suburban the setting, the fact remained that they were a military family.

Most families made regular pilgrimages to visit their civilian relatives, and wives and children often lived with relatives, temporarily, if the father was sent overseas. For the most part, however, military brats perceived civilians as an interesting species of people who were not allowed access to the post or facilities like the commissary and PX. Civilians weren't a part of the hierarchy of rank and, consequently, were rather difficult to define or understand. They were simply different; they weren't military.

We'd say, "Oh, look, there's civilians on base."

It was not unusual for military brats to preface sentences

with "When we retired" or "When we got out." For parents, retirement was a time to reap what they had sown, to settle down, collect retirement benefits, and consider a second career. The family life-style changed dramatically when the father's military career ended, and military brats were, without exception, affected by the transition. They were being transferred to civilian life.

PAULA HOLMES

The Civilians: I thought they were from another planet or something. In our household, they were like the Catholics.

My dad always said that military kids were good kids. "You just don't find better kids than military kids." I remember thinking, well, some of them probably aren't so good.

Your eyes are so opened up when you finally get out and look back on military people now. It's amusing, to me, anyway. What a small world we lived in, very sheltered. When you'd move, somebody would take your hand and say this is your house, this is where you buy your clothes and your new things.

Not only was I in that sheltered environment, but I was close to my family because of the insecurities that I had about the world out there. It frightened me to think of getting out on my own. It was a long, drawn-out procedure—I moved away, I moved back home, and when I was three thousand miles away, my dad was still trying to push me around, make sure that I was doing the right thing.

Before my dad retired, they tried to send him to Greenland, by himself, and he decided to retire. He said, "There's no way I'm going without my family." When he retired, he went through a real state of confusion. I'm curious if other men handled it the way that he did: he lost weight; he had some serious medical problems, I think, as a result of worrying. He's always been a very high-strung, worrying type. My dad was fifty when he retired, and he was still too young to do nothing, but too old to start a new career. He took off that uniform and it was sort of like who was he?

191

BARRY JENKINS

Civilians were like television: all that stuff on TV was for them; it wasn't for us.

Sometimes in the towns we lived in, we were looked down on. We always had this feeling of being second-class citizens. My mother encountered bad attitudes about Navy people, people saying, "Blah, blah, military family." I always remember that feeling.

The old man: I think the Navy provided him with a lot of answers to his problems. It took care of his family; it took care of a lot of questions about what he was going to do with his life. When my dad retired, they had that big deal, the ceremony. Here the guy had done twenty-two years in the Navy, and they had a little spiel. They did have a little ceremony: the guys in the squadron crossed swords and they walked under it as he did his thing. I always felt like it should have been a bigger deal. I had really long hair, and I felt particularly good about that. There I was among the Navy, and I was looking like a dirt bag in their eyes, which made me feel wonderful.

I suppose retirement was hard for him, but he did it. He bought a sailboat and he turned into this mellow guy. You wouldn't have recognized him. It was surprising.

CATHY ATCHISON

Because my father joined the Air Force when he did, when I was in third grade, I had lived a civilian life. You ran into civilians who had lived in the same house for fifteen years or hadn't ever been out of the city where they were born. I guess I felt that they didn't have as broad a perspective on what the world was about.

TIM BROCKWAY

There was a self-contained, aristocratic feeling among military families. Our parents were aristocratic military people with high values and higher education and all that. From that point of view, you could really feel a class difference. I am a coach now, and I've worked with kids who go to private schools, and when they refer to kids in public schools, they have the same point of view. They don't really know what the kids in public schools are like, but they're sure that they all carry knives and do drugs. Us and them; it's not based on much understanding.

Having to leave the military and become a civilian was not a pleasant prospect for the people in the military. In one sense, civilian life was harder than being in the military, where you have your quarters and your medical and everything taken care of. On military bases, everyone has their job, and has to do it. I can see why that's attractive to people.

My dad didn't want to retire, but they were going to send him on a hardship tour to the Aleutian Islands, and we wouldn't be able to go with him. He didn't want to go, and we didn't want him to go. He wasn't able to appeal to anyone, and I think he was very disillusioned, because he had given his whole life—more than just his life. He had given up everything to be in the military, and expound its virtues, and risk his life. And when it came right down to it, they didn't give a fuck who he was.

Of course, I thought, It doesn't surprise me. But I think it really surprised him that they weren't going to help him out. It was a pretty cold, impersonal thing in the end.

We were all so glad when he got out. I actually count that as the beginning of our family. That was the first time it really felt like we would have a chance to have a family. Before that, I don't think I ever saw my dad very much.

PETER VARGAS

Civilians weren't as important. They were real low in the pecking order. They were "just civilians." We were special, we were the elite in school, and we were treated differently by the civilian kids. It was mostly detrimental to many relationships because we tended to pull ourselves away. And either because of jealousy on their part or whatever, it tended to make them resent us a little bit, so there was a schism between the civilian kids and the military kids that was always there.

We went back to the base, back to our homes, to the security of that barbed-wire fence that went around the base; and we were safe from everything that was outside the base. We were sheltered. We were in and out, but they had to put up with us because we lived there.

ANNE HEYWOOD

We lived in a small, industrial town near St. Louis, and the civilians in that area were kind of looked down on; they had a blue-collar image. Civilians were considered to be people who weren't with us. They were a different species of people, even when we lived in other, more affluent areas. From very early on, I knew that not everyone was in the military. We usually lived in neighborhoods off base and got to know other kids who weren't in the military, and it was very natural. I think only in Missouri did we look down on them, because they seemed to be ignorant, not very well educated, cliquish, exclusive towny people.

My dad had an awfully hard time retiring. He still is very depressed, off and on. He just can't tolerate not having that authority that he had and the structure. He worked part-time in sales, and he just couldn't tolerate being the peon. It was too humiliating for him. He was a career man, and he worked his way up from the time he was eighteen years old, so it was his whole life. He's had a pretty hard time.

JOHN ROWAN

As I grew up, it felt more like a club, to be military, and I knew that other military kids would understand things that civilian kids didn't understand, like what it was like to move a lot and meet new people. And also world events, especially as they related to military strategies. We were in Florida during the Cuban blockade, and I think that the military kids had a more in-depth understanding of what was going on than the civilian kids had. All the base housing had one room in the center of the house that had no windows that was typically used as a storage room, but it was understood that it was also a bomb shelter—as if it would have done any good—but that's what it was.

Particularly in Florida, the base kids were more inclined to stick together. It was a very rural area, so there was quite a bit of difference; I had quite a few friends from the local area, but there was quite a sharp division. You could pretty much tell by looking at kids if they were military or not—by their clothes and haircuts and speech.

BRAD HOLMES

The town outside the base in California was rough and was notorious for gangs and street violence. Anytime the Air Force kids came off the base, the chance was there to get into trouble with "the town kids." Although I never got into any fights, I always thought I was going to get into one, so I was always acting like a tough guy.

When he retired, my dad really changed careers. He went into graphic arts. He wanted to do that; before he got into the military he was an art student. He took a lot of art classes before he retired, and then he got a job in that field right away, after retiring. It was a little different; it didn't pay very well, no authority, but he liked it a lot. And he never wanted to be known as colonel, didn't want to wear his monkey outfit to military day or whatever. He talked about that.

TERRY McCULLOCH

My dad was forty when he retired. He had twenty years of service. I was fourteen when he retired. We were living civilian when he went to Vietnam, and when he came home, suddenly we were military again and were living back on base. Then we moved back to Albuquerque for good when he retired. It was a weird time: being civilian, leaving, and then being civilian again.

The military will place you, when you retire, in a civilian job. My dad went to the job placement center and then went to work at a finance company, selling loans. He did that for about a year, and he hated it. So eventually he took the test and he became a civil servant at the veteran's hospital, and he was perfectly comfortable doing that.

When my dad retired, he went to an extreme of "I'm a civilian now, so I'm going to be mod." He had sideburns and he let his hair grow a little puffy on top and longer in the back. He used to wear those wide ties. Big huge knots at his neck, and loud ties, and he was mod, real mod. When he got out, his biggest complaint was "I don't have anything to wear to work" because he had always had his uniform. He and my mom went shopping and bought all these sports jackets and these ugly polyester pants that he picked out. It was hideous. And white shoes. Why do they always wear the white shoes immediately when they get out? You can always tell an ex-military man: if he's retired, he wears white shoes. That was their idea of what being civilian meant.

In Albuquerque, we were living a civilian life. We put a label on it. The people around us weren't military. Our closest friends in Albuquerque were retired military, too. They turned out to be our best friends. It was like they knew; they were like us.

We used to go out to the base and party once in a while. We'd kind of sneak on base, I guess because we could, and even though we didn't live there, we had some friends who did. We always kept that little connection, still, even after we were out of it.

DEREK LOWE

Suddenly I became aware that we were in this environment. The thing that triggered that was going to Fayetteville, North Carolina. It's a pit, the literal Army town. I remember this little town, where people were real conscious of the fact that you were in the Army and behaved in certain ways toward you because you were in the Army. That's when the contrast became apparent— that I was part of a little tribe here—the contrast between the civilian world and the military life.

When you think about the Army's mission, to fight communism and all that—the most socialist organization in the United States is the military. It's utter socialism in action. It's almost a classic socialist utopia. I think it began to strike me as a very interesting contradiction when I was a teenager. I wonder how many people in the Army—well, I'm sure they don't even think about it. I'm sure they think of themselves as being in a real unique role, and that's why their life-style is sort of insular. I thought it was an interesting paradox, though.

Civilians don't understand the depth of the involvement in the military life-style, how pervasive it is. Civilians have that sameness, the continuity of people in their lives, growing up in one place, knowing people for years.

After my dad retired as a sergeant major, he went to work for the civil service. He recently retired again for the second time. Basically he never left it, from the time he was seventeen.

I'm not good with resources; you have unlimited water and electricity on most bases. To this day, I love to take long showers, and it comes from not ever having to be conscious of utilities in the military. I'm conscious about electricity, but we would go back and live with my grandparents, and of course they were always telling us to turn the lights out and shut the refrigerator and things like that.

I work in a hospital now, and civilian hospitals don't smell like Army hospitals. That ether smell—I don't know what it was, the stuff that they painted the walls with or alcohol.

NANCY KARACAND

We were the military, and there was a certain pride in that. These other people were just the plain old civilians. I never envied them; it was almost as if being a civilian was just plain.

Sometimes I felt sorry for them. I couldn't imagine having to live in the same house, in the same town, for years and years. I always felt, in a way, like I was the advantaged one and they were disadvantaged. I can't remember ever wishing that I could have stayed in the same place all along.

It was always clear to me that I was not one of the town kids. In fact, we moved to Mississippi when I was nine, and still, as a senior in high school, I wasn't a town kid. I was always a military kid. There I was almost eighteen, and there was still that distinction. Very much so. I was never one of the town kids.

We got to go the commissary, and it was always a big thing. My mother always used to say, "Oh, I went to Delchamp's the

197

other day, and you wouldn't believe the food prices. Thank God for the commissary!" Thank God for the base; what would we do without the base; and my God, what would we do without the hospital.

The house that my dad bought before he died was a few blocks from the main entrance to the base, so we had easy access to the commissary and the PX and the hospital. My mom did move, later, but she's probably never been more than a mile from the base.

RHONDA HEALEY

In our neighborhood in Los Angeles, to tell people your father was in the military was unheard-of. They couldn't imagine what your father did in the Navy, and I really didn't know either, because he was in college and that was unbelievable at that time as well. Parents didn't go to college, so to have a father who was in the military and was also a student: he might as well have been a Martian. I was a little confused about it, too. Other kids didn't know what to make of it, and my teachers were uncomfortable with it.

My dad came to school in uniform one time, to pick me up after Brownies or something, and I can remember these kids just being wide-eyed and in awe and not even talking to me. I remember walking out like Queen Elizabeth with my father. Their fathers wore suits and ties and I found that real different. I still fall in love with a real good suit. I can't imagine being impressed by a uniform at this point in my life.

ROBERT BLAKE

When you were on a post, you felt like you were part of the service, not quite, but almost as if you were in uniform yourself. There were post rules that applied to everybody, and you just obeyed them. Of course, there was reveille and the various bugle calls that you would hear. When I was not on a post, I felt particularly different.

I realized what my father was, and I knew that most people were civilians. But particularly with the Marine Corps, I felt like a member of a minority religious group. Everybody else's father was a civilian, and my father was the one in the service.

It wasn't like I was living in an enclave somewhere. Living on a military post came late enough in my life that I didn't think that was the real world and everything else was the phony world. I felt that the real world was the civilian world and that our part was that we were policemen, in effect, to keep the civilian world safe.

During the summer after I graduated from high school, two of my friends and I took the Marine Corps recruit rifle and pistol course at San Diego. We lived on the rifle range there and took the Marine Corps course, including qualifying. Our fathers paid for the ammunition and paid for our subsistence, so it wasn't costing the government anything. They had three extra recruits, except that we didn't get kicked in the pants the way the recruits did.

It hadn't soured us on military service per se, but I noticed that not one of us joined the Marine Corps. One of my friends was commissioned into the Army and was killed in World War II, and the other went to the Naval Academy and made a regular Navy career for himself, and I became a Naval Reserve aviator in World War II.

ELIZABETH SPIVEY

When we were growing up, my brothers were allowed to have toy machine guns, and Air Force planes, and remote-control planes, and GI Joes, and Army men, and all of that. And as soon as my dad retired, we moved to the suburbs, and the neighbors were horrified that my parents would let their children play with militaristic types of toys. Of course, the neighborhood kids were fascinated with them, and they were always over at our house, playing with them, but the other parents would never buy them for their kids. It seemed like military families didn't have the compunction about that, about the military toys.

My parents were really reluctant to retire, because they didn't know if he would make it in civilian life. There's a security in military life, and he wasn't really ready to retire. They were going to send him overseas after Wright Pat, but enough was enough. He didn't want to do that. He was worried, but he's been very successful in civilian life, and it turned out to be a good decision. He didn't want to go overseas.

Somehow you maintain a link to the military, even after you retire. My parents live near an Air Force base, and they still go to the commissary and the PX once a week, just like they did before he retired.

MARY CHANDLER

What? You mean everyone *isn't* in the Army? Mostly civilian life meant your father didn't wear a uniform, you couldn't shop at the PX and the commissary, and you stayed in one place all your life. Civilians might as well have been a different species for all I felt I had in common with them.

It was a gradual realization for me to notice that civilians existed beyond the chain-link boundaries of the post, and at that time, I assured myself that all those people used to be in the Army. Later, as my older siblings headed to college, not West Point, I was shocked to realize that a person could go straight from being an Army brat to being a civilian without having to wear a uniform for a few years. I suppose I was about twelve when this sunk in. I remember it being a realization along the lines of being told about menstruation: one of those melancholy realizations that completely alter your universe.

My father retired the same month I graduated from high school and settled extremely permanently. Immediately after retiring, he single-handedly built a house for himself and my mother. When this task was finished, he split his time between volunteer work for a charity organization and an arts group, which is still how he continues to spend his time. You see, my father debunks the civilian myth that Army colonels retired to high-paying corporate jobs. Ha, ha.

I went to college and continued to use my PX and commissary privileges until they ran out and finally lost all contact with the military, except that I have married a man who was himself in the Air Force for five years, long before we met.

SHEILA WRIGHT

If your dad is in the military, you are, too. There's no two ways about it. You will conform to military rules and standards, and that's it. You can't be what we used to call "normal people." We used to call anybody who wasn't in the military "normal."

Once in a while my grandparents would come and visit, and the kids used to say, "Oh, you've got civilians in your house." And I'd say, "Yeah, it's my grandparents." And the kids would ask, "Oh, was your grandfather in the military?" I'd say no. Your whole family was supposed to be in the military.

When my dad retired, we were so happy. We didn't want to move, but we were happy that Dad was retiring and we weren't going to go to France. Nobody wanted to go to France. It was a real tough time, the first two years he was out of the service. It was horrible. It was the hardest time in our lives, I think. I refused to have anything to do with my dad for years and years, and it all started after he retired and became this tyrant at home. My dad's an alcoholic, so I think not having anything to do all day had a lot to do with it. My dad was the one who worked. He wasn't the type to say, "I will never let my wife work," because I can remember my mom working back when I was real little, so it wasn't that we were brought up thinking that women stayed home and had babies and men worked. But then all of a sudden my dad was in control of the house and to this day, he considers that women's work.

GAIL EMERSON

I did think of the military as the people who had access to the perks of the military, could go to the commissary and the hospital on base, and were under that umbrella. The civilians were everybody else.

SHERRY SULLIVAN

We never had to live in the military housing, with the paper-thin walls. Even when I got married, I didn't want to live on post, so we lived off post, except in Germany. We lived in quarters that were built for Americans in the German section, so that wasn't too bad. You can just get tired of military, twenty-four hours a day. Sometimes it's kind of nice, though. They'll say, "Halloween will be held from 7:00 to 9:00 P.M." At least you'd know that people wouldn't be coming to your door late at night.

LINDA WINSLOW

I didn't know that other fathers didn't wear uniforms. To see a man in civilian clothes looked funny. It was probably in Germany, when I was about nine, that I figured it out. My dad had German civilians working for him, but up until that time it was them and us, who could use the commissary and who couldn't.

I was in the Civil Air Patrol at Fort Bliss. It was Armed Forces Day, and we were allowed to wear our uniforms. I was the equivalent of a corporal in the Civil Air Patrol, but I had my uniform on and I was frightful. And I invited my civilian girlfriend to come on base, and I was flipping salutes to all the officers, and she was going, "How do you know how to salute? You seem so mature in that uniform!" Maybe, in a sense, the military was a way for me to feel grown up.

I think it shocked me when I got older and realized that people my age were in the military. I always thought the grown-ups did that, not somebody my age. That's what Dad did. The grown-ups were the military.

DEBBIE WEST

I haven't seen my dad too often since I left home, and that's been a long time now, over half my life. I've never seen my father in a pair of Levi's. Only recently have I seen him in jeans, and they were sailor's dungarees, with the patch pockets and the slightly belled bottoms. He's always going to think of himself as a Navy man. He likes it, he likes the uniform, he likes the association with that. An anthropologist would call it "real attachment to the all-male group."

BILL FLYNN

We came across a lot of people in the military, people who found that the military was more than just a career or an occupation. It was everything to them. You knew that all of their lives they were going to be real gung ho.

But that wasn't the case with my father. When he retired, he put it behind him. He carried the good with him: the good manners, the good relationships that he had established throughout his military career. He's just a regular guy. We tease him now, because he's got longer hair than we do.

BEVERLY TAYLOR

My father retired after I graduated from high school. My grandmother and mother and I started off, by car, to go to the West Coast so that I could start college and my mother could find a house, and my father was to retire and join us.

I regret that very much: that I didn't see him in the exercises for his retirement, because he was up for general when he retired. I'm sorry that we weren't there for him. I think that was terrible. It's like someone graduating from high school. At the time, I was so unaware of that; I was a very immature child. They were taking me back to college, and I just sort of packed and went.

HELEN PIERSON

Before my dad retired, my mom was always home. When he retired, she went to work. Everything changed a lot. I don't have a lot of fond memories of Dad in the military, and probably even fewer after he got out of the military, because he changed so much.

My parents got divorced, and I'm not sure the military life didn't have something to do with it, because when a man has lived in a structured environment like the military where everything is very regimented, it's very hard for him to come out and adjust to civilian life. A lot of them start drinking more, and

203

it's very stressful. They have to go out and find a job and live in a neighborhood where the neighbors don't have to keep their yards cleaned up. In the Army, you had to have your yard just so. They would inspect it, and if it wasn't kept up, they would send you a letter about it. If you got more than three letters, then you'd have to move off base; at least that's the way that I remember it. We always had a beautiful yard, so we didn't have any problem with that.

I remember helping my dad shine his shoes, and my mom sending his shirts out to be ironed, and the brass—never seeing your dad in anything else. He also wanted to go to the military hospital. I wouldn't want to go there; I just hated that place. My dad, though, was so military, even though he had been out of the service for all those years. He was still so very military that he would not go to a civilian-run hospital or civilian doctors. He died last year, and he was buried in his uniform, so that was kind of neat. I think he would have liked that.

JEFFREY TAVARES

After he retired, my parents had to really move to get caught up with the people who had been with IBM or someplace like that for twenty years. They couldn't afford the first house that they bought: my father had twenty years, but they had to buy a thirteen-thousand-dollar home. It was nothing; it was an old farmhouse. They had a lot of work to get to where they are now, and they didn't have that twenty years to do it. I think they had to work twice as hard to get to where they are now.

I didn't get to stop the "yes, sir, no, sir," until about a year after they retired, and the relatives stopped that, because I'd be saying "yes, sir," to them, and they'd go, "You don't do that here. You're not in the Army anymore."

So then I told my dad, "You've got to figure out what you want. I can't have the relatives telling me I don't have to say 'yes, sir,' and you expecting me to." In the military, there was no problem; I was expected to do that.

I went through a rebellious stage after my dad retired. If I was to look back on it from another perspective, I would say that I was the perfect kid. I had my hair above my ears, and every two weeks, I went and got a military haircut right along with my dad. I didn't deviate from what my parents said; I did exactly what I was told, except for the normal kid things, mainly because I didn't know that you could do other things.

My parents finally retired and I went to a civilian school and saw all these things the other kids were doing, and I was still having to get my hair cut. My dad would traipse me off to the post every two weeks. I didn't get my hair touching my ears until I got into Boy Scouts and avoided my father for a whole summer: I was always going on a hike and couldn't go to the barber with him. I went to summer camp and that really opened my eyes, because then I figured out that you could be a good kid and still be rebellious. When I finally figured that out, it was like opening a cage. I went out of that cage real quick. There was definitely a rebellious point in there.

CAROLINE BAKER

We lived the civilian life that year my dad was in Korea. We lived near my grandparents, and we went to a regular civilian school, and when I got out of school I would walk over to my grandparents' house and spend the afternoon until my mom got off work. That was different for us, living off base and going to a regular public school and having the relatives around.

When my dad retired and they bought their house, it occurred to me: why do they call us brats? It was a shock to me to find out what civilian kids were like. Military kids were well behaved; we weren't allowed to be bratty. There were a few, and they had reputations. I can't imagine where they came up with that term "brats." The civilian kids were the brats.

We still went to the base a lot after he retired, just because we felt more comfortable there for a long time, through that transition to civilian after being in the military. We went swimming and bowling and went to the movies. We'd still drive out to the base, so that Mom could go to the commissary there and we could take ceramics and do hobbies. I don't know if it was the cost, because it was so much cheaper to go there, or the familiarity. When we were older and started going to civilian movie theaters, I couldn't figure out where the National Anthem and the flag were. It seemed like there was something missing. Whenever something wasn't the way I felt it should be from my past, from the military, it seemed like something was missing. I wanted to see that flag up there when I went to the movies.

11

There's No Place Like Home

Both of my parents came from military families; my mother was born in Virginia, my father in Hawaii. The concept of a "hometown" was always elusive to me, though. My mother's parents had retired in Hawaii, and my father's parents had settled in Virginia. For a long time, I felt a vague loyalty to both places without fully understanding why my father's parents lived in the place where my mother had been born, and vice versa.

When my father retired, I vowed that I would never move away from Albuquerque. My parents exchanged knowing smiles at my declarations that I had found my home for once and for all. They had chosen Albuquerque as their permanent home; I had merely ended up there with them. I eventually moved away, and New Mexico became just another place on the list of places I've lived, although I feel stronger ties to Albuquerque because I lived there the longest. As a child I thought that every place we lived was the best place until we got to the next place, a belief that certainly made living in places like Fort Riley, Kansas, more pleasant.

BRATS

In a way, I am from all of the places I've lived. The fact that my memories are attached to so many different places is the legacy that compensates for my vagabond life. When I hear cicadas, I am transported back to hot Kansas afternoons that stretched on forever, with the horizon a mirage of GIs marching on parade grounds that were bleached blond from the heat. Coppertone suntan lotion conjures up Hawaii, a straw beach bag, jets from the base roaring overhead while we played under the graceful leaves of a banana tree.

My parents established a family tradition of moving that has taken hold on some level; I have four brothers and sisters, and only one of the five of us owns a home. The thought of buying a house occurs to me from time to time, but I have never felt compelled to sign a mortgage that specifies that a plot of land is "mine."

Moving has become more complicated for me now, however, because I have a son. I want him to have roots, a sense of being connected to a place. I am caught in a situation that encompasses both the typical parental desire to give my child the things I never had—specifically, a hometown—and my belief that I wouldn't trade my experiences for a hometown, my conviction that I have come out ahead, in spite of and because of my background.

My son's favorite bedtime ritual is listening to stories about my childhood. I tell him about the beaches in Hawaii, the snow in Virginia, and the tornadoes in Kansas, and he doesn't find the fact that I have lived in so many different states unusual. It's only when people innocently ask me where I'm from that I run into trouble. When I sit on the edge of my son's bed and tell him the stories, it all seems to make sense.

When I asked military brats where they were from, they gave me the complete, unedited versions of their varied responses to that question and explained that when the question comes up in a social context they tend to equivocate. They say that they're from the place where they lived the longest, their last stop, or their actual birthplace. "It depends on my mood." "If I want to go into it, I will, but usually I just say Georgia."

Once they had given me the lists of places where they had

lived, I asked them what "home" meant to them. I met many people who told me that they had always been intrigued by the idea of life in a small town, an idyllic white picket fence kind of existence, the ultimate all-American "home." But on a personal level, home was abstract. Military brats had grown up calling a succession of different places "home," and that experience of creating a home, anywhere, gave them an ability to be selective and even arbitrary in their definition of home.

"Home to me is not a dwelling. Home is more like a feeling."

"I don't really feel like I have a home. Maybe Florida will be home."

Many military brats' parents had maintained close ties with their original hometowns, and the exposure to that kind of surrogate hometown seemed to have given them a more enduring sense of permanence, a secondary set of roots that were firmly planted in the distant soil of home. There were also families who, for one reason or another, had no specific hometown to which they returned, and the military brats from these families had an almost clinical interest in what it must have been like to grow up, quite contentedly, in one city, one neighborhood, one house.

Military brats were slightly envious of people who had not moved around. But I also heard echoes of the military recruiting ads: being in the military had been an adventure. People described hardships to me at great length, but I noticed that the stories of hardship were anecdotal, tales of survival. When it came right down to it, they felt that the benefits had outweighed the hardships. Sure, a hometown would be great. But the majority of military brats felt privileged, enriched by their transient pasts.

"I still think that people who were born and raised in one place are kind of deprived."

MARSHA KATZ

Recently I saw a show on television that mentioned Fort Benning, and I told my husband, "That's where I was born!" I have no memory of the place, because we were only there for a month. I don't even know what the place is like.

My whole family is like that; we're all from these kind of obscure places where my father was stationed for short periods of time, and we all tell people that we're from those places. As far back as I can remember, my mother has always been carefully guarding our birth certificates, because it's just such a hassle to get new copies. She had the five of us kids in five different places, including overseas.

Recently we moved across town, and my kids just fell apart; they were so traumatized. I told them about all the moves that I ever had to make and that I had felt the same way, and one of my daughters said, "Well, you're not in the Army anymore! Just because you did it doesn't mean that we have to." I guess I just expected them to be able to adjust, just like I always had to. It really jolted me when she said that. My kids just naturally expect to have a say in things, and I never did. It really surprised me that my kids would feel that way; it wasn't like I was moving them across the country and forcing them to leave their friends forever. They didn't see it that way, though. They had a really tough time.

RICARDO COTTRELL

When I was younger, I used to brag about moving. And now I find myself sneaking it in, here and there. I just say I'm from Delaware, but I live here now. I've spent twice as much time here as I ever did in Delaware. I don't look at one place as my home. If, if, if . . . if I remarried, maybe then I would have to settle down. That might have been part of the reason my marriage didn't work. It was always this tugging thing. I was stuck.

I'm attempting to get a job with a company that will send me overseas. You can do three months at a shot. It's like the total gypsy life. I'm chomping at the bit to get in there, but I'm holding back because I have an eight-year-old daughter. She lives with her mother, here in town, and I just won't be able to see her as often as I would like to.

I was talking to my mother the other day, and she said that from her viewpoint my sister and brother and I came out ahead of people who grew up in one place. And I have to agree in that respect. If I had to do it over again, if I had any say in it, I would. I think I was pretty lucky. I feel much more broadened. I know that the earth's not just this one small town, or one small state, or one small country.

At the end of the movie *Bladerunner*, one of the characters is dying and he says, "I've seen things you people wouldn't understand." And sometimes I feel that way. How can I tell a person what the streets of Madrid smell like, after the rain, at dawn? I can't.

BARRY JENKINS

I was always a little envious of kids who didn't grow up in the military. I don't necessarily feel like I'm from anywhere. I still felt like the West Coast was my home for the first two years after I moved here, but homesickness is not something I suffer from a lot. I don't feel like New York is my home, either. I always feel like a bit of an outsider.

When I moved away from home, I moved around a little bit, just out of necessity. I don't like moving from house to house, even in the same town. I finally got into a place and said, "I'm staying here, I ain't going nowhere." I was in that house for four years: that's a lifetime record.

Then I moved to New York, and everyone kept saying, "You're so brave!" and "You're out of your mind!" It didn't scare me; what scared me to death was being stuck in that rut in that town.

But I'm not going to stay here forever either. That's kind of funny, too. I think, where will I go? A year ago if you'd asked me, I'd say, I'm going back to the West Coast. Now I don't think I would. I don't know where I'd go, if I had the choice and the money. Conceivably, I could go anywhere now and work out of anywhere I wanted to, but I have a real tendency to stay put, just to want to stay put, just so I don't go off, doing that crazy stuff.

CATHY ATCHISON

I don't refer to being born in Salt Lake City. Sure, that's where I was born, but it doesn't sound right for me to say I'm from Salt Lake City.

211

Certainly there are benefits to growing up in one town, and having the same people around you most of your life, and being involved in their lives in a way. As a military brat, you just can't get involved in people's lives, if you know what I mean by that. There are drawbacks to that kind of life, but I think that's the case with a military life, too.

There are definite benefits. I think flexibility and adaptability are two things that military children gain; on the other hand, one of the things that they lose by all of that moving is a depth of participation in the community. You cannot participate in the community with the depth that someone can who has lived there for fifteen or twenty or thirty years.

Surely it is easy to pick up and move and settle in somewhere, but the roots take a long time to grow. I'm pretty well rooted now, but it's taken—I've been here for seven years, and I was coming home when I moved here. It may be very difficult for me to move now.

HELEN PIERSON

I tell people that I've lived in Texas; North Carolina; Arizona; Georgia; South Carolina; Germany; Washington, D.C.; Illinois; and Hawaii, and their eyes get bigger and bigger. I say that my dad was in the service, so I'm from everywhere.

People have a hard time understanding that you have moved so many times, and they're like "How could you have done it?" I just tell them that I knew no other way, and I had no choice.

I don't think I would move again even if I had to. I would really have to think about it. I hate to say never, but I can say no, not now.

I felt like I missed something, not having roots some place. Some place to call home. I noticed it when I went to visit my relatives down South, and I saw how close they all were. I hadn't seen these people in twenty years, and I'm the outsider. I felt regret; I would have liked to know what life would have been like, having such a close family, and if I would have been different if I had had that, and if my family would have been different. Now that I'm getting older, I kind of wish we hadn't moved around. I wish I would have had that stability.

PETER VARGAS

Whenever I fill out a job application form or something, I see those words *permanent address,* the set of words that every military brat knows. Permanent address. Texas comes to mind, always, first, even though it's not my permanent address anymore. My permanent address now is where I'm living now, but Texas comes to mind, always. Now it's wherever I hang my hat, I guess. I'm from wherever I'm living. This is my home now; I'm from California now. I've been here long enough; I feel like a native.

My mother has an address book with about ten pages for the *V*s. She could have one page for every letter, except *V* for our family. Because I moved around, and my sister was the same way. My sister lives in the same city that my parents live in. They retired, and she was lucky enough to go through senior high and college all in the same place. She has that camaraderie with the local civilians that I never had, and I'm jealous of that. She married one of the local football heroes. She has reunions that she goes to and she knows everybody, and I missed that. But nonetheless, she's changed jobs an awful lot, and she's moved with her husband a lot. I think he's been a real stabilizing influence on her. I'm sure she's ready to move every year, almost.

Family life, aside from the immediate circle, was not all that important to me and still isn't. There's a whole side of the family that I almost ignore, because I rarely ever saw them or talked to them, and there's a sense of guilt from that. I don't correspond with people as much as I should. When I'm away from them, they're not there. The wall that you erect to get rid of your past life goes up even to separate you from family and friends. They're not here; I'm here. I think of the way that I look at the outside family as a disadvantage. The other side of that is the way that the immediate family is all-important.

BRENDA ROWAN

I'm happy here, and we've lived here for four years, but we're ready to move. That pattern still exists. We're thinking about moving. I kind of wonder, well, when is this going to stop? We're hoping that this time we'll just settle down. Neither of us is afraid to go to different places, and take risks, and meet new people.

I usually say that I'm from Chicago, and my father was in the Navy, and we traveled around a lot. I don't consider my home to be anywhere, not even Chicago. I would never go back there to live. I just don't consider any place to be home.

I like to clear the decks, I guess because my father was like that. I can only take so much junk lying around and then I give it to Goodwill or throw it out. In fact, I enjoy doing that every once in a while: just go through my stuff and toss things out. I have three or four boxes of childhood dolls and just stuff from my past. I do get very attached to certain objects, though, like this chair that we have, and my Oriental art collection. I have certain things that I'm very attached to, and I keep moving them from place to place.

JOHN ROWAN

Often, I tell people I'm from Boston, because that's where I was born. I don't go into the fact that we only lived there for six months. At different times in my life, my answer has been different places. My answer depends on whether or not I want to engage in any conversation about it. If I do, I'll say Hawaii. That's where I lived the longest, and it's the place I know the best. Or I say I've moved around a lot; that's another response that comes easily.

Home is probably the camper that I put on my pickup truck. I guess I haven't found it yet. I liked Hawaii a lot, but I don't know if I consider it home. I think if I had to pick a place, and I had to go there and not be able to go anyplace again, I'd probably pick Hawaii. I lived there for twelve years altogether. That was the longest that I've lived anywhere, ever.

I don't really hang on to stuff, consciously, although I seem

214

to accumulate a lot of junk. I have moved my collection of chess books from Hawaii to here and back again twice, about three cardboard boxes, but mostly I prefer to get rid of everything. With each move, though, it seems we've had more to drag along with us. When I first moved to Hawaii, I literally had everything I owned in my backpack, and it's been a little more each time. I still feel like it would be no trauma for me to move and take absolutely nothing.

PAULA HOLMES

I'm from everywhere, and people say, "What?" I've been in California for sixteen years, so really it is home, now. But it still doesn't account for that other part of my life.

I don't want my kids to go through what happened to me. I wanted to move before our daughter started kindergarten. We moved here when she was two, and we probably will move again, but it will be in California.

People look at me funny because they don't know about my background, and I didn't know how sensitive I'd become. I didn't realize it until I talked to another mother and told her how happy my daughter is in kindergarten, and she said, "Did you think she wouldn't be?" Without having to get into all of it—I don't want to have to get into it with just anybody—I just kind of rationalized and stopped it right there. I said, "Well, I had considered private schools." I agonized all summer over where to send my daughter to school, and other people just seem to make the decisions so easily.

Maybe I'm going overboard. I'm always talking to her teacher, "How's she doing?" I want the teacher to know who I am. I work in her classroom once a week, and if there's a problem, I want to know about it right away. I asked her, "Does she have any friends?" And the teacher kind of looked at me funny and said, "I haven't noticed her being a loner."

It's very important that the kids have roots. If Rachel just mentions the names of one of the friends she's known since she was two, I will find a way to get together with them, because I want her to know that even though those people are not a part of her daily life, she can still see them sometimes. I will bend over backwards to drive over to the old neighborhood to visit kids that she knew when she was little.

TERRY McCULLOCH

Until about four years ago, I had a hard time defining home. I said I'm from Albuquerque, but I was just born there; I don't live there anymore. Home is where I am.

People are absolutely fascinated when I tell them how I got to Seattle. I had never been here, and I didn't have a job here, but it sounded like a neat place to live. I didn't know anybody here, but I had the name and phone number of a friend, so I got in the car and drove up.

I'm strong and independent. I have no fear. My childhood gave me all the confidence that I needed to do all the traveling that I wanted to do, and I'm really glad that I did. I still have the bug. Tell me in a minute that we're going to do some traveling and I'd be ready; I'd love it. That's probably one of my greatest loves, travel.

I lost a lot of the benefits of childhood, of growing up in one place, with my grandparents down the road, and aunts and uncles and cousins around. They're all strangers to me. I don't know those people.

Having such an intense, hard life with just your parents and your sisters around was a strain, and eventually, I had to break away. I couldn't handle the pressure anymore. I think that's really kind of sad, because I can see how close my husband's family is. It's a real shame. I go to see my parents maybe once every two years or so. It's starting to stretch out more and more between visits.

I envy other people. I envy the fact that my husband can go to the store and nine times out of ten, he runs into someone he knows, or he runs into a friend of someone he knows. He's so deeply rooted in this place that he doesn't even question it. He knows the place. Around every corner there's a memory. I think that's why his childhood is so vivid to him, because he can pick

216

out memories everywhere he goes. He remembers everyone, whereas to me my childhood is a blur.

That was our way of life. That was the only way we knew. We were just ignorant of the Beaver Cleaver type of life. You can go either way: you can be really incredibly dependent on your family, by living that kind of life-style, or you can be the opposite, like me, and say I just can't handle the pressure of this family and take off.

RANDY MARTIN

I was into drugs really heavy for years. I had friends, and there were certain things that they would not do. I couldn't understand them; I thought they were chickenshits. I look at it from another perspective now. It dawned on me one day that it was their hometown, and that for them to go down, and get busted, would be a big disgrace to their families. I finally wised up to that. I eventually got busted, and my family never really knew about it. I was able to keep it under wraps because they lived so far away. I realized that if I had been around my family, I wouldn't have been doing half the stuff I was doing. There was no way.

BRUCE HUTSON

I always hesitate when people ask me where I'm from, and then I say, "Well, what do you mean? Where was I born, or where did I come from most recently?" And that usually starts a conversation. I was born in Texas, but I've lived in a lot of other places, too. It's like opening the floodgates, that subject. It's case by case. If I'm into it, I'll go into detail, but if I'm not into it, I'll just say I came here from Alabama.

When I came back to go to the University of Kentucky, I met people going to school there who'd never left the state. To me this was a new place, another new adventure, something else to deal with. I always felt self-conscious about saying I had just moved there from Europe.

"Where'd you go to high school?" I'd say Kaiserslautern

217

American High School. "Well, where the hell is that?" It's in Germany and I lived there for four and half years. Or it would be "What did you do over the summer?" And people would say, oh, after graduation, I went to Myrtle Beach or Florida. "Where'd you go, Bruce?" And I'd go, oh, Monaco. It wasn't a big deal; you just hopped in the car and drove there.

Well, when you're young, there's no urgency. You think, "Well, that was fun. Next!" What's next? And then two more years someplace else, and okay, that was fun. Next!

Some people I've talked to who were not military or didn't move around a lot wondered if that would influence your psyche or how you grow up. Do you become a real scattered person, or are you real grounded, or what? They ask me, "Was it a good childhood? Don't you feel left out that you don't have this hometown?"

Well, how can I feel like I'm missing something that I never experienced? I still feel this real fondness for the way I was brought up, because that's the way that I was brought up.

Sometimes I meet people who did grow up in one town. They don't have the scope. When they're faced with something new, it's hard for them to adjust to it. And for me, I love new things; I love change—not all the time, sometimes. For the most part, when something new comes up, it's great. I have been used to so much change that things don't really traumatize me a lot. I realize that, well, that's the way it is, and I move on to something else.

I hate it when people try to tell you that part of growing up means becoming boring, or losing your sense of humor, or becoming stable, or what they consider stable. Getting your Colonial furniture and a split-level house, or whatever the thing is now—the ranch-style house. I can't do that.

People keep asking me, "Where are you moving next, Bruce?" I don't know. I like it here. This is the nicest place I've ever lived. I've lived here for a year and a half. It's just wonderful. I could call this home. In fact, I do call it home. But if somebody came up to me and said, "Okay, Bruce, you're going to move to Los Angeles and do this and that," I'd say, "Okay, why not? Next week? No problem."

NANCY KARACAND

I never know what to say when people ask me where I'm from. I can't give a simple answer like most people can; I don't want to be bothered with going through the whole explanation each time. I'd rather say I'm from New York, because I don't care for Mississippi, and I generally don't want to claim the place. And if I say that I'm from Mississippi, then people say, well, you don't have a southern accent, so then I have to go into a whole explanation. I could just say I was from New York and maybe get away with it, but then people say, oh, where did you live in New York, and then I have to admit that we moved away from New York when I was a year old. It just gets so crazy I don't even want to answer it.

It's hard now. I don't know what to call myself, because I really haven't cut my ties with Alaska yet. There's still that part of me that wants to say I'm from Alaska. I guess I enjoy the differentness that being from Alaska gives you, because there's a feeling that, gee, you must be kind of unusual, that you would choose to live up in Alaska.

Home is where I am right now. It's as much where I am, right now, as it is any other place. Each place I've lived in since I left Mississippi has felt like my place.

When I go to visit my family, there's no fondness or affection for the Gulf Coast. Sometimes when I'm visiting, I think, yeah, this really is a beautiful place, but generally when I'm there, I don't have a sense of being "home." It's just where my family is.

I've lived in eighteen different places, different dwellings, since I got out of college, since I was twenty years old. Oh, God, that sounds terrible! Eighteen moves in fifteen years! I never thought about it that way. I knew that I moved a lot. But the last three or four years, I've been aware of a kind of nesting urge. My living situations have been more stable than they were in the past. I lived in one place for two and half years, although I did move to another apartment within the building during that time. I guess maybe that's not much more stable.

I moved here in October, stuck around for five days, and then I took off for a few weeks to reconnect with all the people I hadn't seen since I moved to Alaska. I could not wait to get back here and get an apartment and settle in. I was living with my boyfriend, and he would have been glad to have me stay with him forever, but I was like, "I've got to get my own space, I've got to get settled, I want my things." It used to be that my things could be three or four items, and I could take those things out and feel at home. But in the last few years, it's much more a sense of really wanting some solid things to make a place my home, really wanting to nest more.

RHONDA HEALEY

I was born at Tinker Air Force Base in Oklahoma. I don't think we lived in Oklahoma for nine months, maybe not even six months, after I was born. They just happened to land there in time to deliver the baby. It was a real temporary thing, although I am a Sooner fan. I still root for the Sooners, but there is no good reason for it, no rational reason.

I did envy people who were born and raised in one place. In fact, I married right out of high school, and I think that a major part of my attraction to the man I married was the fact that he had lived in just two houses in the same town, and his family had a business with their name on it. He knew everybody in town and they knew him, and they all had gone to school together, and I thought that was wonderful. What I came to see was how limiting it is. His experiences were limited, his views on life and relationships were narrow, and consequently the marriage was very, very difficult. It probably lasted longer than it should have. It was just untenable. I wasn't content to stay there, and he couldn't imagine anything else.

What I see now is that when you're born and raised in one place, you gain something in continuity, but you lose a lot in experience. I think I would rather have my children be a little more experienced than be so narrow, even though I am really guarded about continuity for them. I want them in the same school, the same Cub Scout den, those kinds of things, just for that comfort zone. But I don't want them to be narrow-minded. If I can figure out a way to do both somehow, we'll do that.

MICHELLE SLOAN

My husband lived in two houses all his life. A lot of his attitudes used to irritate me. I guess it's because he's been in the same place for so long, and he stereotypes things.

I rearrange our furniture all the time. My mother's always rearranged her furniture all the time, too, and I guess it's because you get used to moving all the time. You don't want everything to be the same all the time; it's boring. My mother-in-law thinks it's funny, every time she comes over it's something different. Her house is always the same.

CAROLINE BAKER

I think that I feel very settled and feel like this is home. Then again, in my growing-up years with my family, we were in the military moving around until I was twelve. So two-thirds of my life with my parents was in the military, moving around, then I was really only settled for about six years, until I left home when I was eighteen. But I have been here, in Virginia, ever since then.

We were all here for a while, but after about five years, my sister and my brother left the area. Then my parents left about a year ago, so it's like "Where did everybody go?" They all ran off and left me. I'm the only one left. I thought, How can you do this to me? I felt abandoned, especially after my mom and dad left. I wanted to call someplace home, and they all got up and left.

SHEILA WRIGHT

I was born in Nebraska, and of course we had to settle in Nebraska. I couldn't be born overseas like my sisters. I don't consider Boston to be my home; I'm just living here. That's my home back there. Nebraska is where every milestone in my life happened, since I was a teenager, so that's been my home for fifteen years.

Ever since I moved away from home, I see my parents' home as my roots, and those are my only roots. I don't feel grounded now at all. I'm moving every year or so. I'd like to be grounded, and settled, and be like other people, but I don't know if I can ever do that. It's always been beyond me to be totally settled. If I bought a home and I wanted to move in a year, I couldn't. That's real difficult, knowing that you want to be settled but you just can't do it. Part of you says, "No, that's not acceptable; you have to be prepared to move."

My sister and I are the only ones from our family who aren't married, don't have kids, and don't own homes. We're the only ones who didn't settle in Nebraska. We came to Boston, and we're kind of like hoboes, continually moving, never staying in one place very long. It's interesting that we're the ones who broke away and stayed in the same mold that we started out with, moving around and not being settled. I wish I could do that: get married, have children, live in one house, have grandchildren and still be in the same house.

When we moved to Nebraska, I was real envious of my friends because they had grown up there. They had never been outside the state. Then as I got older, I realized, you know, I'm pretty lucky to have been able to see as much of the United States as I did. I didn't just stagnate in one area; we lived all over the country: North, South, East, and West.

GAIL EMERSON

I was born in Maryland, but I only lived there for three months, and then I've just been moving around a lot ever since. I really don't know where I'm from, because the place where I came from, my grandparents are dead and nobody lives in that house anymore. I don't know, really.

We've lived here longer than any other place that we've lived. This is my home now: it's the home that I choose, and it's the place that I've lived the longest. I feel comfortable here. Certainly it's not my familial home, but I consider it my home. There's really no other place that I've lived that I consider my home.

I guess I kind of liked moving around, and I sort of accepted that this was the way that things were. It's been necessitated by my husband's work. I had each one of my kids in a different state. My oldest went to several different schools, because we moved to different areas, but he had his whole school career here. My kids didn't move around nearly as much as I did. I don't think it really bothered me, and I don't think that my kids suffered that much.

My husband and I lived in a small town in Pennsylvania for about six years. You could walk all around the town, and it was a nice feeling; it was a very secure and sheltered feeling, and there were some very good things about that. But I wouldn't say that, oh, I would have much rather have grown up in a small town than to have grown up the way that I did.

I'm glad that I had the experience of living there, and I saw what that's like. And believe me, it's different than spending six years in a city. When you live in a small town, you really get more of a feeling of belonging than you do when you live in a big town. You know people, you belong to a church and hear all the gossip, and those things make a difference. But I really don't envy other people. I wouldn't change it.

ELIZABETH SPIVEY

I say I'm from Iowa, because that's where we ended up. My parents live there, and my brother lives there. I don't keep in touch but I know people there, and I guess I feel that I could go back and strike up old friendships again.

I jumped at the chance to move, though. I came out to Denver sight unseen. I just felt that it was time to get away from my parents and live an independent life. We always lived close enough that I felt that we were under their watchful eye, so it was great to move. It turned out to be a good move; we really like it here. I never dreamed that I would be living in Denver, Colorado. It was off the face of the earth, as far as I was concerned, until we moved here.

I wouldn't have wanted to have been born and raised in one place. It seems like no matter where you move, there's some good to be found in any community. I'm sure I could name a couple of places where I would not be happy living, but I think just about any place you can make a home and be happy. I would not feel bad about moving around a lot with my daughter, although I want my daughter to know her grandparents, and I'm going to make the effort to be sure that she knows her grandparents more than I knew mine.

GEORGE DEXTER

My home is Albuquerque. I might just point out—and I think that this is a common experience for people who live in the Army—when I was appointed to West Point, Florida was my legal residence and that's what it was when I turned twenty-one. I kept calling Florida home for a long time, but I never voted or paid taxes in Florida.

But when we got married, and we came out here to Albuquerque, we decided at that time that we liked it and thought we'd come back to retire here. We were in Okinawa when my unit was sent to Vietnam; I had to declare and send Katie home. We decided that Katie would come home to Albuquerque with the kids and see if she still liked it, and my brother could help her out while I was away. And she did, so we took out residence and started paying taxes.

JACK LEMONT

I really can't pinpoint my wanderlust. I want to blame it on my dad, I guess, but then maybe it is just part of me. I still haven't found what I'm looking for, like that song says. I'm still looking for something.

To this day, it depends on who I am talking to as to where I am from. Since I live out here, I have more Texas pride. Everyone knows me as the guy from Texas, because I have the accent, and it is kind of a novelty in this area. When I lived down in Texas, I would tell them I was born in California, and I consider myself a native Californian with pride. It's my only way of being different. I didn't want to be lumped in with everybody else.

There are those people who are the kind to say this is the best place to live—there is no other place—and put down all other areas that they haven't been to. It is scary the first time, but moving kind of knocks down the wall of wondering what is out there, because you have seen it or been through it before.

224

My mom didn't want me to move, of course. When she was young, she moved out to California, and it just wasn't an accepted thing, especially for a girl. If you were from a small town you stayed there, got married, and had kids. My dad was from the same town, and they ran into each other out in California and got married.

I don't see my brother ever moving, and my sister is the same way. They will be local. I can't see them ever leaving. Me, I'm just checking things out, looking around. I've always been a late bloomer, late to do things, just getting them out of my system later than I should. But it hasn't cost me anything yet. Just see what happens.

MARK DENTON

I was an altar boy at church, and they had an evening service, and it was pretty casual. You could call out the hymns that you wanted to sing at the evening service, and we'd always sing a dozen hymns or so, requests from the audience.

We had just gotten our orders to come back to the States, and we were leaving that week. So they asked, "What would you like to sing?" and I raised my hand and requested "God Bless America." I don't think there was a dry eye in the place. We were going home, and everybody knew that, and nobody else was going home.

The interesting thing was that during the time we were in Germany, we were on a post, surrounded by Americans. I mean, we could have been in New Jersey. We were surrounded by everything familiar, and yet we weren't in the United States.

After all of that traveling about, all of my life, I've decided that I don't want to move. I've been living in my house for four and half years. I'm going to stay here for a long time. This is my home. I've got my own yard; I've got a garage. This is mine. I'll stay here at least ten more years.

JULIE MEDINA

I remember the last house that we lived in in Washington, D.C., very well. I just got a chance to see it again, and it sure doesn't

225

look like it did when I was a little kid. I was so shocked. I remember a big house, really well kept, with a long flight of stairs and a long porch.

I had a little room upstairs next to the chimney. My mom turned it into a beautiful little room with white satin curtains that made a little door, and they put a clothesrack underneath the shelf for my clothes. Dad found a tiny white and gold vanity at a garage sale, and it was like treasure to me. I had my own room, even though it really wasn't a room.

This place seemed so huge to me when I was a kid. I went back with a friend, and we were driving around, looking for the house, and I kept telling him the house has a staircase and a porch, and a driveway—just like that house, only it looks better than that. When we drove away, I realized that was the house. The fence had been pulled up, and someone had dug up all the big oak trees that were in the front yard. It was terrible. After all those years, I remembered the address as 200 Oakleaf Road, and it was 2300 Oakleaf Road. It sure wasn't like I remembered, but it was so special to be able to go back there and see that house. It has haunted me my whole life.

JEFFREY TAVARES

I don't have a previous home; this is my home. My dad would always talk about Kentucky as being home, because that's where he was born. I always felt kind of funny about that. I would think, where am I from? The only thing I could think of was Transit.

DEREK LOWE

My family's home is in Louisiana, and I am connected to my extended family there. I do have a hometown, so I didn't miss out on that part of it.

This is the longest that I've lived anywhere. It's the first place I've called home, other than an Army post. This is the most stability that I've ever had. I decided last year that when people ask me where my home is, where I'm from, I'm going to say

Seattle. Because, for me, this is home. This is the first place I've felt like it was home.

I can't go to Fort Lewis, and that really disappoints me, that the post is closed now. Not that I ever did, that much, but every now and then I'll have this security craving, to go and drive around or something, like some nut.

I went out to Fort Lawton one summer day, really golden and crystal clear. It was just like drifting back into a dream, to wander onto the old post like that. I really indulged it: that feeling of drifting back to another time; the memories of running across those big, open Army fields, and that sense of security that I had as a kid, running free on the post. And I tried to bring that back, and it was just euphoric, practically. I just sat there and tried to bring that back, that feeling.

We were never stationed at Fort Lawton, but they're all the same, in some way. Going there brought about the acknowledgment of that intense association that I have with the military. That quality of feeling at home really exists more on a post. It's actually a physical feeling, when I am on post, of suddenly relaxing and, at the same time, feeling encompassed.

12

Once a Brat, Always a Brat

I sat down one night and figured out that I had lived in twenty-two different houses. I mentioned the figure at work the next day, and my co-workers' eyes widened. One of them said, "Well, one day you just won't show up at work and you'll call us and say, 'Guess what? I moved again.'" The same co-worker came to my house a few months later, looked around, and finally said, "Gee, you've got some nice furniture." I suppose he had imagined that I had a knapsack with my belongings in it and a bedroll in the corner.

I was married to a man who had spent his entire life in the same neighborhood. When the local economy in his hometown went bad, I brought home out-of-state newspapers and we even briefly considered moving to Alaska, the final frontier. He eventually found a job in California, and I was able to pack up our belongings and move—again.

I have continued to move, not just across town, but from one state to another. I have moved for jobs, for school, and I have moved on a whim, simply because I got restless, tired of a place.

228

The ironic thing is that I hated moving when I was a child. The familiar rituals that we followed at each new house were comforting, though, and I soon forgot how our voices had echoed in the last, empty house. I used to get a horrible feeling in the pit of my stomach when I said good-bye to old friends or introduced myself to new people, but somewhere along the line, to my mother's great relief, I outgrew my shyness.

Now I have friends all over the country, despite the complications of distance. But I have made and broken many promises to stay in touch with people. I have left some places, some people, without ever looking back.

I have the soul of a nomad, a gypsy, and I suppose that I can attribute some of it to my own personality, and the rest to my family and my peripatetic upbringing. Despite my mother's encouragement, I think that I gave her the most trouble with my failure to adjust to moving, but as an adult I have moved more than any of my siblings.

If "willing to relocate" were a military job description, I'm sure that I could have made an ideal military career for myself. Despite inheriting or assuming my parents' wanderlust, though, the genes for a fine, unquestioning soldier seem to have bypassed me. For some reason when I'm told to do something, I like to do exactly the opposite. Bucking authority: it's called mutiny in the military, and they don't look kindly upon it.

When I left home, I cut my ties to the military. Now I decide if and where I want to move, and when I move, I stack the cartons in some out-of-the-way corner and I update my telltale résumé that never fails to raise eyebrows in interviews. I am no longer a dependent; I am a civilian. I traded my ID card for a driver's license that rarely has my current address on it.

When I asked people how their lives had been influenced by their military family background, the overwhelming reply included some variation of "I am adjustable and adaptable." One woman said, "Adaptable in the sense, that—well, I've always used the phrase 'you sink or swim.' "

The military brats I met are swimmers. They had moved across the country and around the world, been yanked out of schools, left friends behind, and stoically never tired of the process, and they saw their ability to adapt to change as an advantage and a strength. They had adjusted before, and, if necessary, they would do so again.

Repeatedly, people mentioned a quintessential military brat, a child who had been aggressive, outgoing, resilient, and well adjusted. The people I met described themselves as introverted, hesitant, and shy, but they had always felt that somewhere out there was a mythical kid who never had problems.

Military brats who had maintained childhood friendships were the exception. Most, like me, date their friendships from the time they joined civilian life; the friends they made during their military years tended to "fall by the wayside." Adjusting and adapting to new situations had not really prepared any of us for dealing with the ebb and flow of long-term relationships with people outside our immediate families.

"It was easy to make friends, and it was easy to give them up. And that's carried over, and that's made things difficult. If I don't see somebody for a year, they're out of my life."

Military brats had developed an idealistic image of friendships and talked about people who had grown up among one group of friends with a combination of envy and curiosity.

"I get a kick out of my wife talking about her school days with friends. She'll be talking about something she did with so-and-so, and then they went over to somebody's house and did that. Me, I can remember stuff like that, but I couldn't tell you where it happened. What state was that?"

The people I talked to had faced the normal challenges that mark the transition from child to adult, decisions regarding education, careers, and marriage. For military brats, adulthood also signaled the nullification of their ID cards and the end of their status as dependents.

Many post–World War II generation military brats, despite their exposure to the security and benefits afforded by a military career, had not opted for military careers for themselves. They described the civilian world in "us versus them" terms, yet they embraced the opportunity to join "them" as soon as they reached adulthood.

"You saw things firsthand that a civilian kid would never see.

I wonder if the children of cops are particularly prejudiced against law enforcement? Or the children of teachers against teaching?"

Careers and job security were major issues for many of the people I interviewed. I felt that my own rather haphazard work history was vindicated when I heard others describe their careers. Even those who had been employed by one company for an extended period of time cited frequent job changes within the company; others expressed specific fears of being stuck in a dead-end career gridlock. Military brats were, after all, accustomed to seeing the adults around them study, train, move, and promote—without actually changing jobs. In civilian jobs, promotions do not mean a change of rank and more impressive quarters, but military brats seem to expect promotions to mean change. They want challenge and at least linear movement in their jobs.

Literature, movies, and even cartoons have depicted, analyzed, criticized, and glorified the military to such an extent that all Americans are familiar with its stereotypes: the baby-faced soldier, the snarling drill sergeant, the colonel with ramrod-perfect posture. Dependents, for the most part, have been referred to as "military wives" or "brats." Although it is possible to find snarling drill sergeants and bratty children in the military, the widely recognizable stereotypes are just that: caricatures of the individuals who make up the ranks of the military.

As a child, on bad days, I was quite capable of being a brat, but I have always known that there was a difference between being a brat, plain and simple, and being an Army brat. I have always been an Army brat.

The label *brat* is not unlike "stupid," or "ugly." It is acceptable to describe yourself in that way, but coming from someone else, it takes on a completely different connotation. It is also similar to describing a person who was born and raised in a place as a "native." In the same way that the native of an area is subtly and inevitably affected by his origins, military brats share a unique heritage. They turn in their ID cards and leave the post, but they were military brats: dependents of military personnel.

MARSHA KATZ

I always had a sense that my dad was doing something important, that he wasn't just a shoe salesman. His job was to protect our country. We grew up on posts, surrounded by cannons and flags, and it was just a more patriotic upbringing. Other people heard about the military in history books or on television, but we were living it.

I guess I didn't realize how much pride I have about it until recently. Part of it has developed as I've gotten older; when I was a kid I was more worried about my own little world, about leaving my friends and things. There were good times and bad times, just like any family has; I think moving around so much made everything seem more intense.

Our family paid a pretty high price for my father's career, I think; we never really knew our relatives at all, not any of them, and we were constantly being uprooted from friends. I don't think that I had a normal childhood, by any means, but at the same time, I have a hard time saying that it was a negative experience. Some of my worst experiences have led to some of my greatest strengths. It took me a long time to figure it out.

LARRY WILLIAMS

It is difficult to determine which aspects of my life are the result of being from a military family and which are the result of the influence of my parents.

I love my family a great deal, but to be separated from them is not as difficult for me as it is for many of my friends from civilian backgrounds. I am very secure in my knowledge that no matter where I am or what I do, if I needed any one of my family, nothing would be too important, nothing. I imagine that it's that way in many families, but for some reason that "all for one and one for all" spirit seems to be just a bit stronger in military families than it does in civilian families.

I am happy with myself and with my life; I could not change a thing in my life without giving up a benefit that went aloing with it. I want the same thing for my kids and my family, but I am a civilian. Somehow, I do not ever think my kids will have what I had, nor will my family ever be the same team that my family was when I was growing up.

GEORGE DEXTER

When we moved to Fort Benning, I really fell in love with the Army. In those days, they were still using bugle calls. My father was the commander of the Twenty-fourth Infantry, which was a black unit. They had three large quadrangles: the Twenty-fourth, and the Twenty-ninth, and then between them, another.

At night during the summer, I would sleep on the sleeping porch, and I could hear the buglers calling Taps at each of the three quadrangles, during the night. I became quite fascinated with the Army, and I went to a couple of demonstrations, and that was when I decided that I wanted to become a soldier.

RICARDO COTTRELL

There would be times, when we moved, before I knew anyone, and I'd have to spend time by myself. I would just get into a book. That's how I started reading. You get a pretty good sense of self when you keep moving around and you're in different situations. You get pretty self-reliant. You become a discerning observer.

I used to read a lot: Cornelius Ryan, Marine Corps history. My father told me that my mother was ecstatic; she thought I was going to become a Marine because I was talking about it when I was fifteen or something.

My brother is in the service, and I don't think he is really happy in his job, but he's going for twenty years so he can get the retirement. He keeps putting his life off into the future: "Well, I'll be set at this point in time." My brother has more of an Oriental type of mind. He saves and he plans and he does it, whereas I like to live my life every day. I'm more instant gratification–oriented, is what it is.

Some of the things I've picked up, I can't say that everybody would get this out of it. You see that a life span is a small thing and that history is a very large thing. Nothing is really permanent. To think that is an illusion.

BARRY JENKINS

My dad used to say to me, sort of to challenge me, "You'll never join the military because you don't like being told what to do," as if that were a negative trait. And I'd say, "You're goddamn right." I told him I like giving orders, but I don't want to be an officer. I don't like taking orders—I don't like being told what to do. What does that make me, a moron or something?

It's funny, though, because I do have a certain regimentation that I can work under, and that's helped me, especially in a business like this. In the entertainment business, if you don't keep tabs on how they run things, it'll get away from you, and people take advantage of you. If you don't have the ability to organize and sort of regiment things to some degree, you ain't gonna work in this day and age. You have to be on the ball. So a lot of that has helped me out. I can be intimidating. Sometimes you've got to stand up and say, "Look mister, we don't operate that way, and, goddammit, here's why." I can lay it out, and they'll say, "Oh, all right." I can come in and say, "All right, it's time to stand to. Let's get going. Stand to, you swabs!" I don't like doing it, but sometimes people won't get rolling unless someone's telling them to.

I have the same tendencies that my dad had. I know that I approach what I do for a living with the same obsessiveness. It is a whole life, not just a job that you punch in for and punch out and leave and leave it behind. It's not one of those things. My dad always brought his work home with him: all his attitudes, all that bullshit. Not only the military side, but his technical side—the gears were turning all the time, you could just see it.

Most of my adult life, I've been an artist, doing what I wanted to do. Never made any money, but that was not important to me. I've always been kind of on the edge. Pensions, security, life insurance: I still don't have any of it. I had that stuff drilled into my head, and, if anything, the more that they drilled it into my head, the more it appealed to me to do something else.

My dad got into what I was trying to do after a while, he really did. I still can't figure it out. He got so supportive it almost scared him. "You'll make it, you're going to do fine." He just figured I worked hard enough at it, which I did. He knew what it was like to come up from the depths with nothing. He retired a lieutenant commander with a lot of honors, so he knew that I was essentially doing the same thing, in a really hard field. I think, if anything, he understood and recognized—and this was the positive side to all this bullshit—that anything you work real hard at is bound to pay off somehow.

I've been doing this Civil War thing. I think in some twisted way, it appeals to my military background. I swore I'd never march around in a uniform, carrying a gun, but that's what I've been doing.

It's fun, but my old man would laugh if he could see this. He'd say, "I knew you'd do it sooner or later." I've got a uniform and the works. It's crazy, but it's really fun. The period is the thing: it's the clothes, and some of the guys learn to write in the old script, and they carry Civil War period coins in their pockets and old pictures and playing cards. Details, right down to your shoelaces and your buttons. All of these guys are really knowledgeable historians. They're not gun nuts; in fact, none of them own guns, aside from the muskets they use.

It took me months to decide to do it. I've always really liked history. It's not really a military thing, but there's that side of me, in the back of my mind, that understands it completely: "Stand at attention; follow orders!" I know what that's all about, only too well.

BEVERLY TAYLOR

I know it shows in my personality now. I have a great deal of confidence. I'm an achiever. I'm a bit of a snob—I really am—and this is just the way that things are, and that's just the way it goes. To me it's perfectly natural, because that's the way that I was

235

raised, and my parents kept me in that kind of situation. And in my adult life, I looked for that kind of thing and I kept myself in the kind of environment that I was accustomed to. It's an attitude, and it's hard to explain how I got it and why I'm that way. But it's just there.

Manners are a big thing to me. I have a hard time being with someone who's not well mannered. I'm just appalled if I stand up to leave a table and the gentlemen don't stand, and I'm twice as appalled if I come back to the table and they don't stand. I always write thank-you notes when we're invited somewhere. That's just the thing I do. I know I've gotten sloppy: you just sort of join the pack after a while. I'm sure my manners now are just barely passable, compared to what they used to be.

My father told me, when I moved here, "Well, you're not necessarily going to meet a man in this area who will stay here." What a stupid, ridiculous thing for him to say to me. Of course I would go anywhere that my husband would go.

TIM BROCKWAY

I felt that I'd already served in the military. I definitely went in the opposite direction. Once I got off that base I never wanted to go back. I just never was attracted to it like my father was. He really wanted to be a career officer, the purest form of positive military service, you know. And none of the kids ended up going into the military. My brother went to West Point, and my dad, I'm sure, was pretty proud about that. But none of the rest of us wanted to do it, and my brother's no longer in the service. My dad is still pleased that the military helped him get to where he is now, in terms of his job and things like that. The rest of us were not interested at all. I'm sure part of him was sad. I know that he was really hoping that someone would be interested in the military. It would seem natural for someone who was so into it and had six kids.

I knew that I wasn't suited for it. I could have made a fine military guy; I just wasn't attracted to it. I wasn't impressed or excited about military uniforms; I just wasn't fooled. I was in the Cub Scouts, and I never got much past that. When I see the crossing guards, it's amazing. You put a little banner across someone's chest and give them a little stick that says stop and go, and it's incredible what happens. It gets into psychology: it's the same thing that happened in Nazi Germany.

DEBBIE WEST

My father tried to talk me into the military, and I said, "There is no way I would ever consider that. I will die first." But you know, I'm close to it; I do stuff for the Department of Defense. I've been at my job for three years. In the last year, I've been on a missile project and that really does bother me. I am looking at every way I can to get off the project. I don't mind working for defense, as long as it's defense.

I'm superpatriotic—I'm terrible—you ought to see me during the Olympics. Every time they play the National Anthem, I'm crying my eyes out. I guess in some ways I never really pulled away from it. But I don't want to be on the real hawk end of it. I have always been patriotic, even during the tough times in the sixties and early seventies. My rage with the country came more with the administration running it.

When my son was a teenager and they started all those recruiting ads, I went out of my way to tell him how erroneous that all was. There was a time he scared me to death—he thought Rambo was god. And I went, "Oh no! This is my fourteen-year-old; my God, what am I going to do?" I was horrified. So I bought him things like *Dear America—Letters from Vietnam,* and I cut articles out of the newspaper, military nurses describing what it's like to send all these boys home in body bags. "This is what war is. Rambo is not real."

I know that he's going to have to register. With any luck he'll sneak through without having to go in. Of course, my father's leaning on him in the other direction. "Your future's in the Navy, son." As my son's standing there in his Mohawk and his Army boots and his camouflage jacket and his earring. He went up there at Christmas one year, like that. It was funny; I could just see the look on my father's face.

I was thinking about other ways that the military experience has affected my life. My boyfriend was born overseas, and his family, even though they're civilians, share a lot of the same background aspects of my family. His father was gone a lot. Bill and I are close emotionally, but on the surface our relationship is not as close as many people's are. We have no problem spending extended periods of time apart, because we're used to it; we're comfortable with it, because it was a fact of our family life. To me that's a real positive thing. I have so many girlfriends who just languish when their men are gone. I don't. Although Bill and I have lived together, we don't live together right now. Probably 50 percent of our evenings we spend together. Our times together are good, but when he's not around, I don't miss him, and it does give me a time to do things on my own without worrying about being home for dinner. So it's really a good relationship.

I am very progressive, by nature. I've always bucked the establishment, in that sense. I have no use for it, really. Conservatism, to me, is only dragging your heels in the face of the inevitable. Change, to me, is the nature of the universe. And anyone who resists that, to me, is only denying what will eventually happen. You might as well get used to it now, because it is going to happen.

Santayana, one of the Eastern philosophers, once said, "Looking forward to the changing seasons is a whole lot happier state of mind than to be continually in love with spring." That explains me. I do look forward to change, as long as it moves in what I perceive to be a forward direction. My mother always said, "Debbie, you're a real extremist," and I am. There is no middle road for me. I go for it.

When I was in Catholic school, Sister Superior once told me, "When life hands you lemons, make lemonade." And I think, all in all, I have made the best out of my life. Let's face it: life could have been a whole lot worse. As bad as I had it, I didn't have it as bad as some of the other people in this world.

PETER VARGAS

During my senior year, my family moved to the Boston area and I went to live with my father, whom my mother had divorced when I was about two years old. I found myself then just immersed in the antiwar stuff and the drugs and everything else that was going on. Prior to that, I had been sheltered, and all of a sudden I had this whole world to look at that I wasn't familiar with. I had been raised in such a strict, disciplined way by my stepfather that my father was a pushover in comparison. I just took over, or tried to. That was my transition into civilian life.

What I found myself doing, before I even graduated from high school, was signing up for the military. Almost immediately after getting out of high school, I went into the Navy. There's a bit of security involved there that's difficult to let go of. I liked it. I've even found myself, in the last few years, missing what the Navy had to offer, missing the camaraderie. Even if you don't know someone, there's a kinship there. I find myself, even today, attracted to the military uniforms, attracted toward the military community in general, because it gives me a feeling like—it's like seeing a cousin who I haven't seen in years, whereas in civilian life I don't feel any kind of kinship toward strangers at all.

I grew up being very idealistic, which is a rough way to grow up. I had to develop a pragmatic attitude about things just to survive; the world is not "just so." I think I had to force myself to become a realist, because in the military, yeah, everything is ideal. You do this, and this is the result, or these are the ramifications, or you don't do it. And for many, many years, I expected that in civilian life and it wasn't there. I think that has a negative impact on children who are growing up in the military, because it teaches them that if you do this, there will be ramifications and results, and it teaches them wrong. It sets them up for a fall. Once you leave the gates of the base, the order leaves.

I was aware of what my father's job was and that it was important, and somewhere deep inside I was proud of him for that, and that pride that he had came to me. When I went into the military, the reason I went in was kind of for two reasons: one was because I was really screwing myself up in civilian life—I couldn't handle the lack of regulations—and then there was a sense of pride. We were in Vietnam, and I thought, well, I want to go and do my part. I think my father would expect it of me, even though he never said that. I think it scared the hell out of him when I did it.

I'm still extremely proud of this country, and it irks me to see a flag that's got tattered edges on it flying from a building: red, gray, and blue. I think that carries over from my having been a military brat. They taught us reverence for the flag. If it hit the ground you got rid of it, because it was no longer a flag. Kids who wore flags over their butts to hide holes in their jeans—that was darn near sacrilege. It was instilled in us from an early age. It's not taught in civilian life.

That loyalty carried over to jobs, into everything. In most cases, it's probably an unwarranted loyalty. One of the things my father instilled in me was perfectionism. I've always felt that if you have something to do, you either do it right and do the best that you can or you don't do it at all. Because if you do it half-assed, then people look at you unfavorably. That definitely comes from the military. I'm afraid that's had a detrimental effect on my life, because if I can't do it perfectly, I feel horrible about it. And if I did it perfectly and it was too easy, jeez, I must have done something wrong, or maybe I didn't do all I could because it was too easy. To do things, to do things well, is a tough thing. I have a problem with that now, because there's an idealistic aspect to everything that I want to be there. It's not really there, but I try to shove it into it.

Job security is extremely important. And when there's a problem, when something threatens that security, it's damn near a crisis. I do everything I can to get rid of the threat to that security.

I'm getting ready to move to another job. Something that has been a part of my life since the military has been this need to move. Every year, on the year, it seems, I'm ready to change jobs. Even if I don't change companies, I change jobs within that company. I create a new job and move into it—a new environment—it's just like packing up and moving. So I switch jobs a lot. For many years, I even moved my house every six months to a year. After a year or so, I feel that I'm ready to move. When there's a problem, it's build a wall and put that behind me; don't think about it anymore. It's not going to affect me—which intellectually, I know isn't true—but emotionally, I feel safe when I've put the problem behind me.

The military taught me an awful lot of pride in my country

and in myself and gave me the ability to be independent, to be self-motivated. I have an ability to look at everything around me objectively, because all my life there has always been that outer circle. We've always been surrounded by something, and I've always been able to look out beyond the barbed wire and the gates of the base and see what was out there. And there's the adjustment part of it: being able to size things up everywhere I go, even if it's just from one town to another, or going camping, or going anywhere. Immediately, the first thing that I do is take everything into account, size everything up, figure out what I have to do to adapt to this particular environment.

I became rule-oriented and it's there now. I'm not spontaneous in any sense of the word. I was so sheltered that without that regimentation, without that order, I feel rather helpless, like bait somewhere, where somebody can hit on me. That's probably one of the biggest disadvantages, is that.

The other is that it's so easy to shut out the past life, to bring up those walls to protect yourself. What is important is now and the future. The past is the past and there's nothing I can do about it. And, in most cases, I have a very difficult time remembering the good times or the bad times. It's just something I put behind me. So every time I move now, I put the old part behind me, and adapt to the new, and keep on moving, keep on trucking.

TERRY McCULLOCH

I've never been one to be real long-term when it comes to jobs. That's one of the worst things about it. If I stay in a job for longer than a year, I'm miserable. I start finding faults with the place or with the people there. I've always liked my bosses, but when it comes down to it, I just don't see myself as a lifer, with twenty years at one job. I don't see myself as coming out with a pension. I don't think I'd ever do that. I can't.

I have to always have the option where I can just quit, maybe because my dad couldn't quit. I have the option; I'm gone. You can't make me stay here. So I always use that every year and a half or so: "See you later!" I find fault with the job, or they find fault with me, or I just get bored and start looking for something else, something better. And I think that all comes down to the fact that I have the option: I don't have to live here, I don't have to work here, I don't have to see you. I don't have to do anything.

NANCY KARACAND

I think that the most formative years, developmentally, are from birth to five or six years old. That's when you form the core of your personality, and it was during those years of my life that we were moving the most. I get a sense that because I was in the middle of the family that I caught the biggest chunk of the moving, and in terms of my adult life, it shows the most.

I have chosen to move a lot. I don't know how long I'll be here. I can never say how long I'll be anywhere. I get restless, and I love new things. Moving here from Alaska was great. Now I've been here for seven months, and I like it, and I'm pleased to be here, but there's always that anticipation of what's around the corner.

I'm giving my notice on my job tomorrow, and I think it's real acceptable for me. If I'm not doing something that I enjoy, I get out. I made a promise to myself that I would explore alternatives. There's no reason that I have to be tied to someone else's schedule.

I think that my life-style is very related to growing up in a military family, because part of it comes out of saying that I don't want to be this, like my father, or this, like my mother. I don't want to be tied to anything resembling the military, as far as having to answer to someone and having my whereabouts and my moves being determined by someone else. I like having the freedom and flexibility to go where I want, when I want to go. I learned that kind of adaptability being a military kid.

MARK DENTON

I had pretty much grown up in Salt Lake, and that move we made to Germany was the most traumatic. My parents tried to make as much light of it as possible, like "Hey, it's going to be something new and exciting!" Bullshit. We were leaving. Having Salt Lake taken away kind of gave me a feeling that nothing's permanent.

My college friends and relationships ended abruptly upon

my divorce from my first wife. I have never associated with those people since; when I divorced, I felt, well, I'm giving up all of that. It's history. It's over, and it's time to move on.

When I bailed out of my marriage, I felt like I had to have a girlfriend; I had to have someone. It took me about a year to realize that I could do it myself: I'd done it before, and I could do it again. It took me a while to remember that I had been through adversity before, and I could face it again, and I could live through it. But God, the first couple of months were hard. I took what I had learned from the time that we were moving around, and I said, I can do this. It was almost like a move, getting divorced.

SHERRY RUTLEDGE

Because the family has to stick together through all the moves, you can end up with a really close family, but the other side of the coin is that you can end up with a dysfunctionally close family. As I described my family, I see it as very enmeshed, and I think that that part of it comes from the fact that we were isolated and never formed real close ties with people outside the family because we moved so much. And I think, in some ways, it reinforced a family system that already had a lot of pathology in it. It was a sick family in some ways, and I know that my father had some serious problems.

I think the fact that we moved gave him the opportunity to isolate us and isolate himself from the outside intervention that might have happened otherwise; let's say if we had gone to the same school for a longer period of time, or if we had formed relationships with people outside the family, whom we could have confided in about some of the things that we struggled with. But because we didn't have some of those ties, it allowed some of the sickness to be intensified. So that's one of the big disadvantages that I can see.

My father didn't give my mother credit for having an ounce of brains in her head. He ran the checkbook; he determined what the money was going to be spent on; he determined whether or not she worked outside the home, what we had for dinner, everything. I think that the military mentality really reinforced that: the male dominance and the inappropriate use of discipline in the family.

The military mentality has a negative influence on the family, in that it tends to breed men who want power and control over family members, particularly if they're dealing with issues of rank at work and dealing with the insecurity of those types of issues. They're that much more likely to come home and use their power at home, if they're not feeling it at work. I saw that clearly in my family.

JEFFREY TAVARES

When I first got out of high school, it was "Don't you have a job? Aren't you going to work?" Finally I got a job, and that settled him down, and then it was "When are you going to get your life going?" My dad put my name in for NCO school and got me a sponsor, and I went, "Uh-uh. If civilian life fails me, then I'll go." It wasn't for me, just no way. And that pacified him.

There was a point in there where I had to prove to my dad that I was going to make it. So I moved away, and I really got my feet off the ground and took off. I don't know what would have happened if I hadn't moved. He finally told me that I'd made the right decision.

Today I have to make a phone call to accept a new job or not. I've been at my current job for ten years. It's really hard for me to make the decision to leave. The job I'm in now is a dead-end street, but the security is there. There's not a lot of security in the new job, but the outlook is great, so it's really a turmoil for me; should I stick it out just for the security or take the chance? That's always been a real problem with my decisions, whether it's buying a car or taking a job: whether I should take the chance, give up my security. But I'm going to take the new job. I'm going to forget about security this time and go for it.

Four months ago we bought a new car, and I had a real hard time with it. Mainly because I was real secure, and I knew my life was going right, and we bought something that we really didn't need. But I was raised that you didn't buy things that you didn't need. I think the military has everything to do with it. The worst thing that could ever happen to me, personally, would be to have to go on welfare. And I relate most everything to that: if you spend over your budget, you'll have to go on welfare. It's either the military or it's welfare—black and white.

I'm a very black-and-white thinker. There are no ifs or ands; either it's this or it's that. That's one of the things I'm working on, that there is room for shades of gray. I think that's more from my father; he's a very black-and-white thinker.

The military was an easy life, the way I see it. They tell you when to get up, when to go to work, where you're going, what you're going to eat, where to shop; they set everything out for you and you just follow that plan. I told my dad it was just a gravy life. You don't think. Not knocking it—I wouldn't knock the service, because it was real good for my father—but the people that I know who are in the service now are go-nowhere people. It's sheltered and it's structured. I think that is the best definition of the military life. Everything is planned. Everything is taken care of.

I was raised older, and I've talked to other people who were raised in the military who feel the same way. Filling in for the father when he's not around, responsibility. And that's hard for a kid to live up to. There's no room to be a bad kid. I relate to older people better than I can relate to people my age, and I've been that way for as long as I can remember. My neighbors tell stories about their son, things he did that I would have loved to be able to do. He got in just enough trouble to keep things stirred up. He's very outgoing, where I really sit down and analyze the situation before I jump into anything. He's off and going, right in the middle of it. To be able to have that ability kind of makes me a little envious. I have to make sure it's the right thing to do, check out the situation.

JACK LEMONT

When I was engaged, I was pretty well resigned to the fact that I wanted to settle down. We lived in a pretty nice area, found a good deal on an older house, and I felt like I could put down some roots there. But after that didn't work out, it kind of ignited the travel bug.

I thought it would be neat to have a job where I could work through the winter and be off during the summer, so I could travel around. I have a friend in Montana, and he is always trying to get me to move up there. I was tempted to swing through there and try it for a while, but it's such a different culture. Los Angeles is almost too fast, and Montana is almost too slow. I'm going to try to find somewhere in between.

MARK STANLEY

I knew what the game was, so they couldn't screw around with me. That's why I picked the Air Force. And I needed a job really bad. I was thinking about getting married, and I figured it was a good way to get training, get some income, have your kids while you're in the service. It's smart: having a baby costs what, six or seven thousand dollars now. My mom told me I cost like a buck and a half or something; they had to pay for their meals and that was it.

The only reason I picked the Air Force was I knew it; I had lived with it all my life, heard what was going on, the games they played, what they could and couldn't do. I knew what my chances were. I had gone in as a CO, noncombatant. The first year the draft didn't catch me; my number was like 189 or something. The second year I was getting real close. I ended up going in when I was twenty.

The war was over in April of 1975, and I got out in March. I was in for two and a half years, and they were cutting back. The ranks were top-heavy, and they had too many enlisted, and they were doing big RIFs [reduction in forces], and stuff. That's one of the reasons I was forced out. It didn't bother me, though.

ELIZABETH SPIVEY

Even today, I get a hankering to move every four or five years. We've lived here for four years, and I really like it here, but I'm ready to move. I don't know if it's a product of being in the military, associated with that. Maybe I would have had this sort of wanderlust, anyway.

246

I don't know if I can blame it on the military, but I've never found a job that I really like. I always hate every job that I have, eventually. I've changed jobs six times since 1981. That's kind of a lot, isn't it? I'm always surprised that the next employer wants to hire me, after that. I just luck out; what can I say? I can't seem to work in one place for very long; I get aggravated and fed up with either the job or the powers that be at the particular job.

I'm not afraid of change; I always look forward to change, and I always think that the next job is going to be the mecca of all jobs, and it will be the answer to my career happiness, though it never is. Revision number 247 of my résumé. I never associated that with my being from a military family. See, Mom and Dad? There are other people out there like me.

I dated a few military guys in college, and I didn't have an aversion to marrying a military guy after my military experience. I have to admit that young officers in their blue uniforms seemed to be very attractive and businesslike and astute. I can't say that I actually sought them out over civilian dates or anything like that. I guess I like men who are very neat, crisp dressers. I wouldn't mind if I were married to a man who is in the military; it just worked out that my husband isn't.

I always think of my being a military dependent as having been a positive thing. Certainly there were hardships that we endured, but I think of it as positive. It was almost like being a member of an exclusive club. I don't mean that haughtily; it wasn't necessarily a prestigious club, that's for sure. *Exclusive* meaning that not everyone was a member. I always felt like we were in the know. I always thought of that as a bonus, a plus. Anybody could be a civilian, but we got to know civilian life and were aware of the military and the military life and moving around.

CAROLINE BAKER

Being so dependent on the military for everything, the total life-style, when you do get out into the real world, it is such a shock. I see that as a disadvantage, now that I'm older and I look back on it.

It did seem to be a close-knit little community, like living in a small town, and you felt like a part of the family, part of the community. My neighborhood is like that, and it's reminiscent of being in the service. I think that can be nice, in a way, but then when you have to move away, it is hard to leave. It's like you're leaving home all over again.

The discipline and strictness that I was brought up with—I think my dad was a little more strict than the rest of them. My other friends, I know, also had the same discipline and rules, the strictness. I see that as a disadvantage now. Before, I used to think that was good because we grew up and we knew how to abide by the rules, how to stay in line. We never got into trouble or got thrown in jail or any crazy things like that, although I did rebel a lot my last two years in high school. I just kind of went wild then, because of the strict control. They weren't going to tell me what to do anymore.

Kids are allowed a little more freedom now, and I think that's good for the kids. Being brought up in that strict, controlled environment is not real healthy.

Of course, that was the only way I knew: it was either black or white. But I am finally beginning to see the gray area, and I know that I do things a little differently with my kids, because I do not want controlled little robots for kids. I want them to be able to be who they are, to be kids. I didn't have the opportunity to mess up as a kid. I think that is one of the biggest disadvantages I can think of for military kids. They are not allowed to be kids.

SHEILA WRIGHT

I swore when we got out of the military that I would never ever get involved with anybody in the military. I didn't want any more to do with that. And my mother said, "Well, you never know." And I told her that if I meet a guy and he tells me he's in the military, I will say good-bye. I don't want that kind of life. The money's not that good, and I don't want to live in poverty. I know that they don't make very much money to support families on.

After I got out of high school, I moved eleven times in almost ten years. I'm going on my twelfth move. I really feel this urge to move. It's so fun to set up a new place and go through your boxes and everything.

I feel proud about it now, that my dad was in the military and he was in Vietnam. When I was young, I hated it. We all did. But now that we're all older, we're glad that we had that experience of moving and living in different places and being a military family.

I know I'm real independent. I can take care of myself. I can go wherever I want and get a job. And if I want to move, I can do that. No problem. If my mother could move that many times, so can I.

I'm real thankful that my dad was in the service, because I learned that anything is a possibility. I don't feel that I have to move into a house and stay there for the rest of my life. If you don't like it, move. That's what I tell my friends; they'll be complaining, and I'll say, "Well, move!" And they go, "Well, I can't, I can't quit my job." They have a justification for everything, but they're still not happy.

So when I decided to move back to Nebraska next year, everyone wanted to know why, and I said, "Because I don't like it here anymore; I want to move." And they said, "Well, that doesn't make sense, to move just because you don't like it." It makes perfect sense to me. People say, "Boy, I wish I could do that." And I tell them, "Do it. Nothing's stopping you."

One of my friends was complaining that her mother interferes in her life, and I told her how lucky she is to have her mother so close. I will never, ever take my family for granted again. I know that I used to when I lived around them. But now I realize what it's like to miss all the birthday parties, and the anniversaries, and the kids being born and all that stuff. It's real hard, to be away from that. You don't know what you've got until you're away from it.

I'm too transient to be married, too young to be married. I'm having too much fun being single. I have had some men, not a lot, but some men in my life, and it drives them nuts, because I change my mind a lot and I move a lot. I was dating one guy for a year and half and I moved three times, and he said, "Sheila, I'm not moving you again." It's real hard to have a relationship when you're moving all the time, when you change your phone number so often that people don't know where to call you.

LINDA WINSLOW

It was funny, because when I was fifteen—I don't know whether it was to get my father's approval or if it was because I was curious—I joined the Civil Air Patrol. If I had known then what I know now, I would have joined the military. But what's interesting is that I was doing very well in the Air Patrol, and when I voiced an interest in going into the military, my father said, "Oh, don't even think about it. There are lesbians in there." And I thought, hmmm. I didn't know what that was, but it didn't sound right.

And after I had been married for seven years, I found out that my husband and I were both gay. Have you met any gay people who were raised military? Okay, I'm a first. Or the first honest person. Looking back on it, I think I probably could have made a real successful career of the military, but I think that I was just too paranoid, either with my sexuality or of what people would think or whatever.

By the time I got married, I wanted out of that whole structure. Then I found out that the structure was just wherever you were in one way or another, but in civilian life it doesn't seem to be as regimented. Plus it seems that with the new consciousness, women's liberation or whatever you want to call it, that women don't have to live vicariously anymore. They can have their own career; they can have their own life-style.

I asked my son, when he was a junior or senior in high school, have you thought about the National Guard? And he went, gasp, no. I went, "All you have to do is weekends and two weeks or join the damn Army. You'll get college money." He wants absolutely nothing to do with it. It horrifies him; it terrifies him. He sees it as having to submit to discipline, and I'm telling him, "That's the best thing for you. I'd like to see you go through boot camp."

So you see what I mean? I don't want my son to be a soldier, but at the same time, I can see the advantages that would come out of it, not just financially but in terms of self-discipline. He seems to have a negative attitude about the military, and I don't know if I put that in his head, subconsciously or maybe consciously. But this is a Navy town, and he sees what goes on. I think he considers himself a free spirit.

We did Boy Scouts with my son, and you know what I found myself doing? I caught myself doing a terrible thing: I pushed my kid in the Scouts. I wanted him to make Eagle, but he quit at Star because we moved, and he didn't like his new troop.

SHERRY SULLIVAN

I went into the service myself, and then I married a serviceman before I got out. So I was first an Army brat, then I was a soldier, and then a military wife, so I've seen all the different angles, and I've had all the different ID cards.

I joined the Army when I was twenty-two. My dad thought that everyone should get married as soon as they were finished with school. They sent me to college, but that didn't work out, because it was something they had chosen for me. When the Vietnam War started and the military needed women, I thought, well, I'll go in and that'll pay for my college, and I can pay my dad back. I went in and my mother said, "I don't want to hear any complaints."

I was homesick. I remember I called once from California, and my mom said, "This is so far! Write a letter!" And I called from Germany when my youngest daughter was born, too, and my mother went, "Oh, no! You're calling from Germany!" I was depressed, you know how it is when you've just had a baby. Some people have their relatives helping out when a baby is born, but I had my baby so far away and had to depend on my neighbors.

I didn't like the moving, but I did like the travel. You have to be careful what you say, because everybody wants to travel. I tell my kids that they were in Germany, and they go, "Yeah, we were babies then." They get mad about it.

But the Army paid for my college. If you join the Army, you get twenty-five thousand dollars for college. That's pretty good. If you don't have a family, you're not married, why not? It's just three years of your life. At least you get a head start.

JOHN ROWAN

If I had stayed in the Navy, I would have had twenty years last year. I think about that from time to time. I think I would have been a different person. I think about that when I don't want to get up and go to work: gee, if I had just stuck it out for twenty years in the Navy.

I think about job security. I sometimes think that it would be nice to stay in one place and have some retirement benefits and stuff like that. The last few times that I've changed jobs, I've thought, okay, this is it; this is really it now. I'm going to stay here for ten or twenty years and have some retirement benefits. And then something more attractive comes along and I jump at it.

DEREK LOWE

The first job I had after I graduated from college was working for the Army. I got a job at Fort Ord and I worked there for about five years. So essentially, every day of my life, I felt I was in the Army until I was twenty-eight. My affiliation with the Army continued. So my life and my job and a large percentage of my friends were military.

I got my degree and went to work for the Army in physical therapy in the seventies, right after the war ended. I was, as a professional, in a real different Army that was opposing Vietnam and was really a kind of slack, very rebellious Army. That was quite a different environment than the Army I grew up in.

Finally, at age twenty-eight, I decided that I had to have another view of the world besides olive drab. I wanted to kind of escape, and I just decided to jump through the looking glass, with no job—I got out of the civil service—and got out here, and this was my first civilian experience. I've been here ten years, actually, as of last month, and haven't regretted it.

I work for the university now, and yeah, there is that sense of job security that is very important to me, although I recognize that it is an illusion, no matter where you are, even in the Army, or anywhere else in the world. But I don't have to worry about the company going out of business tomorrow, and I have a good benefits package.

I initially worked for my friend, but that was an excuse to get out here, and then I went to work for the university, and then I had a period of disenchantment with them and decided that I needed more money and went to work for a defense contractor. Some of those old feelings about Vietnam came up when I found myself working on a weapons operation, and that was real uncomfortable.

I think the Army does make you feel like you can't live without it. I don't regret "being in the Army" until I was twenty-eight, but I wish that weren't such a prevalent part of my life. I think that's kind of ongoing, that security need, and it's kind of a negative. It's so inclusive.

I do miss moving. On one level, it's adaptability, but on another level, it's the habit perpetuating itself. It shows up in relationships. The idea of a relationship lasting more than three years is real difficult for me to fathom. It's like, for me, there's an automatic self-destruct that happens after two or three years. I'm currently in a relationship that's been going on for four years, but last year was real tough. I'm set up to have this wrenching process every two or three years. I accept loss very well. I tend to lose or separate, and it's cut and dried.

I say to myself that this is my home. But it's quite conceivable that I won't live here every day of my life. I really do miss moving and going on that new adventure. I've always found wonderful people wherever I've gone. I kind of feel like there must be all of these people I'm missing out on. It's like this momentum of moving. Your life is in chapters. And you look forward to the next chapter, even if you're enjoying this chapter.

Afterword

As I write this, I am in the midst of another move—a local, "house to house" move. My neighbors see me carrying boxes and they ask the questions I've been hearing all my life. "Are you moving? Where are you going?"

I find myself responding to my son's anxious questions about the move with a bravado that I learned from my parents. At seven, he's young enough to believe me when I stop packing long enough to describe the new house in glowing terms.

Until I began to work on this book, I had not devoted much thought to the military or its effects on my childhood and on my life. After talking to other military brats, I was relieved to find that my wanderlust is not unusual; there are other military brats for whom settling down means spending two or three years in a place. Moving is simply one of the more obvious manifestations of patterns that were established very early in my life.

While I found it reassuring to meet other military brats who move as frequently as I do, I didn't have to look beyond my own family to realize that not all military brats continue to move as adults. There is no "typical" military brat in this book, nor have I attempted to draw any broad conclusions from the interview material. I simply kept asking questions about what it was really like to grow up in a military family.

The singular and most pervasive trait that I found among military brats was an intense curiosity about other military brats. Time and time again, people asked me to tell them about other brats, both in the past tense—patterns and chronologies of moving, experiences in classrooms and backyards, family discipline—and in the present and future tenses, in terms of the ways in which a military background had shaped perceptions, behavior, and attitudes in adult life.

The people in this book tell stories that can be confusing to civilians—a year spent here, a year spent there. As an adult, the military brat's sense of roots and identity is inextricably linked to places—plural—which is not unusual in today's highly mobile society. But the sum total of a military brat background is greater than its parts: more than just a description of moves, it is a common cultural background. Raised in the uniquely insular and transient military environment, brats were continually aware of and affected by the military culture that surrounded them. The assumption that a military background is synonymous with moving and living everywhere is usually correct, and it is perpetuated by the way in which military brats tend to edit and simplify their reply to the question "Where are you from?" But there was more to being a military brat than just the moving. When people describe themselves as "military brats," it serves both as an excuse for their inability to give a hometown address and as an acknowledgment of the military culture and its profound effects on their lives.